S0-AXA-283

"I've contacted the caterer, selected the flowers and picked out the cake," Antonia Decker told her friend.

"I made up the guest list and put our name down for the reception hall," Julia Richardson replied in kind.

"Once I book the church we'll be all done."

"I can't think of a single thing we've forgotten. Can you?"

"Noth—" Antonia looked at her friend blankly. "Well, maybe two."

"Two?"

She smiled sheepishly. "The bride and groom."

Dear Reader,

American Romance is "Goin' to the Chapel" with three soon-to-be-wed couples. Only thing is, saying "I do" is the farthest thing from their minds!

So glad you could join us for the first wedding in this trilogy of veils and vows.

We're particularly delighted that perennial favorite Anne McAllister is kicking off the series. Anne has authored eleven bestselling American Romance novels, and in *The Eight Second Wedding* she has created one of the most charming couples of her career. Not to mention some of the most likable in-laws you'll ever see!

Be sure you don't miss any of the Goin' to the Chapel books in the months ahead.

Regards,

Debra Matteucci
Senior Editor & Editorial Coordinator
Harlequin
300 East 42nd Street
New York, NY 10017

Anne McAllister

THE EIGHT SECOND WEDDING

Harlequin Books

TORONTO • NEW YORK • LONDON
AMSTERDAM • PARIS • SYDNEY • HAMBURG
STOCKHOLM • ATHENS • TOKYO • MILAN
MADRID • WARSAW • BUDAPEST • AUCKLAND

If you purchased this book without a cover you should be aware
that this book is stolen property. It was reported as "unsold and
destroyed" to the publisher, and neither the author nor the
publisher has received any payment for this "stripped book."

For my mother, who often knows best
but is considerate enough not to tell me so.

For Chuck and Susan Huntley,
who know the value of research and a good laugh.

And with thanks to Brett Leffew,
whose knowledge of what roads to go down
kept Chan and Madeleine (and me) from
getting lost.

ISBN 0-373-16533-1

THE EIGHT SECOND WEDDING

Copyright © 1994 by Barbara Schenck.

All rights reserved. Except for use in any review, the reproduction or
utilization of this work in whole or in part in any form by any electronic,
mechanical or other means, now known or hereafter invented, including
xerography, photocopying and recording, or in any information storage
or retrieval system, is forbidden without the written permission of the
publisher, Harlequin Enterprises Limited, 225 Duncan Mill Road,
Don Mills, Ontario, Canada M3B 3K9.

All characters in this book have no existence outside the imagination of
the author and have no relation whatsoever to anyone bearing the same
name or names. They are not even distantly inspired by any individual
known or unknown to the author, and all incidents are pure invention.

This edition published by arrangement with Harlequin Enterprises B. V.

® and TM are trademarks of the publisher. Trademarks indicated with
® are registered in the United States Patent and Trademark Office, the
Canadian Trade Marks Office and in other countries.

Printed in U.S.A.

Prologue

It is a truth universally acknowledged that, when it comes to their children's happiness, mothers know best. And when the mothers come equipped with a Ph.D. in genetics in one case, and years of experience in anthropological fieldwork in the other, the truth has considerable clout.

So when Madeleine Frances Decker was born on that bright summer day twenty-six years ago, her future was all but decided.

Her mother, Antonia, knew precisely what her best friend, Julia Richardson, would say upon hearing the news.

"It's perfect. I told you you'd have a girl. You had to." Julia rubbed her hands together gleefully as she looked down at the tiny girl child nestled in Antonia's arms. "She's lovely. Whichever she picks, they'll have beautiful, healthy, intelligent babies."

"It's hard to imagine her having babies," Antonia said softly, "when she's only seven hours old herself."

"Yes," Julia said. "But it will be wonderful. You said that yourself."

"I know, but—"

"And it's not as if we'll be pushing her toward any one of them," she added conscientiously. "She can have her choice."

Of husbands, Julia meant, for she was herself the mother of the four stair-step sons she and Antonia had decided that in time the unsuspecting Madeleine would be able to pick from.

Madeleine, of course, knew nothing of this arrangement for years. Neither did the prospective husbands: Channing, Gardner, Mark and Trevor Richardson.

There was no point in telling them beforetime. Children, Antonia and Julia agreed, couldn't be counted on to act rationally about serious matters like this. In fact, they could be expected to rebel, a fact which both Antonia and Julia well knew.

There would be time enough, they decided, to inform their respective children when they were older. They would understand better when they were past the childish follies of first loves and adolescent crushes, and so able at last to fully appreciate the scientific, genetic and cultural basis for their mothers' infinite wisdom.

Then, and only then would they be told, and Madeleine could take her choice.

At least that was the plan.

But when Madeleine was only fifteen, Gard Richardson narrowed her choices by marrying Emily Keane a month after his high school graduation.

Julia apologized to her friend. "But I could hardly tell him not to. He's eighteen. He loves her. And," she added ruefully, "there's a baby on the way."

"Madeleine probably wouldn't have wanted Gard, anyway," Antonia said philosophically.

"Probably not. Besides, she still has three to pick from," Julia agreed.

Or she did have until five years later, when Mark joined the navy, went to Australia and, the next thing Julia knew, married a pretty redhead named Kelly Fraser.

"I didn't even know until after he'd done it," Julia called to tell Antonia in dismay. "He phoned us from Perth, for goodness sake, and said, 'Guess what, Mom, I'm married!' I mean, really!" It was the most offended Antonia had ever heard her.

"Don't fret," Antonia said soothingly. "There're still Chan and Trevor."

Julia sighed. "That's true."

And the thought of Antonia's Madeleine and her Trevor made her muster her optimism and a smile. The optimism and the smile had lasted until this past December when Trevor called his parents from Boston and announced his engagement to Marybeth Boone.

"You won't believe this," Julia told Antonia without preamble. "He's given her a diamond. They're marrying in February. On Valentine's Day, would you believe? I never thought Trev would indulge in such romanticism. I really," she confided wistfully, "always thought Trevor was the one. I mean, he and Madeleine both have so much in common. They're both scholarly and intellectual. They're both Ph.D. candidates at top graduate schools."

"Yes, well, it can't be helped," Antonia said. "And there's always Chan."

"Yes," Julia said slowly, "there's always Chan."

Neither of them had deemed Channing Richardson a serious candidate for Madeleine's husband in years.

Julia considered the possibility now. If she hadn't believed in her research so thoroughly, she would have quailed at the thought of her eldest son marrying Antonia's only daughter. Never, not even in her wildest dreams, had she linked Madeleine and Chan. She didn't imagine anyone else had, either.

Still, she reminded herself, genetics didn't lie. Chan and Madeleine should have just as good a chance of having wonderful, talented, healthy, strong babies as Madeleine and any of her other sons would have. And Antonia's anthropological research provided substantial evidence that very often the best marriages were made for economic, social and familial reasons, and not for anything so vague as that unpredictable thing called "love."

Still—and here Julia couldn't help shaking her head—Chan and Madeleine together?

It wasn't going to be easy.

But really, now that she thought about it, it might be for the best. It might be the making of both of them, genetics and cultural determinism aside.

"Let us hope, at least," she said dryly, "that the old wives' tale is true."

"Which one is that?" Antonia asked.

"That opposites attract."

Chapter One

"I have told you, haven't I," Julia Richardson said to her son, who was currently sprawled on his back in the dirt in front of her, "of the advantages of good breeding?"

Channing Richardson spat out a mouthful of dirt and hauled himself to his feet. He didn't reply. The monologue was all too familiar. He grunted, slapped the dirt off his jeans and limped over to fetch his hat.

"I thought I had," his mother went on unconcerned. "And Danny Boy simply proves it." A contented smile wreathed her face as she watched the bull who had just thrown her son into the dirt now trot briskly around the corral with a look of smug satisfaction on his bovine face.

Chan wiped his hand across his mouth, snagged his hat and jammed it back on his head.

"Admit it, Chan, he's a fine fellow," Julia said. "You're just angry that he keeps tossing you."

Chan grimaced. Danny Boy was more than a fine fellow. He was the damnedest hard ride Chan had ever experienced. Every time he came home he made it a point to test his mettle against the young bull, and he hadn't stayed on him yet.

"Just like his father and his father before him," Julia went on cheerfully. She was perched on the corral fence, a spread sheet of Danny Boy's lineage chart in her hand. She smiled at it as she spoke. "And that lovely little mamma cow I picked."

"Ill-tempered hussy, you mean," Chan muttered.

Julia smiled. "Precisely. Exactly what one wants in rodeo stock, isn't it?"

"Mmm, hmm." He'd give her that much. He'd also admit she was the brains behind the success of the entire Richardson cattle operation, both the rodeo stock and the beef cattle they raised in the foothills of the Big Horn mountains of Wyoming. Chan's father, Channing, Sr., called Rick, had done a good job developing the herd left to him by his father. He'd bought good stock, grazed them well and doctored them carefully. He'd even gone to Montana State University to study agriculture and he'd learned a lot.

But the smartest move Rick Richardson had ever made was falling in love with the tall, curvy, chestnut-haired girl with the four-point in his genetics class and having the good sense to encourage her to finish her Ph.D. before he married her.

Julia Richardson knew her way around cattle; Chan had to give her that. She had genetics all figured out. She could talk bloodlines in her sleep. Probably she did, he thought wearily, but he didn't dare ask his father to confirm it.

"You could do as well," his mother said now, climbing down off the corral fence and ambling alongside him toward the house.

He shot her a sideways glance, but kept on walking. "Huh?"

She made a huffing sound. "Don't play dumb with me, Chan Richardson. You know very well what I'm talking about."

Trouble was, he did. When his mother got the bit between her teeth about something, she didn't let up. She galloped right on to the finish, no matter how long it took, no matter how many obstacles loomed in her way. And all the discouragement in the world, which God knew he'd been doing his best to provide, never ever distracted her from her course.

"Bloodlines," she said patiently. "Good genes. Propagation of the species. Children. *Yours,*" she finished pointedly, in case he decided to continue pretending that he didn't know what she was talking about.

He went into the mud room and tugged off his boots. Then he turned on the faucet, stripped his shirt off and plunged his head under the stream of cool, running water. It felt good, he couldn't hear her, and with luck, he thought, she would get tired of waiting until he came up for air.

But he could see the toes of her ropers out of the corner of his eye, and they didn't move as long as he stayed there letting the water sluice over his head. At last, with a groan, he shut the water off, unbent and took the towel she handed him.

"Ma," he said finally, which he should have done in the first place, "give it a rest."

"But, Chan—"

"I'm not marrying some girl just so you can have perfect grandchildren."

"Of course you're not." Julia looked at him askance. "Did I ever suggest such a thing?"

"Yes."

She colored slightly. "Well, you know I didn't mean it. You know I would never presume . . . I just . . . Oh, Chan, she's a wonderful girl. So bright. So clever. Did I tell you she's getting a Ph.D. in philosophy?"

"Fifty or sixty times," he said into the towel.

"She's writing her dissertation now. She expects to have it finished by the end of next summer, I hear."

"Good for her." He scrubbed at his hair, then slung the towel around his neck and made himself look down into the hopeful eyes of his mother. He gave her a wry grin. "She's probably too smart for me."

Julia looked affronted. "Don't be absurd, Chan. You're every bit as bright as she is. Just because you've always profited by less traditional methods of learning..."

A corner of Chan's mouth lifted. "Is that what they're calling 'the school of hard knocks' these days?"

Julia put her hands on her hips and glared at him.

He grinned. "Just kidding, Ma."

"You're far too hard on yourself, Chan, always have been. Now, as I was saying, you two would suit admirably. You're strong and healthy and clever, and she's bright and healthy and—"

"Ma, I'm not a bull."

"You're as stubborn as one," Julia grumbled.

Chan wandered into the kitchen, still bare-chested, the towel slung around his neck. Julia followed him like a determined cow dog trying to bring home a balky steer. He opened the refrigerator and took out the milk, tipping it up and drinking straight from the carton.

Julia looked annoyed but didn't say anything. So much for trying to distract her. Chan wiped his mouth on the back of his hand.

"Ma, we don't live in the same world."

"You're going to New York next week, aren't you?"

Oh, hell, he'd given her an opening. "So?"

"So simply drop in and meet her."

"Yeah, right."

"What have you got to lose?"

"My freedom, if you have anything to say about it. Hell, Ma, what's got into you? You never did this with Gard or Mark or Trev."

"I never had to," Julia said mildly. "They all found lovely girls on their own."

As he remembered it, she hadn't been overly thrilled with any of her daughters-in-law at first glance, though now she couldn't have been happier. And there were five grandchildren, as well, all warming the cockles of her heart. "Well, give me time. I might, too."

He heard a muffled noise that sounded suspiciously like a snort. He gave his mother a level look. Her smile was a mingling of tolerance and skepticism. "Like you found Vivian or Dena or Callie or Brenda or—"

Chan grimaced. "So, I was shopping around. I just haven't found the right one."

"I know that, dear," Julia said patiently. "That's exactly what I've been telling you. But I have. Madeleine."

"Ma, I'm a grown man. I'm thirty-one years old, for God's sake. You can stop telling me what to do. And you can sure as hell stop telling me who to marry!"

"I'm only trying to help," Julia said meekly, dropping her eyes.

Chan looked at her narrowly. He couldn't remember his mother ever sounding meek. She even looked slightly frail, standing there looking up at him. She was close to sixty years old, and he'd never thought about it before. For the first time he was aware that his mother wasn't as unshakable and as enduring as the Tetons. The notion unnerved him.

But, damn it, he wasn't going to marry some woman he didn't even know just to bring the color back to her cheeks!

"It won't work," he said gruffly.

Julia didn't look at him. "I only thought..." she ventured, and he heard it again, that faint meekness in her tone. "Since you're going to New York anyway..."

"That's another thing. New York!" Chan fairly spat the words. "How can you expect me to marry a New Yorker?"

Julia sighed. "All I'm asking right now is that you just go see her."

"And tell her you expect me to marry her?"

"She already knows that."

"She does?"

She smiled, nodding. "Indeed. Antonia thinks it's a wonderful idea."

Chan frowned. "I thought you said her name was Madeleine."

"It is."

"So who's this Antonia?"

"Her mother."

Chan put his hands over his eyes and groaned.

"DID YOU KNOW," Antonia Decker said to her daughter, Madeleine, "that the average Trobriand Island woman marries at the age of fourteen?"

"Mmm." Madeleine didn't look up from the Sunday *Times* which she was reading as she sprawled on the sofa on her Upper West Side apartment. She didn't think it was true, but she couldn't argue. Antonia would cite some obscure footnote that Madeleine wouldn't be able to find to disprove her.

"And," Antonia continued, looking over the tops of her half glasses to catch her daughter's reaction, "that the usual age for marriage among Wapiti women was sixteen?"

"Because they were dead by thirty-two," Madeleine said flatly, which probably wasn't true, either, but what the hell. "So if I live to be eighty, and I want to be married half my lifetime, I don't have to worry for another thirteen or fourteen years, right?" She lifted her gaze long enough to give her mother a smile as wide as it was insincere.

Antonia sighed and tapped her pen on the newspaper. "Honestly, Madeleine, the things you say! You'd think I was hinting!"

"Weren't you?"

"Not . . . precisely."

"You don't have someone in mind?"

Antonia flapped the book review section of the *Times*. "Well, I wouldn't go so far as to say that, but—"

"The same guy you've been trying to push on me for the past year?"

"Channing is a very nice man!"

"I'm sure he is," Madeleine said wearily. "Carlo the butcher on the corner is a very nice man, but that doesn't mean I ought to marry him."

"Carlo the butcher on the corner has nothing to do with this!"

"You're telling me," Madeleine muttered. "And neither does your Mr. Richardson, Mother. Because I'm not getting married."

Antonia pursed her lips. "Utter drivel," she said. "You know you will."

Madeleine shrugged her off. "In my own good time, then." She wasn't going to argue with her mother about that, either. No one had ever won an argument with Antonia Decker. "I have a dissertation to write, remember?"

"Of course I do."

"And if I don't get it done by the end of next summer, I'm not going to get hired at Chamberlain, am I?"

"Probably not, but—"

"So, I have work to do."

"Well, I'm sure I have no intention of stopping you," Antonia said, an injured tone to her voice, turning back to the book reviews.

Madeleine smothered a groan. It wasn't fair. Mothers should either be nagging, moaning pests or dedicated, hard-edged professionals; they shouldn't be both!

But then, when had Antonia Decker ever done what she was supposed to do? Madeleine wondered.

Ever since she'd realized that her mother was not exactly like other mothers, that she was somehow more clever, more competent, more insightful—more everything, Madeleine thought wearily—Madeleine had been struggling to live up to her parent and yet make her life her own at the same time.

It hadn't been easy. Antonia Decker was her generation's answer to Margaret Mead. She'd written at least half a dozen definitive studies of tribal cultures. She could speak languages most people hadn't even heard of, and yet could melt into the background so easily that sometimes people forgot she was there.

Madeleine didn't forget. Ever.

There was a time that she'd wanted to be just like her mother, do fieldwork like her mother, get down to the nitty-gritty of the way cultures and individual people interacted like her mother.

But then she grew up. She met reality. And she knew it was never going to happen. She wasn't her mother. So she had to find herself. She changed her major, opting for philosophy, because dealing with abstract constructs seemed about as far as she could get from living in a hut. Antonia was hurt, there was no doubt about it.

But Madeleine stuck to her guns. Still it was no accident that she was writing her dissertation on free will.

This was not to say that Madeleine didn't love her mother. She did.

It was impossible not to love Antonia Decker. She was sweet, sincere and smart, and, since the death of her husband almost twenty years before, she'd loved her daughter more than anyone on earth. She wanted what was best for Madeleine, and Madeleine knew it.

She just wished her mother wasn't so certain about what was best.

Who on earth was this Channing Richardson paragon, anyway?

Why him?

Of course, since she was small she'd been hearing stories about her mother's dearest school chum, Julia Gardner, the absolutely brilliant geneticist who, against all rhyme and reason, had fallen in love with some handsome cattle baron out west. She'd heard about how Julia had taken her Ph.D., but then turned down a job at Princeton and left the hallowed ivy-covered halls of academe to marry him.

Madeleine had frankly wondered just how intelligent Julia could be if she had really done such a thing. But Antonia didn't seem to find it odd, so Madeleine didn't remark on it.

Nor did she remark on the long, detailed letters that came every six months or so about Julia's four wonderful sons. Mostly she didn't listen to them. Sometimes, when one was living with Antonia, earplugs seemed the greatest invention of the twentieth century.

Now Madeleine wondered if perhaps by wearing them so often she had missed something early on. For it wasn't until Christmas of last year that she'd learned that her mother expected her to marry one of the wonderful Richardsons!

"We had hoped to give you a choice," Antonia had said almost apologetically when it was first mentioned.

"Thank you very much," Madeleine replied dryly, but her sarcasm was lost on her mother.

"Still, it shouldn't matter over much," Antonia went right on. "In most cultures marriages are economic and social arrangements to begin with. For the good of the tribe, you know? And they work out just fine."

Madeleine had wondered at the time if strangulation was too good for her mother. She wondered if Antonia would even know why she was being strangled. She wondered if, in her mother's mind, free will was anything more than a philosophical construct.

Over the next nine and a half months, Madeleine had endeavored to teach her what it meant. She'd resisted all mention of Channing Richardson. She'd walked out of rooms when Julia's letters came. She didn't want to know. She didn't want to hear.

Antonia's attacks didn't cease; they simply became more subtle. There was the invitation to accompany her to another Richardson brother's wedding on Valentine's Day.

"No," Madeleine replied succinctly.

"Oh, but, you could take a look at Chan and no one would be the wiser."

"No," Madeleine said again. "Besides, what if I went and decided I liked the one who was getting married? Would you want me to stand up and say so when they asked for objections?"

The fact that Antonia actually seemed to consider the possibility seriously sent Madeleine scurrying from the room.

She didn't attend Trevor Richardson's wedding. Neither, she discovered later, did Channing.

"Business," Antonia had said when she came home from Boston. "He had business that weekend. He couldn't come."

"Maybe he was avoiding me."

"Don't be ridiculous," Antonia huffed, but she looked decidedly uncomfortable, and Madeleine grinned.

Still, she hoped that this sudden push to marry her off would blow over, that Antonia would find a new culture to study, a new construct to explore, and that she would forget all about introducing Channing Richardson to her daughter.

She was out of luck.

Though they lived on opposite sides of town and only met regularly for Sunday brunch, which should have forestalled a lot of this name-dropping, Antonia wasn't averse to picking up the phone and dropping the occasional hint. Madeleine did her best to turn a deaf ear. If it wouldn't have made the rest of her life considerably more difficult, she would have considered wearing the earplugs full-time.

In June Antonia took a group of college students on a physical anthropology field trip to an archaeological site near Shell, Wyoming. She tried cajoling Madeleine into coming along. Madeleine declined. "Your friend Julia lives out that way, doesn't she?"

"You're becoming paranoid, Madeleine," Antonia complained.

"I wonder," Madeleine said. And though she did feel a bit paranoid, several weeks later Antonia let slip that indeed she had run into Channing.

"He was just there overnight on his way to Idaho. Such a good-looking man," she said. "Medium height. Just a little under six feet. But good strong bones. He'd be perfect for you."

Perfect biologically, she meant. Perfect intellectually, perhaps. But perfect emotionally?

Madeleine wondered if such a man existed. She'd never met one—had never met a man who touched her soul, reached her heart, made her think that life without him would not be complete.

Of course she never said such things to Antonia. If Antonia believed in heart-and-soul commitment, she never said so to Madeleine, either. She talked about culture and kinship, mores and traditions. And when she talked about a husband for Madeleine, she just talked in terms of the anthropologically and genetically perfect man.

Until now Madeleine had let her talk. It had been easier than saying what she felt. Besides, she had other things to think about: philosophers' works to study, supporting evidence for her thesis to compile a dissertation to write so she'd be qualified for a job at Chamberlain.

But now that the genetically and anthropologically perfect man had a name, she had a problem. This constant blather about Channing Richardson reminded her of things she hadn't thought about in a long time.

Not since Scott.

She'd never told Antonia about Scott. She'd never told anyone about Scott—or more to the point, her feelings about Scott.

Scott Barlowe: her candidate for the perfect mate. A little bit taller than medium height. Good strong bones.

Antonia would have liked that. So would Julia.

So had Madeleine as a matter of fact.

Scott Barlowe was a beautiful man in any woman's estimation. Blond-haired. Blue-eyed. Intelligent. Very clever, indeed, though Madeleine hadn't realized it at the time.

The time had been her senior year at university. She was taking a seminar in anthropology under one of her mother's oldest friends, Kimball Griffin. Scott was Kim's graduate assistant and quickly became Madeleine's mentor.

It seemed like destiny to a closet romantic like Madeleine.

And, romantic that she was, she'd fallen headlong in love with Scott Barlowe. He was everything she'd ever dreamed her perfect man would be.

Scott would, she was sure, become for her what her father had been for her mother. They were even in the same field! She remembered only vaguely the time that her father had been with them. But what she did remember seemed enchanted, a wonderful dream of a family living and loving and sharing their work and their play. She'd never been happier than in those early years. She knew Antonia hadn't, either.

She'd hoped to recapture that joy with Scott. She even dared envision them doing second-generation studies in Bali, following up the work done by her parents.

And Scott had encouraged her.

Or maybe she just thought he had.

Actually she realized now that he was far too self-centered to have ever thought about encouraging anyone else. Madeleine was significant to Scott as long as she helped him.

Help him she had. She'd slaved for him, done hours and hours of research for him, work he never seemed to have time to get to himself. She cooked meals for him and ironed shirts for him and made small talk at faculty-grad assistant teas and potlucks for him. She wore frilly Victorian dresses for him because he thought they looked feminine. She even, fool that she was, slept with him.

And then, because he asked her to, she wrote her mother a letter on his behalf. Antonia was chairing an international committee on anthropological research, and Scott was desperate to secure a post-doctoral fellowship in Paris. Madeleine thought it would be a wonderful place for a honeymoon.

Scott got the fellowship.

Madeleine got the boot.

"Come with me?" She could still remember the astonishment on his face when she'd suggested it. She could still remember her chagrin growing as he'd smiled and shaken his head. "Don't be silly, Madeleine. Why would I need you?"

Why indeed?

Even now she could still feel sick in the pit of her stomach, if she let herself think about Scott too long.

So much for the man of her dreams.

She hadn't had one since. Didn't want one. Didn't trust herself to find one—let alone trust Antonia to do it.

In September, for the first time since Christmas, Channing Richardson's name didn't come up.

Madeleine held her breath.

Had her mother given up? Found a new enthusiasm? Forgotten? Was it too good to be true?

By mid-October she began to breathe more easily. Her dissertation was starting to take shape. A good part of the research was finished. She was beginning to organize the first draft.

Late in the month she felt confident enough to call and invite Antonia out to dinner for her birthday. It was a risk, but one she felt she could take.

"Friday?" Antonia sounded doubtful.

"That's your birthday, isn't it? Why? Do you have other plans?"

There was a hesitation, then, "No, of course not. I'd be delighted."

Madeleine frowned at what seemed to be a sort of vague reluctance. "Are you waiting for a better offer, Mom? Has Dr. Steele come back from Pago-Pago?"

Her mother's first love interest in almost twenty years, Dr. Jeremiah Steele, had been researching in the South Pacific all year. And though far less had been said about him than about Channing Richardson, Madeleine knew her mother missed him. He was the only man she could remember her mother looking twice at since Lothar Decker's death.

"Jeremiah won't be back until the end of the semester. I would love to have dinner with you," Antonia said briskly. "Shall we go to Lazlo's?" It was her mother's favorite, a tiny Hungarian restaurant on the Upper East Side.

"Wherever you want. It's your birthday."

"Would that you were always so amenable," Antonia said dryly.

"Would that your interference in my life only extended to telling me where to eat!"

Antonia laughed. "Seven o'clock?"

Which meant, Madeleine thought now, that she had two hours to find that damnable missing reference card she'd been looking for all day, then bathe, wash and dry her hair, dress, and get across town.

It was raining and she was soaked by the time she got home. Her long dark hair, which often demonstrated a mind of its own, seemed to have become positively scatterbrained today. The front frizzed and curled outrageously while the rest cascaded in springy, soggy tangles halfway down her back.

She dragged her bike up three flights of stairs, stowed it in the entry hall, shed her coat, dumped her overflowing backpack on the sofa and kicked off her shoes. Then, shaking her head and scattering raindrops across the room, she went into the kitchen and put the kettle on for a desperately needed cup of tea.

While the water was heating, she went into the bathroom and turned on the tap for a bath. Then, tugging her sweater over her head, she went back out and punched the button on her answering machine.

"Mad," said a cheery female voice. "It's Alfie. Hot date tonight. I need to borrow your slinky black thing. You know, the one with no back."

Madeleine grinned and shook her head as she unzipped her damp jeans and began wriggling out of them. Alfie, her upstairs neighbor, had been with her when she'd bought the "slinky black thing."

"It's you, Mad," she'd enthused. But in the six months she'd had it, she was beginning to believe it was more "Alfie." Certainly Alfie wore it more often. But then, Alfie had more hot dates.

Kicking her jeans off, Madeleine ambled toward the closet in the bedroom, half catching the sound of her mother's voice as the next message played. Was Antonia canceling? she wondered.

She grabbed the slinky black dress off its hanger and returned to the kitchen in time to hear her mother say, "...see what I mean. See you tonight, then."

So she wasn't canceling, Madeline decided. And whatever it was her mother had wanted, it could wait until she saw her.

Alfie's voice came over the machine again. "Mad, for heaven's sake, it's three o'clock. Can I borrow the dress?" And again after another beep, "Mad, now it's four-fifteen. I know I told you it was a hot date, but am I going to dinner naked?" And finally, panicky, "Mad, damn it! Where the hell are you?"

This last was followed almost at once by the one shrill ring of Madeleine's doorbell.

Trust Alfie. She must have been listening for Madeleine to come in. Or perhaps she was hearing her own voice echoing up through the paper-thin plaster that separated her floor and Madeleine's ceiling. Clad only in her bra and a pair of skimpy black panties, Madeleine carried the dress with her to answer the door.

She opened it and thrust out the dress simultaneously, saying, "Here. You might as well keep it. You wear it more than I do."

It wasn't Alfie.

It was a cowboy.

Chapter Two

He took the dress, holding it out away from him as if she'd handed him a live grenade.

"I don't think it'd fit me," he said.

Horrified, face flaming, Madeleine snatched it back, hopped behind the door and peered from around it to glare at him.

"Who the hell are you? What're you doing here? Where's Alfie?"

He grinned then. It was a slow, lazy grin. The epitome of what Madeleine would have expected of a cowboy grin. It revealed itself one tooth at a time, until it shone with amused arrogance while she stood and sputtered.

"My name's Chan Richardson. And I'm here because I promised my mother I'd see if you were worth marrying." He looked her over once, more thoroughly. "I'm sorry, but I don't know anybody named Alfie."

Madeleine managed an inarticulate noise and slammed the door shut in his face, then leaned against it, her heart pounding. *God,* she thought desperately. *Oh, God.*

She heard footsteps on the stairs, then Alfie's voice. "Hi. Are you looking for Madeleine?"

"Actually I think I found her." He was laughing, damn him!

"I thought I heard her come home." Alfie banged on the door. "Mad! Open up!"

Never, Madeleine thought frantically. *Never again. I am never coming out of this apartment. Not ever.*

"Mad!"

Madeleine didn't move.

"She's . . . er, indisposed," she heard Chan offer after a moment.

"Huh?"

"Undressed."

"Undressed?"

Madeleine pressed her palms to burning cheeks. Oh, merciful heavens, worse and worse. She knew what a mind like Alfie's could make of a statement like that.

"Just a minute! Hold your horses, Alfie, I'm coming!" She grabbed her jeans off the floor and struggled into them. Their clamminess almost defeated her, but at last she succeeded in hauling them up her legs and zipping them. Then she dragged her sweater over her head, picked up the dress and yanked open the door.

Chan Richardson and Alfie stood side by side staring at her. Chan was still grinning. Alfie looked amazed.

Madeleine thrust the dress at Alfie. "Take it. Keep it. I don't care. Just go away."

Alfie shot first Madeleine, then Chan, uncertain glances. A worried smile flickered across her wide-eyed face. "S-sure, Mad. Thanks." She backed hastily toward the steps.

As she went her gaze turned to one of speculation, and just before she disappeared around the landing, she made lip-smacking gestures in Chan's direction, grinned hugely at Madeleine and mouthed, "He's yummy."

Madeleine wanted to die. Or kill. Whichever.

Her gaze traveled back to Chan. He hadn't moved an inch. He was still studying her avidly and she felt almost as naked now as she'd been at their first encounter.

So she did the only thing she could think of under the circumstances; she did an equally thorough appraisal of him.

Her mother was, unfortunately, right—at least insofar as the physical perfection was concerned. Channing Richardson was of medium build, probably an inch or so shy of six feet. But every bit of him was lean and well-muscled. Madeleine could tell that much from the way he filled out the faded, but well-pressed jeans and the long-sleeved pale pink shirt he wore.

Pale pink? No anthropologist would be caught dead in a shirt of that color. Only a cowboy or some other very confident male would dare!

His eyes were blue. Deep blue, like the sea, and still alight with amusement as he regarded her steadily. His hair was thick and dark and recently cut. It looked like the sort of hair that cowgirls would line up to run their fingers through.

One thing was perfectly clear: he didn't look like the sort who needed his mother to set him up with a woman, still less to find him a wife.

His grin had faded somewhat now, but the bemused expression remained. She could just imagine the impression he was forming of her. It made her stiffen and glare.

"It wasn't funny," she said abruptly.

"Yes, it was." A corner of his mouth quirked. "You must not have been expecting me."

"No kidding," Madeleine muttered.

"Your mother said she'd call."

"My mother?" Oh, good grief, was that the message she'd missed?

Chan grimaced. "Sorry. I thought she'd ring and you'd be expecting me. I talked to her last week."

"Last week?" Antonia had known Chan Richardson was coming for a *week?* She remembered her mother's vague hesitation on the phone. Suddenly things were becoming clearer.

He nodded. "My mother, well, she knows how to pressure a guy, so I—" he shrugged "—thought what the hell? I might as well do it since I had to come anyhow."

"On business?" Madeleine said, her tone halfway between sarcasm and skepticism as she looked from the black felt cowboy hat he held in his hands to the fancy tooled boots he wore. But her doubts were apparently lost on him.

He just nodded quite seriously, and she frowned.

"What business are you in?" she asked finally.

"I ride bulls."

Madeleine blinked, certain she hadn't heard him right. She looked at him more closely.

"I thought only popes wrote bulls," she ventured after a moment.

"Not write. Ride. I *ride* bulls. R-I-D-E. They never said? No, of course they didn't. They wouldn't." He gave a half sigh, half groan. "Damn them, anyway. I ride rough stock in rodeos. Bulls. I'm riding in a rodeo upstate tonight and at Madison Square garden tomorrow."

Madeleine just looked at him, mind reeling.

A rodeo cowboy.

Channing Richardson—her mother's notion of her perfect mate—was a *rodeo cowboy?*

Chan shifted from one foot to the other. "Look. I'm sorry if I startled you just popping up like this. I did tell 'em to warn you."

"She didn't warn me," Madeleine said tightly.

He nodded. "Figures. Your mother's probably as devious as mine."

For an instant a current of rapport arced between them. Madeleine almost smiled at him. Then she remembered who he was, who her mother—and his—wanted him to be and she said firmly, "They're nuts, both of them."

Channing Richardson bobbed his head. "They are."

"Completely loony."

"Yep."

She looked at him cautiously. "We're agreed?"

"You bet," he said fervently.

"But even though we think they're out of their minds, we've respected them. We've done what they wanted—we've met, right?"

"Right."

"And we've discovered that a philosophy student and a rodeo cowboy have nothing in common."

"Nothing."

"So this is the end of it." It wasn't a question.

They looked at each other. Madeleine thought she'd never seen eyes so blue. She looked quickly away.

"Good," she said briskly.

And Chan took a deep breath. "Amen." He set his hat back on his head and tugged down the brim, then slanted a grin in her direction. His gaze flickered back to meet hers for just a second before he turned away. "So long," he said.

Madeleine said, "Goodbye."

She shut the door before he reached the steps, then stood quite still and felt a shudder run through her as she listened to his boots clatter down them.

Finally, when she heard the outer door bang shut behind him, she tugged her sweater over her head and dropped it onto the floor. Then she tried to unsnap her jeans. Her fingers were trembling.

So that was Channing Richardson.

Not precisely what she would have expected, she thought, peeling the jeans down her hips. What in heaven's name had her mother and Julia been thinking of?

Genetics, she answered herself at once. Good breeding. The good of the tribe. Bouncing, healthy grandchildren. Lots of them. All the things loony, over-educated mothers thought of.

But without warning, a split-second vision of herself and Channing Richardson doing what needed to be done to make those bouncing, healthy children flashed across her mind.

"Stop it. Don't even think it," she commanded herself.

The last thing she needed to do was get tangled up with a cowboy, no matter how lovely their potential offspring would be. Besides, Chan Richardson obviously didn't like the notion any more than she did.

"Like?" she could hear Antonia saying now scornfully. "What does *like* have to do with anything? Marriages have been built on far less than *like.*"

"Free will," Madeleine muttered desperately to herself, heading toward the bathroom. "Free blooming will. Just remember that."

She didn't have to do what her mother wanted her to do. She didn't have to be the person her mother thought she should be. She took a deep steadying breath and let it out slowly, deliberately shutting out visions of Chan Richardson's remarkable blue eyes.

Channing had come. Channing had gone. Channing hadn't conquered.

It was done, over, weathered, survived. Nothing else could go wrong for the rest of the day.

The bath tub was overflowing.

HE'D SEEN FENCE POSTS with more shape than Madeleine Decker. He'd seen lifelong Rastafarians with less hair.

Granted she had milky white skin and big green eyes, but they weren't enough to redeem her. And he didn't care if she did have pert small breasts inside that lacy black bra that just begged to be cupped in his callused hands—that didn't mean he wanted to see her again!

She didn't like him.

He knew the way women looked at guys they liked, and Madeleine Decker had looked at him the way his mother would look at a cow pie on the kitchen floor.

Well, fine. He hadn't exactly been overjoyed to meet her, either.

Hell, it hadn't been his idea, he thought that evening as he strode into the rodeo grounds and made his way toward the back of the chutes. He'd have been just as happy to come to New York, ride the bulls and hit the road again without ever going near his mother's precious Professor Madeleine Decker.

And he'd tell his interfering parent so the next time he talked to her!

But right now he couldn't think about Madeleine Decker any longer. Or what he'd like to tell his mother. Right now he had to get his mind fixed on what really mattered—the eighteen-hundred-pound, one-horned Brahma he was going to be riding in less than an hour—a dipping, twisting brindle sadist called Banana Split.

"Hey, Chan." Wiley Nichols, one of his traveling partners, looked up from taping his ribs. "Me an' Gil an' Dev looked for you when we left the hotel. Where'd you go?"

Chan dropped his rigging bag and hunkered down to open it. "Did a little sight-seeing."

"Still?" Wiley grinned and shook his head. "You been here often enough I reckoned you'd seen everything by now."

"Not everything." Madeleine Decker's near-naked body, for instance. He hadn't seen that before.

And he needed to forget it now.

Chan took out his rigging carefully, hanging it on the fence, checking it over thoroughly. It was habit, it was necessary. He smoothed his hand over the rope, then took out his knife and picked out bits of flaking rosin, loosening them, then tugged on the rope gently, testing it and his strength against it, feeling the tension, the give.

Then he took it down and began to rosin it anew. When he had it rosined to his satisfaction, he did the same to his glove, slipping his fingers into it, working them around, flexing and stretching, taking his time, then getting the palm tacky, too. He clenched and unclenched his fist, making the leather more supple with the heat of his palm, feeling it grip and pull.

"What d'you know about ol' Mr. Banana Split?" he asked.

Wiley laughed. "Not much. Lasted about two seconds on him in Pendleton. Spins goin' out of the gate. Real tight and fast, man. Damn fast."

"To the right?"

"Nope. Left at first, but then he switched back, came right into my hand. Didn't want me to get too comfortable." Wiley grimaced.

"He'll try to sucker you," Denny Bailey put in. "Did it to me back in Cheyenne. Ducks his head way down, too, then like to take your head right off. Feel like you're goin' right over the top, then wham."

Chan knew what he meant.

"He's a hell-raiser, that one. But you stay with him and you'll get some bucks—the dollar kind," Denny said, grinning at Chan while he taped his shoulder.

Chan nodded. "Here's hoping." He shoved up his sleeve and started taping his wrist.

They were up to the calf roping. He could hear the announcer commiserating with a guy who'd missed with his second loop. He finished his taping, pulled his cuff down and snapped it. He could hear them bringing the bulls in.

He rubbed his palms down the sides of his jeans and closed his eyes, shutting out the announcer, shutting out Wiley, Denny, even Madeleine Decker's breasts.

Now, in his mind's eye all he could see was the brindle Brahma. He could see the bull as clear as he would when he rode him, could feel himself settling down on the bull's back, felt the tension in those surging muscles, the restlessness, the waiting.

He imagined his hand wrapping the rope, feeling the press of it against his palm as they tightened the slack. He could feel himself shrugging forward, settling in, taking hold, wrapping that one last loop.

He nodded his head.

The gate would open and it would begin.

With his whole body Chan felt the explosive power as he would feel it then. He anticipated the spins, the twists, the ducking head, the jumps. He thought the ride all the way through, his body shifting, adjusting, compensating as he envisioned it. Again. And again. And again. Right down to the moment when the buzzer would sound and he'd jump, landing clear and lifting his hands in triumph.

"Let's go," Wiley said, "'s time."

Wiley was up first. Then Denny. Then Gil Trabert. Chan could see his one-horned brindle bull being put into chute number 4. It went in easily enough, stood quietly. But that didn't mean much. Sometimes it meant the worst. It wasn't standing around that brought out the worst in a bull, it was having someone on his back.

One of the later riders began to help Wiley pull up the slack. Chan moved onto his own bull, leaning over the top of the chute, studying him, watching the hump move, watching the big head turn, the eye glint and roll. He dropped his rope down alongside the bull. Gus Campbell, a bronc rider, fished it through and tossed it over. Chan threaded the rope through the loop so it fit snugly. He heard the roar when Wiley's chute opened, and the almost instant groan that meant he'd hit the dirt.

Chan barely noticed. He had problems of his own right now. Or opportunities. Three quarters of a ton of them twitching and quivering right below him. He slipped his fingers into the glove and flexed them, then bound the glove tightly around his wrist.

"Do better'n I did," Wiley said, climbing up to lean over the fence. He wiped a smudge of dirt off his jaw.

Chan flashed him a faint grin. Out of the corner of his eye he saw Denny's chute open. The crowd roared. He straddled the chute as the buzzer sounded again.

"76," the announcer proclaimed. So Denny was now the man to beat.

"Steady, ol' fella," Chan said quietly as he settled down onto the brindle's broad back. Gus pulled up the slack. The rope tautened against Chan's gloved hand. The bull's muscles quivered under his touch.

"Tighter," he said and Gus pulled again, with Wiley helping.

Suddenly the brindle lurched sideways, mashing Chan's knee against the rails, then kicking the gate hard, making it shudder and clank. Chan ignored it, rubbing his hand along the rosined rope, warming it, then taking another wrap around his hand. Nothing was going to shake that grip loose. Nothing at all.

He sucked in his breath. He didn't hear the crowd, didn't see Gus or Wiley or anyone else. Saw only the patch at the top of the bull's hump.

His muscles tightened, the adrenaline flowed. Between his legs he could feel the warmth of the bull's hairy hide as he shifted and tensed. The power of the bull flowed up between the animal's back and his own legs, as if they were one.

They needed to be one, he thought grimly, monkeying his rear end forward, wedging his body against his hand and laying his forearm into the curve where his torso met his thigh. Toes out, heels in, to get the most contact, he gripped the bull with his legs, settled himself, got centered, tightened his grip, tucked in his chin.

"Ready?"

Chan nodded.

The gate swung open. The bull bunched, jumped, spun.

Time was never more relative, Chan had realized years ago, than when you were riding a bull. Eight seconds was nothing; it was an eternity. The world was a blur and yet, if all was well, he was never more focused.

Banana Split came out of the chute spinning. And Chan spun with him, let himself follow the line of the bull's spine, not fighting the tilt, going with it, yet prepared, ready for the snap back, ready for the duck, ready for anything.

And he got it. The quick jerk. The lunge forward to try to unseat him, then the snap back of the bull's head. He clung. The bull sunfished, twisting so that he and Chan lay almost horizontal. An instant later the brindle snapped back, hooking his horn around, trying to lift Chan right off his broad back. He stuck right where he was.

The bull twisted again, dropped his head and kicked out with his back feet. Twisted. Kicked again. Chan dug in his heels and gripped with his thighs to stop himself from being flung right over the bull's head. His hand slipped slightly and he clenched tighter. Not now. Not yet!

And then he heard the buzzer.

He opened his fist, felt the rope slip away, pushed off as the bull came back up again. That was what he wanted— a clean dismount, to land on his feet, to tip his hat to the crowd.

He almost made it. It was that last little kick that did it. The hoof caught him in the ribs as he bailed out, knocking him sideways into the dirt. He hit and rolled, lost sight of the bull entirely. But he could feel the force of the hooves right through the dirt. He jerked his head around, caught a glimpse of the clowns and rolled away from them. Then, grabbing his hat, he scrambled to his feet and headed for the fence.

"Give that man an 84," the loud speaker bellowed into the auditorium. "Richardson has an 84 and the lead!"

Hanging on to the fence, just now beginning to feel the throb in his ribs from the bull's last kick and the pain in his knee where he'd hit the chute before the ride even began, Chan grinned.

HE WAS STILL GRINNING when the phone rang in his hotel room in the city the next morning.

"Well?" Julia's voice said into his ear.

"84. I won."

"Lovely," his mother said. "Very nice. What about Madeleine?"

Chan, who'd managed to forget Madeleine Decker entirely in his pursuit of some fairly extravagant celebrating after last night's win, suddenly remembered her, breasts and all. His grin widened. "Saw her yesterday after-noon."

"And?"

He shrugged and felt his ribs protest. "And nothing. I met her. I said hello. I left. That's what I said I'd do."

"Chan." She was using her disapproving mother voice.

"You thought maybe I married her?" he teased.

"Chan. Didn't you at least invite her to dinner?"

"What for?"

"To be polite. To get to know her."

"I don't need to know her."

"What does that mean?"

"It means she's not my type."

"Chan," Julia began to protest.

"She's not!" Regardless of how tempting those breasts were, regardless of those big green eyes. "Ma, she's a col-lege professor, for God's sake."

"She's a graduate student."

"Same difference."

"Yes, but—"

"And she's a city girl."

"She was raised in a rice paddy in Bali."

"You know what I mean."

"I'm beginning to," Julia said quietly.

Her sudden acquiescence caught him off balance for a second. Then he said, "Well, then, you understand."

"I do. And maybe you're right." Her voice sounded al-most gentle now, consoling.

"I am."

"I really wouldn't have thought she was too much woman for you, but—"

"*What?*"

"I do understand. It's nothing to be ashamed of, Chan-ning," she went on in the same mild tone, just as if he hadn't yelped so loudly he'd wakened the four other guys in the room.

"I'm not ashamed!" he shouted.

Wiley lifted his head off the pillow and squinted disapprovingly at him. Devlin Gray, another bull rider who sometimes traveled with them, looked over blearily.

"Wha'dya do? Knock some girl up?" Kevin Skates, the rookie bull rider, wanted to know.

Chan glared at him, hauled himself out of the bed, ignoring his aching ribs and bad knee, and dragged the phone into the bathroom where he could have some privacy. Gil was asleep in the tub.

"And you have no need to be," Julia went on in that same damnably soothing voice.

Chan shut his eyes and rubbed his hand against his forehead. "Ma—"

"Just because you didn't finish college—"

"Ma, it has nothing to do with college!"

"Of course it doesn't," she said, which he knew was exactly the opposite of what she meant.

"Wha'dya wanta go to college for?" Gil mumbled.

Chan carried the phone back into the bedroom, tripping over somebody's duffel bag in the still-darkened room. He winced, hopping over to jerk open the drapes and let in the late-morning sunlight. He'd forgotten that all they had was a view of an airshaft. At high noon they got maybe fifteen minutes of sun. He left the drapes open, anyway.

"And just because you feel self-conscious about being a country boy—"

"I am not self-conscious!"

Julia sighed. "It should have been Trevor. I knew it should have been Trevor. I should have stopped the wedding," she said sadly.

"Don't be ridiculous," Chan snapped, furious. "Trev loves Marybeth."

"Love isn't everything."

"It's the only thing!"

There was a pregnant pause during which Julia said nothing at all and Chan realized exactly what it was that he had said.

"Oh, hell. Don't mind me," he muttered, raking a hand through his hair. "I'm half-asleep. I must be dreaming I'm Vince Lombardi."

"Poor Chan," his mother commiserated.

"Damn it! Stop that!"

She made a tsking sound. "Don't swear, Channing. I just want you to know that I understand. Don't worry about it, dear. You tried."

"I didn't—!"

"You can't help it if she's too much for you. Go back to sleep, darling. You need your rest if you're going to ride well today." She hung up.

She hung up! Chan stood there, apoplectic. How dare she hang up? He strangled the telephone, wishing it were his mother's neck.

Damn her, anyway! How could she insinuate such a thing? How could she possibly think that some weedy, small-breasted, jade-eyed *graduate student*—his mind twisted the words with a vengeance—was too much woman for him?

He said something as rude as it was succinct.

"Shuddup," someone mumbled. "Can'tcha let a guy sleep?"

MADELEINE COULDN'T believe her luck. They'd spent the whole evening together, she and her mother, and Channing Richardson's name hadn't come up.

Not once.

Of course she'd had to do some pretty fancy conversational footwork to keep her mother occupied with other things. She'd dredged up more anecdotes about past birthdays and asked more scintillating, penetrating questions about Antonia's latest research than she ordinarily asked in a year. She even asked cogent questions about a book on south-sea island puberty rites that her mother was telling her she ought to read, although she didn't care about it in the least.

When she finally caught a taxi back home after the birthday dinner they shared at Lazlo's and the requisite post-dinner brandy in Antonia's apartment, she'd had every right to congratulate herself.

Now she woke and yawned and stretched and wiggled her toes, glorying in the late lie-in she'd promised herself this Saturday morning.

Of course she would have to get to work eventually. There was still the missing reference, after all. But she could take her time going through her desk, and if it wasn't there, well, she could go back to the library at NYU and try to find it again.

After all, she didn't have anything else planned all afternoon. And no one was going to pester her about Channing Richardson.

She rolled over, anticipating another half hour's snooze.

There came a knock on the door.

Madeleine frowned, then dragged herself out of bed and pulled on her robe. It was probably Alfie, come to return the dress and regale her with the story of her latest heartthrob.

She padded out to the living room and opened the door.

"I've brought you a copy of the book," Antonia announced, brushing past Madeleine into the room.

"Book?" Madeleine stared after her blearily.

"On puberty in the Marshall Islands." Antonia waved the book in her face. "You were so interested. You did want to read it, didn't you?"

"Well," said Madeleine. "Um," she said.

"I was certain you would."

"Er...of course."

"Or—" Antonia's brows lifted above the tops of her glasses "—were you just expressing interest to avoid talking about what's been bothering you?"

Madeleine gave herself a little shake. "Bothering me? Nothing's bothering me. What makes you think something's bothering me?"

"You didn't even mention him."

Madeleine felt a distinct sense of foreboding. "Him whom?"

"Channing, of course."

Who else? Madeleine thought heavily. "What about Channing?"

"He came by yesterday, didn't he?" Antonia took off her coat and gave every indication of settling in. She marched into the kitchen and put on the kettle.

Madeleine followed her and turned it off again. "So what if he did?"

"I wondered why you were such a scintillating conversationalist last night," her mother said. She smiled like the Cheshire Cat. "I didn't think about Chan until this morning." She turned the kettle back on again.

"I don't quite make the connection," Madeleine said irritably. "And I don't want a cup of tea, Mother."

"But I do."

"You don't drink tea."

"It is never too late to begin," Antonia said loftily. "Tell me, dear, what did you think of him?"

Madeleine scowled. "What was I supposed to think? I mean, my God, Mother, he's a *cowboy!*"

Antonia smiled. "I wondered if you'd notice."

"How could I not?" Madeleine said darkly. She got down a cup and saucer for her mother, thumping them onto the counter with rather more force than was actually necessary.

"Scared you, did he?"

"Scared me? Of course not!"

"Of course not," Antonia mocked lightly. "How long did you talk to him?"

Madeleine reached for the sugar bowl. "Not long," she said to the cupboard.

"Did he like your apartment?"

"I don't know."

"He didn't say?"

"He didn't come in!"

"You didn't invite him in?" Antonia was clearly horrified.

I was naked, Madeleine wanted to shout. "I was getting ready to have dinner with you. I didn't have time. He showed up completely unannounced."

"I left a message saying he was coming," Antonia said in a wounded tone.

"I missed it."

"Well, even so, I would have understood if you'd called and said you'd be late."

"We had reservations."

"You should have brought him along."

"I didn't *want* to bring him along!"

"Ah, I see." Antonia perched on the bar stool at the kitchen counter and regarded her daughter pityingly.

Madeleine scowled. "What do you see?" she muttered after a moment.

"You really are afraid of him."

"The hell I am!"

"Don't swear, darling."

"I'll swear if I damned well please! And I am most certainly not afraid of him! What a completely ridiculous notion!"

"He's not at all what you're used to." Antonia went on as if Madeleine hadn't protested at all. "Strong, tough. Not exactly your standard professorial type."

"That's for sure. But it doesn't mean I'm afraid of him," Madeleine said grumpily.

Antonia's brows lifted. "No? Well, perhaps not. But you're doing a marvelous imitation of it." Then she smiled gently. "I suppose I should have guessed."

"What's that supposed to mean?"

"Well, you've always led a rather sheltered life where men are concerned, and—"

"I have not!"

At that outburst Antonia did blink.

"How can you say such a thing," Madeleine protested, "after Malcolm and...and Douglas...and...well, after Malcolm and Douglas." She wasn't mentioning Scott. Antonia had been out of the country during her months with Scott. She wished she hadn't brought up Malcolm or Douglas, either. Nerdy Malcolm and tweedy Douglas weren't in Channing Richardson's league, and both she and her mother knew it.

"Malcolm," Antonia echoed. "And Douglas." As if that said it all.

Madeleine was glad her mother didn't know about the fool she'd made of herself over Scott. She squared her shoulders. "I am not afraid of him, Mother."

"Whatever you say."

"I'm not!"

"Fine, you're not," Antonia said agreeably. Too agreeably, damn it. "Perhaps it's yourself you're afraid of."

Madeleine slapped her palms on the counter. "For heaven's sake!"

"Well, we do all have these biological urges, dear."

"You're afraid I might jump his bones, you mean?" The words came out at almost a squeak.

Antonia smiled blithely. "You said it, not me."

Madeleine could do nothing more than make an inarticulate sound in the face of that remark. Her face was flaming. Her fists were clenched.

"Perhaps," Antonia went on, "it's more that you're afraid to be around him? Afraid you might like him just a little?" She gave her daughter a teasing smile.

Madeleine didn't deign to reply.

"Well, it does make one wonder."

The kettle whistled. Antonia lifted the kettle and poured herself a cup of tea, concentrating on trailing the tea bag around in the water, letting Madeleine fume. "Sure you wouldn't like one?"

Madeleine snorted.

"Suit yourself. I wonder what Julia will say when I tell her." Antonia removed the tea bag and added a spoonful of sugar to the cup. "Well, I daresay she'll understand," she said sadly after a moment. She sipped the tea and made a face. "She knows it should have been Trevor."

"It shouldn't be any of them, Mother," Madeleine said firmly.

"But you wouldn't have been afraid of him."

"Mother!"

Antonia sighed. "Well, if you don't want the book, I'll just take it with me." She slid off the bar stool and, fetching her coat, started toward the door, leaving her tea on the counter, still steaming.

Madeleine stared after her, dazed. "What about your tea?"

Antonia waved an airy hand. "Oh, you're quite right, dear, as usual. I don't much like it."

SOMETIMES YOU WHIPPED the bull. Sometimes the bull whipped you.

Last night Chan had got an 84 and a win. Tonight he got kicked in the head.

At least that's what they told him happened.

He didn't remember. Didn't remember anything from the time the chute gate opened and he and a dun-colored bull called Clint's Revenge burst out into the arena, until he came around in the medical room with some doctor shining a light in his eyes and asking him his name and the date and where he was.

Where he was...?

Hell, even when he hadn't been kicked in the head, it could take him a while to remember where he was. It wasn't like he stayed in one place very long, was it?

"Concussion," the doctor decided. "You really should go over for X rays."

"Don't need 'em," Chan muttered, lifting a hand, wincing as he touched the lump on his temple. His head spun, and he felt sick when he lifted his head. "I'm fine," he said.

But he began to wonder if he was, when the doctor disappeared momentarily and his face was replaced by another one.

An unexpected one. A decidedly female one framed with oceans of springy dark hair. She had milky white skin, a smattering of freckles and wide green eyes which stared down at him.

He shut his eyes, disbelieving. He had never hallucinated before in his life, but he supposed there was always a first time.

Carefully he opened his eyes again. She was still there, peering down at him doubtfully.

He squinted, doubting, trying to focus. He lowered his gaze to her breasts.

By damn, it was her!

"I've been thinking," Madeleine Decker said.

Chapter Three

"Huh?"

"I said I've been thinking," Madeleine said briskly, "and I think we need to prove it to them."

"Who?" he said, still dazed.

"Whom," Madeleine corrected absently. "Our mothers, of course."

"Huh?" At this point monosyllables were all he was capable of.

"We need to prove to them that we don't belong together."

He tried to bring her into focus. "How?"

"By being together."

"Huh?" All right, so he wasn't doing justice to this conversation. But what the hell did she expect, busting in here like this, talking about God knew what?

He tried to focus again, but suddenly there were two of her. *Two Madeleine Deckers?* God Almighty. It was more than he could stand. He closed his eyes again.

"Excuse me, miss." The doctor's voice cut in. "I need to get an ice bag on his temple."

"Oh. Of course." She stepped out of the way, and Chan felt a towel wrapped around ice press against his temple, over his eyes.

"Hold this," the doctor said.

Somebody did.

"Hey, doc, c'mere. I think maybe Trabert's punctured his lung."

The doctor moved away. Chan lay there, the cold towel pressed to his temple, covering his eyes, as he listened to the shuffling of feet.

"Lie down here. Get his shirt off," the doctor said.

The cowboy coughed, making a gurgling sound.

"Call for the ambulance."

More feet shuffling, a door banging shut, then open again. Metal sounds of a gurney being wheeled in. "Here. Careful with him."

"I got 'im."

Chan heard Gil curse.

"Careful, I said," barked the doctor. "Come on. Move it."

More thumping and shuffling. Another door banging. Then silence. Almost.

"God," Madeleine said. Her voice was right next to him.

Startled, Chan reached up and pushed away the hand that held the compress to his head. It was hers.

Their gazes met.

There was only one of her again, thank God. One was more than enough. He tried to remember what she'd said. Something about being together?

No, she couldn't have. He must've imagined it.

He frowned. "What're you doing here?"

"I told you. We need to talk. Are you all right?" she asked him for the first time. He saw a sort of perplexed concern in her eyes as she looked down at him.

"I've been better."

She pursed her lips. "I don't know why you aren't dead. It's a damned stupid thing to do, riding bulls."

"Nobody's asking you to do it."

"Nobody should ask anybody to do it."

"Nobody does."

Their gazes locked again.

God, his head hurt. He let out a long breath and shut his eyes and moaned.

"Don't faint," Madeleine said urgently. "You can't faint."

He opened his eyes again and regarded her blearily. "Why not?"

"Because . . . because I'm the only one here."

"So leave."

"Don't be an ass, Richardson. I'm taking care of you."

"The hell you are!"

"I am. I'm putting on the compress. The doctor handed it to me. What was I supposed to do? Hand it back?"

"Give it to me." He held out his hand.

"No." She held it against his temple again, glaring at him as if she expected he might try to fight her for it.

If he'd thought he'd have won, he would have. Tonight, though, all bets were off. He didn't have the strength to fight a kitten. It hurt even to glare at her. He had to shut his eyes once more.

"Don't—"

"I'm not going to faint," he growled, his fingers plucking irritably at the plastic on the cot. "Stop worrying. I promise I'll tell you if I'm going to."

"Thank you."

"Don't mention it."

He didn't know how long they stayed there that way. He didn't faint precisely, but he had trouble keeping his eyes open, and he might've dozed.

Next thing he knew, the doctor was back saying, "Rodeo's over. Everybody's gone. Everybody but you, that is, Richardson, and my roper with the broken fingers. I really think X rays would be a good idea."

"An excellent idea," Madeleine put in.

"I don't need—"

"But I suppose, perhaps, you'd need to have brains to see that," she went on over his protest.

"Fine," he snapped. "I'll get X rays."

The doctor flashed him a quick smile. "Good. You'll go with him, won't you?" he said to Madeleine. "St. Luke's-Roosevelt, all right? I'll just give them a call to let them know you're on your way. I've got to see to the roper, so if you'll excuse me..." And he was gone, leaving Chan and Madeleine alone again.

Chan wished like hell the doc had taken her with him. "I can manage on my own," he said gruffly.

Madeleine got up and moved away, but she didn't leave, just stood watching him, waiting. Daring him, undoubtedly.

He gritted his teeth, trying to muster enough willpower to get himself vertical. Finally, slowly, carefully, keeping his head as steady as he could, Chan levered himself to a sitting position.

The room spun giddily. His fingers tightened on the edge of the cot.

"Go see if Wiley's out there," he commanded.

"Who's Wiley?"

"My buddy. Short guy. Red shirt. Brown hair. And a black eye," he added as an afterthought.

"He went with the punctured lung."

It figured. Wiley and Gil Trabert had been down the road together a time or two, and Trabert was in worse shape then he was. "Never mind, then. I'll get a cab."

"You'll fall over before you reach the sidewalk."

"So step over me."

"God, you're a jerk, Richardson. Come on." She grabbed his arm and steadied him as he shoved himself to his feet.

"'m all right now," he said, trying to shrug her off.

"Sure you are," Madeleine said in a tone that meant exactly the opposite. She started hauling him toward the door.

"I need my rigging bag."

"I've got it."

Chan grumbled, but she didn't let go of him all the way down the corridor out of the building and onto the sidewalk.

The noise was deafening. Cars zipped past, buses lumbered and blew out exhaust. Horns honked, sirens wailed. Underfoot the subway thrummed. His head felt as if someone were pounding a jackhammer right into it.

Madeleine raised her arm and flagged down a taxi. "In you go," she said and scrambled in after him before he could protest. "St Luke's-Roosevelt," she told the driver.

Chan leaned his head back against the seat and shut his eyes, not opening them again until Madeleine said, "Here we are."

Carefully he eased himself out of the cab. "Thanks." He started to fish in his rigging bag for his wallet, but Madeleine had already paid the driver.

"This way," she said and took him by the arm and towed him down another long corridor. Chan let himself be towed. It was easier than fighting with her about it.

Emergency rooms, he'd discovered long ago, were pretty much the same wherever you went. In New York City that was still true, only more so.

There were more people, more knife wounds, more gunshots, more broken bones, more blood, more paperwork, more waiting.

Chan filled out everything he could, then sank down on a cracked plastic chair, closed his eyes and let it all wash over him indifferently.

Madeleine sat beside him. Every time his eyes flicked open he could see her, straight as a fence post, next to him, breathing shallowly, knotting her fingers in her lap until at last they called his name.

Thank God they wouldn't let her come with him to get his head X-rayed and the cut on his temple bandaged. "So long," he said and smiled as they led him away. He looked forward to coming back and finding her gone.

When he did an hour later she was right where he'd left her, still sitting rigid as a poker. She looked up and watched as he crossed the room toward her.

"Thought you'd've left," he muttered.

She shook her head.

"Somebody nail you to the chair?"

"My mother."

"*What?*"

"She would have wanted to know why I didn't stay."

He frowned at her. "Why would you even tell her?"

"I wouldn't have to. She'd know."

It was said with such fatalistic simplicity that Chan couldn't doubt it. Besides, he knew his own mother was capable of the same omniscience.

"Are you finished?" Madeleine asked him.

"Gotta wait for the results. Feel free to leave."

Of course she didn't. She opened the magazine she'd been holding and began to read again.

Chan slumped once more onto his chair. It was another forty-five minutes before the nurse came toward him.

"Good news. Your cranial X rays show nothing, Mr. Richardson," she said.

Chan blinked. Madeleine's lips twitched. She tried unsuccessfully not to laugh.

The nurse looked at Madeleine reproachfully. "It still isn't a laughing matter, you know. A blow to the head is always serious. He needs quiet, rest, someone to wake him periodically. Can you do that?" she asked Madeleine doubtfully.

"No, she can't," Chan said firmly before Madeleine could say a word. "I'm not her problem. Thanks."

He hauled himself to his feet and started for the door, hoping he could lose Madeleine in the crush, but when he got outside she was right there next to him.

"Where's your hotel?" she asked.

He considered not telling her, but it didn't seem worth the effort. He gave her the name. She flagged another cab, got in beside him and accompanied him to the hotel.

"You know, you're a lot like a cattle dog of my dad's," he said as they hurtled across town in the late-night traffic.

"From you I suppose that might be a compliment."

A corner of his mouth lifted. "Take it any way you want. Suit yourself."

"I usually do."

Probably she did, he thought muzzily. She sure as hell seemed to be getting her own way tonight. Why was she bothering? What was it she'd said earlier about proving something to their mothers? Something about being together?

"What'd you mean?" he asked now. "Proving what to our mothers?"

"I told you, I've been thinking."

"Sounds ominous."

She ignored him, going on. "I don't know about yours, but my mother seems to think I'm scared to have anything to do with you. She thinks my not inviting you in means I'm somehow afraid of you." She gave a short half laugh, which showed exactly how she felt about that notion.

Chan felt unaccountably nettled. "And of course you're not."

"I most certainly am not," Madeleine said forcefully. "I considered ignoring her, but my mother is hard to ignore." She sighed as if she'd had a wealth of experience trying to do just that. "So I thought if I spent some time with you, I'd prove it to her. And at the same time I'd be able to prove how unsuitable we are."

Chan tried his best to follow her thinking. It might have had something to do with being kicked in the head, but he wasn't sure he was accomplishing it. "So that's what this is? Trailing around after me tonight?"

Madeleine gave him a pained look. "Hardly. One evening would never prove anything. According to my mother, a truly reliable field study takes at least two to three months."

Chan stared at her. His head pounded. *"Two to three months? What the hell are you talking about?"*

Madeleine spread her hands. "Spending time together."

"Two to three months?"

"I'm not any more thrilled about the idea than you are, believe me," she said flatly. "But I don't see any other alternative. Anyway it might work now that you're injured..."

"I'm not injured."

"You have a concussion. You have a bandage. You look pretty injured to me."

"Well, I'm not. It's nothing. Not the cut. Not the concussion. I've had 'em before."

"The effects of concussion are cumulative," Madeleine informed him. "You need rest. You could stay and—"

"I'll rest on the plane. I'm riding in a rodeo in Texas on Wednesday. I'm going to New Mexico next weekend. It's the way I earn my living. I don't earn if I don't ride."

"I see." She was sitting very still, her hands folded in her lap as the taxi hurtled down Broadway.

Chan slanted her a quick glance. "Good."

She sighed. "Well, if you won't consider taking a couple of months off from getting kicked in the head and stay here in New York, I guess there's only one thing to do."

"What's that?"

"I'll come with you."

CHAN THOUGHT Madeleine must've got kicked in the head, too. Nothing he said made the slightest impression on her. He told her she was nuts. She ignored him. He told her she didn't know what she was getting into. She said she could guess. He told her she wouldn't last a week.

She fixed him with a hard-eyed stare and said, "You want to bet?"

Finally, as the taxi arrived at his hotel, he thought she'd come to her senses because she agreed that it was perhaps not a great idea.

Then she looked at him and challenged, "Do you have a better one?"

He didn't.

Ideas were not Chan's strong suit at the best of times. He was a man of action, not speculation. And tonight he felt at a bigger disadvantage than ever.

He fumbled for his wallet and handed her twenty dollars.

"What's this?"

"My share. You can go home in the same cab."

She handed it back and got out instead. She stood on the curb, holding his rigging bag, waiting for him while he paid.

Dev and Denny passed them on their way out. "Hey, Chan!" they greeted him. They scrutinized Madeleine thoroughly, and their grins widened.

"Nice goin', Chan," Dev said, winking broadly.

"We won't be in early. We promise." Denny grinned.

Chan glanced at Madeleine, trying to gauge her reaction to their innuendo. Was that just possibly a faint scarlet on her cheeks? Whatever it was, her expression didn't change a bit.

Probably didn't even recognize sexual innuendo when she heard it, he thought glumly as they walked to the elevator. Probably preferred books to men. Books with footnotes and annotated bibliographies.

"Don't you think this is a little risky? Coming with me to my room?" he challenged her with as much rakishness as he could muster.

"Should I?" She said it in such a flat, disinterested tone that his own cheeks warmed.

Damn her self-possession, anyway. He scowled and looked away, staring at the doors, determined to ignore her. He could see the curve of her breasts out of the corner of his eye. His jaw tightened.

She didn't say anything else, simply came along with him until he'd unlocked the door to his room. Then he paused and looked down at her. "Coming in?"

It wasn't precisely an invitation, more of a dare.

"Is anyone else here?"

"Not a soul." He gave her a wolfish grin.

"Then I will."

And in she came, stepping carefully over the rigging bags, saddles and piles of all the dirty clothes that five men could accumulate, given a couple of days.

"They said to stay with you," she reminded him and started to move some of the clothes off the chair so she could sit down.

"I'll do that." Chan bent down to shovel some of the clothes off the chair, but his head throbbed and he stood up again, wincing.

"You shouldn't bend over," Madeleine said. "I'll do it. You go to bed."

He looked at her, nonplussed. "Go to bed? With you here?"

"You're afraid I might attack you?"

"Yeah, sure." He just wished he was feeling up to par. He'd enjoy it more.

"Then do I make you nervous?"

"Of course not."

"Well, then . . . ?" She sat down and looked at him expectantly. When he still didn't move, she sighed. "The nurse said you needed someone to keep an eye on you while you slept, Richardson. Until someone else gets here, I'm staying."

"I'll be fine."

Madeleine didn't reply, simply folded her hands in her lap and sat there, looking placidly up at him.

Chan's fists clenched and unclenched. He didn't suppose, the way he felt, that he could pick her up and throw her out, but God knew he was tempted.

Finally he muttered, "Swell, stay. I'm taking a shower," and stalked into the bathroom and shut the door.

He needed a shower. He had dried blood on his hands, dust all over him, and though he was more or less immune to it now, he knew he reeked of dirt and sweat and essence of bull.

By rights the smell of him alone should've driven Madeleine Decker away. But he didn't have a doubt she was camped out in his hotel room for the duration.

In fact she was probably timing him and would burst in to rescue him from drowning, if she thought he was taking a moment longer than necessary.

If he didn't feel so lousy, that might be interesting.

HE WAS TAKING forever. She had visions of him drowning, falling over, concussed, and perishing just feet away. She had visions of his strong-boned face capped by wet dark hair, visions of his lean, hard-muscled naked body, visions of...

She needed to stop having visions, that was certain!

Jumping to her feet, Madeleine paced to and fro, side-stepping the rigging bags, the duffels, the beer and beef jerky and potato chips and scattered piles of clothing, trying not to think of Chan Richardson's body, clothed or unclothed.

This was not the way she'd planned this evening at all.

And, whether it looked like it or not, she had planned it, had planned it well.

She'd fumed for hours after her mother's accusations. She'd denied both to her mother and herself that she could possibly be afraid of Chan Richardson. He was just, well, not the sort of man she knew or understood. Not that she was a connoisseur, but he was a *cowboy,* for God's sake!

But just because she wasn't used to men like him, it didn't mean she was afraid of him—or of spending time with him. She just couldn't see any point to doing so.

But the longer she'd thought about it, the more she'd realized that she would never convince Antonia of that.

Unless—

No. She'd rejected the notion out of hand. It was stupid. It was ridiculous. It was more than that. It was preposterous.

But in the end, it had been the only thing she'd been able to think of.

If she was ever going to be safe from Antonia's lingering doubts, speculative glances and knowing smiles, if she was ever going to convince Antonia—and herself—that Channing Richardson was not her perfect mate, she would have to offer to spend some time with him.

And walk away from him.

And there was only one way to do that.

She'd bought a ticket to the rodeo. Just to see him after, talk to him, convince him to go along with her plan.

She certainly hadn't intended to get stuck with him for the rest of the night!

But when the doctor had asked her to look after him, she hadn't had much choice. She knew as sure as anything that her mother would, one way or another, discover that she had been there. And there would be hell to pay if she left her mother's friend's son uncared for.

Plus, he hadn't agreed yet.

Maybe he wouldn't. She brightened at the thought. She hadn't considered that possibility. But if Chan said no, she'd be off the hook. *She* would have volunteered. *She* would have dared. *He* would have said no.

The more she thought about it, the more likely it seemed. Surely he wouldn't want her tagging along after him for two long months, getting in his way, cramping his style with the women he really preferred.

She thought about what sort of women a man like Chan Richardson might prefer. Sweet airheaded women who would bat their eyes and tell him what a big strong man he was, undoubtedly.

Well, she wasn't good at that. Even when she tried. Just ask Scott.

Damn it, why was he taking so long?

Of course he'd been a mess, Madeleine was willing to grant that. Bloody and dusty, with a grimy streak of some unspeakable substance on his cheek, he had definitely needed a shower. But even if he'd fought every battle of the Thirty Years' War he ought to be clean by now.

She moved closer to the bathroom door, listening to see if, over the noise of the water, she could hear him moving around. She couldn't.

She tapped lightly. "Ahem."

No response. She chewed her lip a moment, then tapped again, louder this time. "Er, Richardson?"

Still nothing.

Another of those blasted visions assailed her. The naked body one. She pressed her fists against her eyes. The water drummed on.

A peek wouldn't hurt. Just one peek to see if he was upright and, presumably, breathing. Nothing more. If he wasn't, she'd call 911. If he was, she'd simply shut the door. It wasn't voyeurism; it was good sense. He had, after all, sustained a blow to the head. Besides, she'd seen a man's naked body before.

She turned the doorknob slowly, easing it open. Steam wafted out. She poked her head around the corner of the door. There was a translucent white shower curtain with a body behind it. The body was upright and, presumably, breathing. It was also lean, well-muscled and decidedly male.

She didn't shut the door.

It was fair play, she told herself. After all, he hadn't minded taking a good long look at her yesterday. So what if she'd had on a few more clothes than he did. He had a shower curtain.

Besides, it was research. Her mother wanted her to marry this man, for goodness' sake.

A woman couldn't even consider such a thing until she'd checked out the goods, could she?

But even Madeleine couldn't make herself believe that. In fact, she blushed just thinking it and shut the door as quickly and as silently as she could.

Then, wiping suddenly damp palms on the sides of her slacks, she went to sit back down in the chair. She tried to think about what she would do tomorrow, the run in the park she and Alfie would take, the bread she would bake, the chapter of her dissertation that she was working on.

She couldn't do it. Her mind seemed to have more free will than she did—or more determination. All it wanted to do was think about Channing Richardson naked. And there seemed to be nothing she could do to stop it!

She scanned the room for some distraction and grabbed a magazine that was falling out of one of the duffel bags, but naked women were not the sort of distraction she needed. Immediately she stuffed it back.

The water stopped running. She could hear him moving around now. He bumped into something, cursed. She half stood, then sat down again and knotted her fingers together.

"Are you all right in there?" she called and was annoyed at how shaky her voice sounded. She wondered what was the matter with her, then remembered she hadn't eaten any supper. She was probably weak from hunger.

"Terrific," came an answering masculine growl.

"You don't . . . need help?"

"No, I don't 'need help.'" His voice mocked her. "I told you, go away."

"And I told you I'm... not going to." The last three words faded a bit as the door opened and Madeleine was confronted with Chan semi-dressed. He was barefoot, his jeans zipped but not buttoned, his shirt hanging open, treating her to a slice of bare, lightly furred chest. She swallowed carefully; her mouth seemed suddenly dry.

Chan looked at her wearily. "Well, I suppose I can't throw you out."

He sank down onto the bed, his feet on the floor, his forearms resting on his knees. He ducked his head, then straightened up quickly, as if the position had hurt him.

Madeleine steeled herself against feeling sorry for him. As he had pointed out, no one asked him to ride that bull.

"So," she said briskly. "What do you say? Shall I come with you?"

"I get a choice?"

"Well, I'm certainly not going to invite myself along. Of course you get a choice."

He didn't say anything. He didn't even move. She couldn't tell for a moment if he was thinking or if he'd fallen asleep sitting up. Then slowly he opened his eyes and fixed her with a fuzzy stare.

"No," he said. "I don't."

Madeleine looked at him with wide-eyed innocence. "What do you mean?"

"I mean, no, I don't get a choice. You're setting me up. You're willing to come along so you look good to your mother and to mine. I say no, I look like a chicken."

He was more astute than she'd given him credit for. "Well, I assume that means you want me to come then," she said airily, or as airily as she could through tightly clenched teeth. "It really doesn't matter to me."

He sighed and shut his eyes and was silent so long that she thought he really had fallen asleep.

"Richardson?"

He opened them once again and met her gaze. His face was absolutely expressionless, but his eyes were curiously bright. Slowly he nodded his head. "All right, Decker. You wanta go down the road with me. You're on. We'll do it."

Chapter Four

Wyoming, seven months later

He never thought she would.

When he'd said yes clear back last October, he'd thought at worst they'd get it over with right then, and it sure as hell wouldn't take two months. But if she wanted to come to Texas and New Mexico with him, let her, he'd thought. It might be good for a laugh. And when his head felt better, he was sure he could think of other things it might be good for. Compatibility tests, if you please.

The thought had made him grin even though his head still hurt.

But Madeleine had said no. She'd said they had to do it properly. Scientifically.

"Under controlled conditions?" he joked.

But she'd been absolutely serious. "If we want them to believe us, yes."

And coming with him then was out of the question. She had her dissertation to work on—research to do, data to collect, evidence to find. She could do it in six months, maybe seven.

"The end of May," she'd told him. "I should be ready by the end of May."

"Next summer? You're nuts. That's my busiest time of the year."

"The busier, the better. You'll be out of my hair, I'll stay out of yours. But Mother won't have a thing to complain about."

Mother had no right to complain in any case, to Chan's way of thinking. Mother was answerable for the whole mess.

But he hadn't said so then. His head ached. He wanted to sleep. And hell, in six or seven months chances were she wouldn't even remember.

When he called home for Mother's Day, he got the shock of his life.

"Madeleine Decker called," Julia told him, bemused. "She says she'll be at the ranch at the end of the month. She says you can pick her up here." She paused. "What are you up to, Chan?"

"Up to? Me?" His voice had changed when he was fourteen, but you wouldn't have known it to hear him then. "I'll call her," he promised.

He did. Right then. From a roadside phone booth in Idaho.

"Are you nuts?" he blurted without preamble as soon as she answered the phone.

"No, I'm sorry. I'm Madeleine," she said, absolutely deadpan. "And who are you?"

"This is Chan Richardson," he said through clenched teeth.

There was a sigh. "Why am I not surprised?"

He ignored that. "What the hell have you been telling my mother? What's this nonsense about meeting me at the ranch?"

"Well, in two weeks it'll be the end of May. Where do you want me to meet you?"

He still couldn't fathom that she was actually coming. "You're not serious. You're not coming."

"Of course I'm serious. And I'm coming. We agreed."

"But—"

"Chickening out, Richardson?" she asked sweetly.

His teeth came together. "Like hell I am."

"Then where?"

He looked over his shoulder at his camper, full of his traveling buddies, Wiley, Dev, Gil, all watching him with curious, speculative grins. He shut his eyes.

"End of May?" he said hollowly. He counted two weeks down the road. "Vegas."

"Las Vegas!" She sounded like he'd suggested Sodom or Gomorrah.

"What's the matter with Las Vegas?"

"Have you got a few years?"

"Too tough a town for you, Decker?"

He heard a sharp, explosive breath. "Never mind. I'll be there. No problem. I'll let you know what time I'm arriving."

A TIME THAT WOULD be here in less than twenty-four hours from now.

"This is crazy," he complained to his mother. He was pacing around her kitchen, feeling as if the hound of hell was nipping at his heels. He'd purposely stopped in on his way to Vegas, ostensibly to take another shot at staying on Danny Boy, but actually in the desperate hope that she'd tell him what a bad idea it was, how wrong she'd been, and then maybe she'd volunteer to call Madeleine Decker and head her off at the pass.

She said, "You can't know how delighted I am, Chan. When Antonia and I heard, we thought it was an absolutely brilliant plan."

"Absolutely nuts," Chan corrected. "Can you imagine what it'll be like, dragging some...some...*professor* all over the place?"

"Enlightening, I should think," Julia said brightly. "For both of you. You'll get to know each other so well."

Chan groaned at the thought. "She'll freak."

"I doubt it. You might be surprised."

"The only thing that'll surprise me is if she lasts longer than a week."

Believing Madeleine wouldn't last more than that was the only bright light in Chan's life at the moment. It sure wasn't his spot in the standings. He was barely in the top fifteen. Nor was it the way his ribs and shoulder felt, which was as if that last bull in Montana had ridden him rather than the other way around.

He never should have tackled Danny Boy this morning. He flexed his shoulders and stretched painfully, then did another lap of the kitchen floor and kicked at the rag rug underfoot. But really his muscles weren't the problem. The problem was Madeleine. Julia watched, bemused.

"You're enjoying this," Chan accused her.

"A little."

"A lot."

His mother laughed and slid off the stool. "Well, yes. It's been a long time since I've seen you unnerved by anything."

"I'm not unnerved."

"Aren't you." It wasn't a question.

He gave her a wry smile.

She smiled gently back at him. "I love you, Chan."

"You sure as hell have a funny way of showing it. You never set up any of your other sons."

"I never got the chance. Perhaps if you'd been quicker off the mark—"

Chan said a rude word.

"Don't swear, dear." Julia reached up and ruffled a hand through his hair exactly the way she'd done when he was no taller than her waist. "You're taking this much too seriously. I didn't mean this to be a great trial, only a good way for you to get to know a woman who might be right for you."

"*Madeleine Decker?*"

She gave a self-conscious little laugh. "You know me and my charts."

"There's more to marriage than charts, Ma."

She nodded. "You're absolutely right. The most important thing is love."

"And you set me up with Madeleine Decker, anyway?"

She hugged him once more and stepped back and brushed light fingers against his cheek as she looked up into his eyes. "*You* set you up," she pointed out. "Antonia and I only suggested the possibility that you might like each other."

"That's all you did, huh?"

Julia had the grace to look slightly abashed. "It's not as if it's forever, Chan. Only a little while."

"Two damned months!"

"You chose the time frame," she reminded him.

"*She* chose it. Scientifically."

Julia smiled. "There is something to be said for science, Chan."

He snorted.

"And Madeleine is a bright young woman."

"Madeleine is a pain in the a—neck."

"Give her a chance, Chan. Who knows? You really might fall in love with her."

Chan rocked slowly back and forth on his heels and didn't say a word. There was no use arguing about an absurdity like that.

BACK IN OCTOBER June had seemed centuries away. Or years away at least. Far enough so that for the longest time the reality of spending two months with Channing Richardson had been but a dim threat clouding Madeleine's horizon.

Any number of unforeseen things could happen between late October and the end of May, she'd assured herself. Chances were she would never have to spend all of June and July with Chan Richardson.

Unfortunately nothing unforeseen did.

The world didn't end. She didn't fall madly and senselessly in love with anyone else—or even marry someone else whom she wasn't madly and senselessly in love with.

Her perfect man was as elusive as ever. Not that she'd gone looking for him.

She'd been too busy.

Still she might have been able to conveniently forget about their agreement if Antonia, like the Chinese water torture in human form, hadn't dropped Chan's name into every conversation, and then met Madeleine for brunch on Mother's Day with a tall blond man in tow.

"I know you remember Scott Barlowe," she said, oblivious to Madeleine's suddenly pale face. "You wrote me a letter on his behalf several years ago."

"Of course she does," Scott said smoothly and touched his lips to Madeleine's icy ones, then slipped an arm around her to give her a squeeze. "How's my Madeleine?"

Fortunately for Madeleine, she hadn't had to answer.

Antonia had gone right on. "Scott just got in from Bali last night. He's been there all semester doing research where Lothar and I were. And he's going back when Jeremiah and I go next month. But he called me last night to catch me up on things, and I knew since you spent so much time there as a child, you'd want to hear, too. Isn't that nice?"

Mute, Madeleine nodded.

The waitress took their order and disappeared. Scott smiled and talked about Bali. He talked about places she'd been as a girl, people she knew, things she'd seen. A pitcher of Bloody Marys arrived. Then their eggs Benedict. Scott talked on, enthused. Antonia questioned eagerly, her eyes alight.

And Madeleine listened—and yet somewhere deep inside, she didn't listen at all.

He'd gone to Bali, she thought. Just as she'd dreamed. He'd gone to Bali and—

"—this summer, Madeleine?"

She blinked, aware that her mother had spoken to her. "What?"

"I said, why don't you bring your dissertation along and join us this summer? Jeremiah and me. And Scott. I'm sure Scott would be glad of your company, wouldn't you?"

"Absolutely," Scott agreed and gave Madeleine a fresh glimpse of the smile she'd once been in love with.

Madeleine looked at him, she looked at her mother. She thought about her hopes, her dreams, the ashes they'd become. And she knew she would die before she raked over them again. Both Antonia and Scott smiled at her encouragingly.

"I can't," she said.

"Can't?" Scott echoed. He actually looked disappointed.

Antonia frowned. "You can't? Why not?"

"Because," said Madeleine rashly, "I'm doing what you've been after me to do for months, Mother. I'm going down the road with Channing Richardson. I'm giving your perfect man a chance."

AND NOW, heaven help her, here she was.

She had sublet her apartment, sent her cat and her slinky black dress to live with Alfie for the summer, packed her laptop computer, her notes and her floppy disks, thrown all the jeans and T-shirts she owned into a pair of duffel bags, told her dissertation director she'd be in touch every week, and, at one forty-five on the last Sunday in May Madeleine Decker had boarded a plane to Las Vegas.

She'd never been to Las Vegas in her life, couldn't imagine a life in which a visit to Vegas would ever be required.

Surprise, surprise.

Chan had agreed to return her to the airport in Cheyenne, Wyoming at the end of Cheyenne Frontier Days. In the interim Madeleine would spend two months— sixty-one days or 1464 hours or 87,840 minutes, more or less—in Channing Richardson's company.

Unless, she thought hopefully as the plane lifted off that afternoon, the plane crashed or he came to his senses before then and simply didn't show up.

No such luck.

When she walked off the plane and into the airport there he was.

She'd come on this absurd journey to avoid Scott, to avoid temptation, to avoid making a fool of herself a second time. She'd come to prove to her mother that Chan

Richardson wasn't the perfect man, either. She'd come to prove to herself that she could easily resist the Richardson charm as well as the Richardson genes and the Richardson handsome face.

Well, she told herself, good luck.

There must be upwards of four million men in New York. She saw hundreds, perhaps thousands, every day, and she couldn't ever remember seeing one like him. Certainly she'd never met one who seemed half as alive, half as vigorously masculine as the man walking toward her now.

With his dark hair peeking out from beneath the straw cowboy hat, with his deeply tanned face and pale blue, ice chip eyes, Channing Richardson looked every bit the handsome, hard, devil-may-care cowboy he was.

Back in New York City, the thought of spending two months with him had seemed annoying but not particularly daunting. But that was then—when he'd been dwarfed by skyscrapers, hemmed in by taxis and buses, kicked by a bull and lying there looking at her bleary-eyed, through a concussed fog.

This was now.

Madeleine's only consolation was that he looked no less thrilled to see her than she was to be here.

He took his hat off and raked his fingers through his hair, ruffling it. Then he slapped his hat down on his head again, tugged it over his eyes and moved toward her with as much enthusiasm as Gary Cooper facing a baddie at high noon.

He walked with a slow measured stride. A gunslinger's stride, Madeleine thought warily. There was a roll to his gait, too, almost as if his hips fitted differently onto his legs.

Damn it, she thought. She was not going to think about Chan Richardson's hips and legs.

He stopped directly in front of her. His blue eyes met her green ones. "You came."

Such enthusiasm was hardly overwhelming. She lifted her chin. "Did you think I wouldn't?"

"Hoped." For a second a heart-stopping grin flickered across his face. "No one ever said *I* had any sense. Reckon I was counting on you."

"Don't," Madeleine warned him.

His brows lifted, then he nodded. "Fair enough. So, you ready?"

As I'll ever be, Madeleine thought. She nodded.

"Come on, then. Let's get your gear." He turned and started toward the baggage claim. Madeleine had to almost run to keep up.

"So, what's the plan?" she asked. They hadn't discussed anything. She had done her best, made lists of what she'd thought she would need, plans for testing their compatibility so she'd have plenty of documented evidence for her mother come August. But she hadn't had a chance to talk to Chan at all other than two brief "I'm-in-a-phone-booth-gotta-run" conversations.

He shrugged. "I'm goin' down the road. You're tagging along."

So he was going to be difficult. "That's not precisely the way I would have put it," she said stiffly after a moment.

Chan slanted her a sideways glance. "What would you call it?"

"A mutual survival pact. Isn't that the general idea? We've banded together so we can convince our mothers not to meddle."

"Makes us sound like a couple of grade schoolers," he grumbled.

"You agreed that it was necessary last fall," she reminded him.

"The more fool I."

"Well, we can certainly call it off," she said. "There's a phone right over there. You just call your mother and tell her you chickened out. Then I'll just ring up my mother and—"

She wouldn't, of course. Her mother would see it as an opportunity to drag her along to Bali.

"I'm not chickening out!" Chan snapped.

"Well, then, we're going. So why don't you just try to be civil?"

"I am civil. You want me to sweep you off your feet? Throw my arms around you? Give you a kiss? Test for compatibility?" He gave her a leer instead.

She backed up a step. "Of course not. But you could show a few manners."

"Maybe I don't have any."

"Maybe you don't."

They glared at each other. Madeleine's chin rose in a stubborn tilt. She refused to give an inch.

Finally Chan grinned and winked at her. "Gonna be a hell of a two months, Mad, ol' girl."

"Don't call me Mad!"

Chan just laughed. "Right, Decker."

They reached the baggage claim, but she didn't see her luggage. She glanced warily at Chan. He was watching the women go by. She could almost see the wheels turning in his head.

"So," she said briskly, "did you ride this afternoon?"

"Huh?" He jerked his gaze back from a statuesque blonde he'd been evaluating. "Er, yeah. I did."

"How did you do?" Madeleine wasn't sure if she should ask that or not. She didn't know what the proper etiquette was for inquiring about the success or failure of bull rides. Frankly she didn't care.

"82."

Which meant what? He must have noticed her baffled look because he went on to explain.

"Out of a possible score of 100. There's two judges and each of them can award a maximum of 50 points, 25 for the rider and 25 for the bull."

"They grade the bull?" She was surprised.

"Yep. That's why you want a rank one."

"Rank?"

"Bad. Mean. Stomp you into the dirt."

"Ah. The worse the bull the higher the score?"

"You got it."

"And 82 is good?"

"Not bad." He glanced at his watch.

"Are we in a hurry?"

"I said we'd have dinner with some friends. Here comes the luggage. Do you see yours?"

"Those two navy duffels."

Chan grabbed them off the baggage carrier, hefting them both easily. Then he headed toward the exit, leaving Madeleine once again to catch up or trail in his wake. But when they got to the door, he stopped and held it open for her.

She blinked, opened her mouth to comment, then thought better of it. But she was still puzzling over his gallantry when they reached the lot.

She trailed just behind him, wondering what kind of car he drove. Something sturdy and macho, no doubt. She made bets with herself as they approached sturdy Jeeps and Ford utility vehicles and anything else that seemed likely.

She would have lost no matter which she bet on. He didn't drive a car at all; he drove a truck.

The truck didn't surprise her. What surprised her was the large camper on back. It was less a truck than a sort of mini motor home.

Madeleine stopped dead. "This isn't—"

"Home sweet home," Chan said. He held the back door open for her.

Madeleine hesitated, this time not in amazement at his chivalry, but in awareness of some very important questions that she had failed to ask.

She'd expected car trips with Chan, yes. She knew "going down the road" meant literally going down the road, traveling from one rodeo to the next, one town to the next, one state to the next.

But she'd also expected nighttime stops complete with motel rooms. *Separate* motel rooms. Space. Privacy. Not twenty-four-hour-a day togetherness in a camper the size of a Shredded Wheat box.

"Don't tell me. You're waiting for an engraved invitation?" His head was cocked and he was grinning at her.

Madeleine shot him a hard glare. Why in heaven's name hadn't he mentioned their living quarters, told her what she was getting into? But then, she imagined him saying, if living quarters were an issue, why hadn't she asked?

Indeed, why hadn't she?

Because she was an idiot, apparently.

Well, yes. And she knew what he'd say if she protested now: "So chicken out."

No way.

Taking a deep breath, she climbed in.

It was bigger than she'd thought. In fact, the back of the truck with its tiny kitchen area, its table and couch and bed seemed almost spacious...until Chan stepped in behind her and shut the door.

Suddenly it became cereal-box-size again. Meal-in-a-cereal-box-size, as a matter of fact.

Chan tossed her duffels onto the couch. "You can make yourself at home. I cleared out some drawers and part of the closet. Just throw my stuff aside if it's in your way. Except my shirts." He jerked open a closet door and she saw a half a dozen colorful, neatly pressed, long-sleeved shirts hanging side by side. He winked. "Gotta look snazzy for the fans."

"I'm sure," Madeleine said dryly.

Chan laughed. "And my rigging bag." He nodded at a dirty black duffel shoved under the table. "Don't mess with it. Otherwise you can do what you want. Later. Now we gotta go."

He brushed past her and settled into the driver's seat, started up the engine and, with the ease of long practice, whipped them out of the parking lot.

Madeleine, still standing in the aisle, was dumped unceremoniously onto the narrow couch.

"You wanta sit down when we're movin'," Chan advised without even turning around. "Safer that way."

Driving slower would be safer, too. "I'll keep it in mind," Madeleine said to the back of his black head.

LAS VEGAS was everything she'd ever imagined—and more. More sky. More mountains in the distance. More hotels. More casinos. More gaudiness. More neon. More heat.

When she got out of the truck to go into the restaurant, she felt as if she was stepping into an oven. Chan didn't even seem to notice. He just locked the door after her and led the way into the splashy Western-style building.

They went through a casino where Madeleine's eyes grew round as the poker chips on the tables as she took in the rows of people clad in everything from plaid polyester to gold lamé, industriously tugging on the handles of slot machines.

She craned her neck to get a look at the gaming tables as Chan led her past. The blackjack dealers really did wear tuxes. She stopped to watch, but it wasn't their tuxes or their red cummerbunds and pleated white shirts that attracted her. It was their hands. They dealt so smoothly with such economy of movement. Her own fingers itched to try it, to learn their tricks. She leaned closer. She wasn't into gold lamé and polyester or high-stakes gambling, but cards fascinated her, the odds, the chances.

A hand grabbed her arm and hauled her away. "More'n my hide's worth if I let you near those tables."

Madeleine blinked. "I beg your pardon?"

"Be like a lamb at the slaughter," Chan muttered. "Come on."

Madeleine cast a longing glance over her shoulder, then allowed herself to be dragged. She didn't think she'd get fleeced—or worse—but she wasn't going to argue with him. Yet.

They reached the dining area and the hostess appeared in front of them. She had a beehive of lacquered black hair, a pound or two of eye makeup and bright pink lipstick. She looked right past Madeleine and batted her lashes at Chan. "I saw you ride this afternoon. You were fan—tas—tic."

Chan grinned. "Thanks. I'm lookin' for some friends. They should already be here. Ah, yeah," he said as someone waved a cowboy hat from the far side of the room.

But before they could proceed, the hostess stepped in front of him and laid a hand on his arm. "You gonna be around later, honey? I get off at eleven." She still didn't seem to see Madeleine.

Chan shook his head regretfully. "On my way, right after we eat."

"Pity," the hostess said. The neon pink lips pouted prettily, then she gave him a coquettish look. "Maybe next time."

Chan grinned. "Could be." He stepped past her.

Madeleine followed, steaming as he steered her across the room. "Are you crazy?" she hissed.

"Bringing you in here? Probably."

"Not me! Her! She was trying to pick you up!"

"No? Really?"

"Yes, really. And you didn't even say no!"

He blinked. Then a corner of his mouth lifted. "It wouldn't have been polite."

Madeleine looked at him, dumbfounded, unable to say a word.

He flashed her a grin. "Come on, Decker. Don't worry about it."

He hauled her through the dining room to the table where his friends already sat. They were nibbling on popcorn, drinking beer and watching the two of them with undisguised interest.

Madeleine, who, if she didn't believe Antonia about everything else, did agree that first impressions were important, pasted on her best, most cheerful smile.

"These are my buddies," Chan said. "Devlin Gray." He nodded to the handsome, dark-haired, clean-shaven cowboy in the corner. "Tom Holden." Holden was blond, with a bushy mustache. "And Gil Trabert."

"The punctured lung," Madeleine said, remembering. She smiled at him.

"What? Oh, yeah." Chan frowned. "You were there that day, weren't you?"

"She was?" Gil's eyes widened. "How the hell did I miss that?"

"She wasn't there to see you. She came to see me."

"Not exactly your type, is she?" Devlin Gray said.

Chan bristled. "Just what the hell is my type?"

At the same time Madeline said, "No, I'm not."

Gil and Tom and Dev laughed, but Chan's scowl deepened. "Very funny."

"So who is she, really?" Tom asked.

"My name is Madeleine Decker. I'm from New York," Madeleine told them.

"So'd you just run into him in the lobby?" Gil asked.

"No," Chan said. "I went to the airport to pick her up. She's traveling with me for the summer."

Three mouths dropped open. Three sets of eyes grew narrow, then wide, then narrowed speculatively again.

"You're kidding," Tom said.

"She's the reason you wanted to be on your own?" Gil's eyes were like silver dollars.

"Well, hell," Dev said. "Are there any more like her at home?"

"No, there aren't," Chan said shortly. He held a chair for Madeleine, then took the one next to her.

"Where'd you find her?" Tom asked.

"My mother gave her to me." Chan leaned back and laid a proprietary arm along the back of Madeleine's chair.

The three pair of narrowed eyes immediately widened.

"Your mother?" Dev choked.

"He's kidding," Madeleine said quickly. She edged forward so she wouldn't have to lean back into his arm.

"Am not," Chan said. "It's the truth. Or do you like your version better?"

Madeleine blinked. "Mine?"

"That you propositioned me?"

"I never!"

"You weren't the one who said you wanted to go down the road with me?"

"Well, yes, but you know very well why. My mother thinks I ought to marry him," she told the three astonished cowboys. "And so does his."

The three jaws dropped farther.

"God Almightly," Tom breathed.

"This is a joke, right?" Gil said.

A slow grin started to spread across Dev's face.

Madeleine shook her head. "It's not a joke."

They looked at Chan. He shook his head, too.

Dev whistled softly. Gil rolled his eyes.

"Well," Tom said, "you came to the right place. You can get married tonight if you want in Vegas."

"We don't want!" Chan and Madeleine said together.

"It's like this," Madeleine said earnestly. "We knew they wouldn't give up unless we proved to them we wouldn't suit, so we thought that if we spent two months together we could compile enough evidence to show them that we were basically incompatible and that the odds were we wouldn't make a good marriage."

All three men stared at them in silence.

Then Dev said, "You and *Chan* thought of that?"

"Why not?" Chan said a trifle belligerently.

Dev muttered something under his breath and shook his head.

"So you're really taking her around for the summer?" Gil asked Chan tentatively.

"Yeah."

"Day in and day out in that truck of yours? Just the two of you?" Tom said. "Compiling evidence?" He grinned.

Chan scowled at him. "That's right."

"And while you ride bulls, what's she gonna do? Iron your shirts?"

"Not on your life. I'm typing my dissertation," Madeleine said quickly.

Dev whistled. "Dissertation?"

"You got a new career as an echo?" Chan said irritably.

"Dissertation on what?" Gil asked her. "From where?"

"On free will. From NYU."

The men looked at each other, at Chan, at Madeleine. They looked at each other again and shook their heads.

"Ho, boy," Tom breathed.

Gil started grinning. Dev rolled his eyes.

"What?" Chan demanded.

Gil's grin widened. "That's a hell of a lot of evidence right there."

Chan looked like he couldn't decide whether to agree. Finally he just picked up the menu and started to read.

"Well, in spite of all this evidence," Gil said with a wink, "you don't think it's, uh, maybe temptin' fate, spending all this time together?"

"You don't reckon that—all those things you don't have in common aside—you might just sort of fall in love?" Dev suggested.

"You don't think your mothers might win?" Tom said.

"Of course not," Madeleine said.

"Hell, no," said Chan.

Gil and Tom and Dev looked at each other and didn't say anything at all.

"Did he pick her up?" Antonia demanded the minute Julia answered the phone.

"I don't know. He hasn't called. And frankly, I don't expect him to. He's not exactly thrilled."

"And you think Madeleine is?"

"Well, what do they know?" Julia said huffily. "They're much too young to have any idea what's best for them."

"I suppose," Antonia said. "To be honest, I'm surprised she's doing this. I thought she'd jump at the chance to come to Bali with us."

"Maybe she thought she'd prefer Las Vegas," Julia said.

"Las Vegas? She met him in Las Vegas?" Antonia hadn't known that.

Madeleine hadn't been exactly forthcoming recently. In fact, ever since she'd announced that she was going down the road with Channing Richardson, she'd been extremely quiet.

Sometimes Antonia despaired of ever understanding what went on in Madeleine's head. When Madeleine had been little, Antonia had always thought they were as alike as a mother and daughter could possibly be. They dug holes, talked to strangers, played poker. In general they enjoyed all the same things.

And when Madeleine had chosen to go into anthropology, she'd even imagined they'd someday be able to share in their fieldwork.

But then abruptly Madeleine had seemed to lose interest. In her last year at Radcliffe, while Antonia was in Ecuador, Madeleine had cooled perceptibly. And though she'd finished and graduated in anthropology, she'd chosen philosophy for her graduate degrees.

"I've changed my mind," was all she'd said to her mother. "I have a right to." Her green eyes had flashed the way Antonia remembered Lothar's used to.

She hadn't argued; she'd tried to understand. But Madeleine wouldn't talk about it, and she'd felt she was losing contact with her daughter after that.

And the deeper Madeleine had gone into the philosophy nonsense, the greater the gap between them. To Antonia it seemed that Madeleine had retreated into a world of logical constructs instead of living real life.

She had nightmares that her grubby tomboy daughter would marry some ethereal flake like that Malcolm character or, worse, old tweed-and-dust Douglas, and shut herself up in some ivy-covered ivory tower for the rest of her life.

That was when she'd started talking about Channing Richardson. Not because she actually expected Madeleine to listen to her, to run right out and marry him. But because she'd wanted to shake Madeleine up.

Julia Richardson's eldest son could certainly be counted on to do that. And if it turned out the way she and Julia hoped, so much the better. But—

"Las Vegas is hardly going to start things on the right foot," she grumbled now. "Madeleine hates tacky."

"So do I," said Julia. "But it's where he needed to be. I can't change the rodeo schedule."

"I know. I know," Antonia soothed. "It will probably be fine." She laughed softly now as she thought about it. "I'd love to see Madeleine's face when she first sees Las Vegas."

"Didn't you win five thousand at the tables when you and Lothar went to that conference there years and years ago?"

Antonia smiled. "Did I! We might have been independently wealthy if he'd ever dared to take me back."

"Well, maybe we should consider it an omen. If your one and only visit brought you luck, maybe Madeleine's visit will bring her luck, too."

Chapter Five

"Your friends think we're crazy," Madeleine told Chan as they were going back to the truck after their meal.

"We are."

"Nonsense. We're just doing what any two sane, sensible adults would do confronted with a pair of bossy mothers."

"If you say so."

"I do. I don't know what else we could have done."

"We could have ignored them."

"Yes, well, that might have worked for you, but..." Madeleine's voice died out.

"But what? You couldn't ignore her?"

"Of course I could. It's just that... Never mind." She pressed her lips together and got a mulish expression on her face, the one that Chan had already begun to recognize as meaning "Forget it, fella."

He shrugged. "They're just jealous."

"Jealous? Our mothers?"

"No, Decker," he said patiently. "Dev and Gil and Tom."

"Why?"

"They wish they were sharing a truck with you."

"Why should they wish that?"

Chan rolled his eyes. He opened the door and climbed in, then let the door bang in her face. Serve her right. She opened it again and followed him in. He felt like he'd gained a shadow.

"Why?" she repeated. "I mean, it's not as if we're doing anything."

He didn't say anything, just looked at her.

Her gaze narrowed. "We aren't doing anything," she reminded him.

He spread his hands. "Not yet."

"What the hell do you mean, not yet?"

"I think I'd know if we were. I'm fully dressed. So are you." He turned and headed toward the driver's seat.

Madeleine grabbed his arm. "Now just a damned minute—"

"No swearing, Decker. It doesn't become you."

"I'll swear if I want to. Just what do you think is going to happen during these two months, Richardson? Perhaps we should get that straight right at the start."

"Should've got it straight a long time ago," he muttered, reaching over to straighten the window blind.

She stepped forward so he had to look at her. "So? What?" she demanded.

He shrugged. "Well, heck. I thought you said we were testing for compatibility." He gave her a bright hopeful leer.

"That does not mean sleeping together!"

"Well, maybe not sleeping, but—"

"Or going to bed together. No sex! Read my lips, Richardson. No. Sex."

"No...sex?" He shook his head sadly. "Then what're we gonna do for two months? Compatibilitywise, I mean?" he added after a moment.

"Trust you to think that the only kind of compatibility is sexual."

"It helps."

"And I'm sure you'd know it."

"Well, I'm not a virgin, if that's what you mean. But I don't think you could call me promiscuous."

"I could."

"I suppose you're some thirty-year-old virgin?"

"I'm not thirty!"

"And you're not a virgin, either, are you?"

By damn, but she could blush! Her fingers were knotting together like they'd like to strangle him. He edged just a little bit back.

"It's none of your business what I am," Madeleine bit out sharply.

"I should think it would figure in our compatibility quotient."

Her eyes narrowed. "What do you know about compatibility quotients?"

He grinned. "Nothing. I made it up. Relax, Decker." He winked. "I don't care if you're a virgin. Probably better that you're not actually. Then I won't feel bad if I'm the first and it doesn't work out."

She positively gaped at him. "Let's get a few things straight right now, Chan Richardson. One, I don't care if you care if I'm a virgin or not. Two, I am not having sex with you in any case. And three, there is absolutely no possibility of it, as you so blithely put it, 'working out.' Got that?"

He was still grinning, damn him. "Loud and clear, sweetheart."

"And I'm not your sweetheart!"

"No, Decker. You got that right. You sure as hell are not."

WELL, THEY WERE OFF to a dazzling start, that was certain, Madeleine thought, staring at the back of his head as they hurtled down the highway into the setting sun.

She'd worried that they wouldn't be able to survive two months together. They'd be lucky not to kill each other before the night was out.

Maybe if they never spoke, they'd cope. The less they said to each other, the better. Time spent in silence was still time. She simply had to keep reminding herself that she was that much closer to going home unencumbered by anyone's notion of a perfect man than she had been two hours ago.

Could they possibly, she wondered, spend the entire two months in silence?

Not and bring home evidence, she decided. If she went home and told Antonia she hadn't talked for two months, her mother would be telling her to check out Trappistine convents.

And anyway, it wasn't silent. The minute they'd hit the highway, Chan turned on the radio. A steel guitar was wailing in the background now, as a man's tenor twanged on about highways and byways and goodbyes and all that rot.

Madeleine gritted her teeth. Could a summer on Bali with Scott possibly have been any harder to take than this?

Well, it was too late to change her mind. She unzipped her duffel bag and began to make herself at home.

Madeleine had made herself at home on coral atolls and in stilt-legged huts. She'd settled into a West Side efficiency sublet and a Navajo hogan with equal aplomb. She'd even spent a relatively comfortable two weeks in a quinzee that she and three college friends had built out of ice at twenty-five below. She was used to settling in wherever she went. But everywhere else she'd been before now seemed somehow safer and more hospitable than this!

She reached into her bag and brought out a small box.

"What's that?"

She looked around to discover that he had glanced over his shoulder at her. "A trick box from China," she said. "No one knows how to open it but me." She set a yellow, furry stuffed animal alongside it.

"What's that?" he demanded.

"This is Leroy. I've had him since I was six."

"Swell."

"I haven't commented on your taste in calendars," she said tartly with a glance at it hanging in the closet. She still wouldn't. They might have chaps and boots on, but she was sorry, they didn't look like any cowgirls she'd ever seen.

"If you've got a problem with it, close your eyes."

"I'll try."

"And stop flitting around back there, will you? Sit still."

"You told me I could move in. It's hard to do that sitting still. Sorry. I didn't realize I was distracting you."

"You're not distracting me!"

"I'll wait if we're going to stop soon."

"We're not going to stop soon."

"Well, then—"

"Oh hell, fine. Move. I don't give a damn what you do."

YEAH, RIGHT, she wasn't distracting him. And if he could convince himself of that there was no telling the amount of self-deception he could indulge in.

As night came on, he should have noticed her less. In fact, he was conscious of every move she made. In her black jeans and black scoop-necked T-shirt, she should have become invisible in the increasing darkness. Not a chance.

In fact, though she still looked for all the world like some damn fence post, all he could remember was that she didn't look like a fence post underneath.

And she said no sex.

Cripes, was she nuts?

She wasn't even a virgin! He could almost understand her saying no if she'd been a virgin. But since she wasn't—

He wondered who she'd had sex with.

She didn't look like the kind of woman who had sex. Well, of course at some point she probably would, but she didn't look like the type who just hopped into bed for a good time. She didn't look as if she knew what a good time was. And when she had sex, she probably wouldn't call it that. She'd call it "making love."

So, then, who had she made love with?

A philosopher? Probably.

And what had happened to him? How come she wasn't still making love with him? What was she doing out here in the middle of the California desert bedeviling an unsuspecting rodeo cowboy like him?

He knew right now that he was never going to survive living with her in this very truck for two months, sleeping just feet away from her, sharing meals with her, knowing she was showering behind that flimsy accordion door.

Not if they couldn't have sex.

Another more vivid vision of Madeleine Decker without her curve-hugging black shirt spun through his head.

Damn. He shrugged his bottom against the driver's seat, trying to find a little more room in his jeans. He really must have been concussed to agree with her harebrained scheme.

She didn't seem to have the same problem. She was just humming away back there like some little broody hen, chipper as you please. He glanced over his shoulder.

Another mistake.

He could just glimpse her silhouette in the evening shadows. Her small straight nose. Her slightly tilted chin. Her breasts.

He jerked his gaze right around and hit the gas pedal. Keep your eyes on the road, Richardson! he chastised himself.

He should've told her he'd meet her in Santa Maria. No, he should have told her not to come at all.

He wished his old man hadn't asked him to check out a bull at Frank Parker's tomorrow morning. They could've stayed at a motel tonight, had separate rooms, a little space, maybe got to know each other gradually.

The way it was now, as the miles rolled by and dusk turned to dark, he felt like the walls of the camper were closing in on him. Even if he didn't glance back at her, even if he turned the radio up so he didn't have to listen to her hum, he still knew she was there.

He could smell her presence even without a glance.

She wasn't wearing perfume exactly. But there was something unique about Madeleine Decker, some sunny floral scent, a freshness that touched his nostrils even now, teasing him.

Forget that, he thought and hit the gas harder.

He flexed his fingers on the steering wheel. He watched the white line and tried to anticipate how long it would take him to get to the next curve. He tried to beat what he thought would be the time. He tried to hum along with the music on the radio.

But damned if she didn't hum louder, too.

He stomped down harder on the accelerator.

The humming got louder yet, became high-pitched and not very tuneful.

"Richardson?" Madeleine's voice drifted up from the back of the truck.

He jerked his head around as she came toward him up the aisle. How could she talk and hum at the same time? Could the damned woman do miracles on top of driving him nuts?

He scowled. "What?"

"The car behind us," she said. "The flashing lights. The siren. I think it's a cop."

SHE COULD TELL he was embarrassed. He tried to sound nonchalant when he got out of the truck to talk to the officer. He even joked a little with him while the patrolman was writing out the ticket.

But he was embarrassed because when he took off his hat to rake his fingers through his hair she could see that the tips of his ears were bright pink. And when he got back in the truck and the light turned on, his neck was red, too.

He tossed her the keys. "Your turn."

"What?" Madeleine stared at him, aghast.

He grimaced. "Your turn. You drive."

She shook her head. "Don't be silly. You're doing fine."

"Yeah, right."

"It's just one little ticket."

"Just one little ticket?" he echoed. "Well, yeah, I guess you could look at it that way." He gave her an odd look. "Though frankly I'm surprised you are." He shook his head. "But even so, it's been a long day. You're bound to do better."

"No."

"No?" His brows lifted. "Is this modesty, Decker?"

Madeleine gave a blithe little shrug, quite willing to have him believe that. "What else?"

"Well, it doesn't become you," he said flatly. "Come on. Show off."

"No, really. You go ahead." Why in God's name hadn't she thought about this?

"You're not afraid it's too big, are you, Decker?" he teased. "It's just like handling a regular pickup. You learn to use the mirrors a bit more. It's not even a stick."

"It's not that," Madeleine assured him.

"So what is it?"

"I just...think you drive really well." One compliment shouldn't swell his head too much.

"Thanks," he said dryly. "I also sleep really well, and I'd like to. Just a couple of hours. I could use a little shut-eye."

She yawned prodigiously. "So could I."

His gaze narrowed. "You're sleepy, too?"

"Oh, yes."

"What've you got to be tired from?"

"I was up at six this morning, packing, settling my cat—"

"Okay, okay." He sighed and turned back to the driver's seat. "I'll give it another hour or two and you sleep. Then we'll trade." He jerked his head. "You can sleep where you are or up over the cab. Suit you?"

"That's fine," Madeleine said softly. She hesitated as he pulled the truck back out onto the road, then knew she had to say something else. "Richardson?"

"What?"

"I think maybe you'd better drive until we find a rest stop and then we'll both get some sleep."

His head jerked around. Then he pulled over onto the shoulder again, shut off the engine and turned to look at her. "Yeah?" His eyes were glittering in the oncoming headlights. "Are you saying what I think you're saying?"

"What do you mean, what am I saying? Which words didn't you understand?"

"The part about us both getting some sleep." His voice gave the words an inflection that told her only too clearly what he was asking.

Her cheeks flamed. "No!" she blurted. "I absolutely do not mean that! Honest to Pete, is all you can think about sex? I meant exactly what I said. Sleep."

"Sleep." Chan weighed that, then shook his head. "I must be getting tireder than I thought, Decker," he said finally, "because for the life of me, I cannot understand why. Maybe you, being a logical scientific type, can explain it to me. How about it, Decker? If I drive while you sleep, why can't you drive while I sleep?"

"Because, damn it, I don't drive!"

OUTSIDE cars whizzed past. One semi thundered by and then another, rattling the windows of the camper. Inside no one said a word, except the radio announcer. Chan reached around and shut the radio off.

"I don't think I heard you right," he said carefully. "You said..."

"I said I don't drive."

"Don't. Drive." He rolled the words around in his mouth, tested them, tasted them. Then spat them out. *"Don't drive?"* He glared at her. "You're kidding, of course."

"I'm not, actually. I mean, I guess I could in a pinch. I drove a Jeep once in Indonesia. And when we went to visit some friends in Australia I drove a tractor once. But I don't... have a license."

He couldn't believe it. Even when she spelled it out, he couldn't believe it. "Why the hell not?"

She shrugged. "I've never needed one."

"Never needed one?" he echoed faintly. "This is the twentieth century, Decker. Practically the twenty-first. The age of the automobile. How the hell do you get around? Or don't you? Maybe you philosopher types just float up above on the clouds. Is that what you do?"

"I live in New York," Madeleine snapped. "I take the bus. The subway. Taxis. I ride my bike."

"You ride your bike. *In New York City?*"

"What's wrong with that? It's far less polluting. Far more ecologically sound."

"You could get killed!"

"Says the man who rides bulls for a living."

"I don't do it in traffic! I don't believe this," he muttered. "How the hell did you imagine you were going to go down the road with me if you can't drive?"

"How the hell should I know?" Madeleine shouted at him.

Chan wanted to shout, too. No, he wanted to do more than shout. He wanted to scream. He wanted to strangle his mother and her mother and that pea-picker geneticist Gregor Mendel and those damned anthropologists Levi-Strauss and Margaret Mead and anyone else who'd ever influenced either one of those batty old ladies.

How could they have thought he was suited in any way, genetically, anthropologically or otherwise, to spend a summer—hell, to spend a *day*—with a woman who couldn't drive? And hadn't even seen fit to mention the fact?

He rubbed a hand over his face. Then he scrubbed at his eyes with the heels of his hands and finally looked up at her again in the darkness of the truck.

She was looking stricken, her face white in the glare of every pair of headlights that passed, and he found himself feeling guilty for exploding at her. She was so airy-fairy she probably didn't even think being able to drive mattered.

Hell.

He flexed his shoulders, rubbed the back of his neck. "I suppose it's not your fault," he said gruffly.

"And whose fault is it supposed to be? Don't tell me you're going to take the blame."

So much for feeling sorry for her. "No, damn it. It's not my fault you can't drive. It's not my fault you're even here. And as far as I'm concerned you can go the hell away."

She took a deep breath and let it out again. Then she said, "I... can't."

"Why not? You're not going to do me a damn bit of good. I can't do all the driving myself. I have to go to Arkansas and Kansas and Texas and Oregon and—"

"I get the point."

"So I need another driver."

"I suppose you do." Her voice was subdued. It was practically the first time he'd heard it that way. She looked up at him and squared her shoulders. "Well, then, I guess you'll have to teach me to drive."

He gaped at her. "Me? Teach you to drive? Have you got rocks in your head?"

"Well, you said you need another driver and—"

"A good driver."

"I'd be a good driver."

"How do you know?"

She looked at him, affronted. "I'm good at everything I do!"

He snorted. "Yeah? Well, you don't drive."

"Not yet. I will if you teach me. Come on, Richardson."

"I said you could come along, fool that I was. I never said I'd teach you to drive."

"What you mean is, you can't."

"The hell I can't. I won't."

"Why? Afraid I'll be good and you'll have to admit it?"

"Afraid you'll kill us both you'll be so bad."

"I won't." She lifted her chin and stared at him, daring him. "I went with you to the hospital, Richardson. I sat for hours waiting in that stupid emergency room."

"Nobody asked you to."

"I guess I'm just a nicer person than you are." She smiled sweetly.

He slammed his hand against the steering wheel. "Damn it!"

"Come on, Richardson. You'll enjoy it. You'll get to boss me around. Yell at me. All those things you know you want to do." She gave him a winning grin.

He raked his fingers through his hair. "We've only got four days if we start tomorrow," he argued. "Thursday night right after the rodeo, I'm heading for Fort Smith."

"I can learn in four days."

He looked at her skeptically.

"If I don't have my license in four days, I'll go back to New York."

"Is that a promise, Decker?"

"If—"

He groaned.

"—you've really made an effort to teach me. You have to try."

"I don't cheat, Decker. Ever."

"Fine." She held out her hand. "Neither do I."

He hesitated, then took her hand. Her grip was strong and firm, her skin soft and warm.

"Deal," Madeleine said.

Chan got back in the driver's seat and drove off in the darkness, muttering under his breath, "I must be nuts."

CHAN DROVE the rest of the night. He was tired, his muscles were stiff, his ribs hurt when he moved. But he drove because he didn't know what else to do.

He had to meet Frank Parker to see a bull at nine, so he couldn't stop, couldn't sleep. But what the hell, chances were he wouldn't sleep, anyway.

Had he really agreed to teach Madeleine Decker to drive?

He wondered if the effects of concussion could linger seven months. Everything he'd done as far as she was concerned was weird as hell.

He didn't let women come on the road with him. He didn't give up traveling with his buddies and take on unknown philosopher-women to make his mother happy. Hell, he hadn't made his mother happy in years.

So what in the devil was he doing?

Losing his mind? Satisfying his curiosity? Scratching an itch?

He wished.

Madeleine Decker wasn't an itch anymore. She was a gawddamned rash. He'd forgotten just how alive, how vibrant, how contentious she was.

But it sure hadn't taken her long to remind him.

He grinned and shook his head. Chances were he'd regret it. He couldn't see much good coming out of tangling with Madeleine Decker for the next two months.

But it was like taking on the meanest, rankest bull in the country. You weren't in it for the payoff. Not really. If you were, you were crazy, because odds were a hundred to one you'd get your butt kicked.

No, you didn't climb on a bull like that for the result. You did it for the challenge. You dug in, hung on and enjoyed the hell out of the ride.

Chapter Six

It was late when Madeleine woke. The sun was already high in the sky. And the truck was no longer moving, so she thought Chan must be asleep.

But when she peered over the edge of the bunk above the cab and looked down onto the one next to the table, he was nowhere to be seen. Only a rumpled pillow and tangled sheets proved that he had been there at all.

She turned and drew back the curtain to get her bearings. The truck was parked on gravel near a garage, alongside another truck with a smaller camper top. Beyond it, on the far side of the gravel, she saw a broad lawn and a low-slung, white wood frame ranch house with dark green shutters. Someone's home. And a very nice home indeed.

A movement caught her eye, and she spied a slender woman in jeans, with long blond hair braided down her back, hanging rows of blue jeans and long-sleeved shirts on a clothesline.

The owner of the very nice home? Probably.

Or maybe the daughter of the owner. She looked fairly young—maybe even younger than Madeleine.

A friend of Chan's?

No doubt.

Madeleine was sure she would meet plenty of "friends of Chan's" wherever they went. He probably had the rodeo cowboy's version of a woman in every port.

Good, she thought. It would keep his mind off her.

She didn't know why she hadn't considered the sex business—she didn't know what else to call it—when she first proposed this insanity.

Well, actually, yes, she did consider it: she just hadn't thought he'd be interested.

Madeleine Decker wasn't the sort of woman that men were interested in. Well, not many men, anyway. Malcolm and Douglas had mustered a bit of enthusiasm. They'd managed the occasional peck on the cheek and nibble on the lips. But they'd much preferred talking with her, arguing philosophy with her, trading quips with her. And that had been fine with Madeleine.

Sex was highly overrated.

She knew that from her experience with Scott.

He was the other reason she hadn't considered sex to be an issue. Scott had certainly wasted no tears when their relationship had ended. In fact, if she were being brutally honest, she knew that he'd probably just made love with her because she'd thrown herself at him.

God, she could still feel the mortification now, five years later, just thinking about it. Well, she was damned if she'd do it again. Even if she was no longer a virgin, Chan Richardson needn't think she was ripe for the picking.

In any case, it looked as though he could have his pick of any orchard he wanted. And from a distance, at least, this one looked considerably more attractive than the hostess in the restaurant.

She thought so, anyway. She wondered just exactly what Chan Richardson found appealing in a woman. Judging from the well-lacquered hostess and this blond, fresh daisy and his broad hints—no, blatant come-ons to her—he had wide-ranging tastes.

Madeleine's jaw snapped shut. She glanced at her watch and was dismayed to discover it was almost ten o'clock. She hadn't slept that late in years.

She stopped worrying where Chan was and started worrying that he'd be back and find her still in bed.

She scrambled down out of the bed, straightened the blankets, gathered clean clothes and disappeared into the bathroom.

There she took a quick shower and washed her hair, then dressed and was just wadding her hair up into a towel on the top of her head when there was a knock at the door.

She opened it to find the blond woman smiling up at her.

"Hi. I'm Lily. I wondered if you wanted to come to the house for some breakfast."

A cheerful welcome from one of Chan's women wasn't exactly what she'd expected, especially after the hostess had looked right through her. But she smiled back. "Oh, er, yes. Thanks."

The other woman actually resembled her name. Slender and strong, yet delicate, too. Her cheeks were smooth and pale, and she wore no makeup at all. Clearly a woman at the opposite end of the spectrum from the hostess. Lily shifted the empty clothes basket on her hip, and Madeleine noticed the wedding ring on her finger. Her eyes widened, then she understood Lily's equanimity.

She opened the door and climbed out of the camper. "I'm Madeleine," she said.

"I know. Chan told me. He says you're traveling with him for the summer." She looked interested, amused perhaps, but not scandalized in the least.

"Writing my dissertation," Madeleine said.

"That's what he said."

"Really?" She was surprised. "Did you believe him?"

Lily stared. "What?" she asked, then started to laugh. "The guys have been getting to you, have they? Don't mind them. They wear their brains below their belts."

"So does Chan," Madeleine said.

Lily laughed. "Is it true your mother and his want you two to get married?"

"He told you that?"

"Sure. Is it?"

"Sort of," Madeleine hedged.

"And you're spending the summer together to see if you suit?" Lily giggled. "I think that's great."

"We're going to prove that we don't suit," Madeleine corrected her.

"Right," Lily said. She opened the screen door and gestured Madeleine into the kitchen ahead of her.

It was exactly the sort of kitchen she'd always dreamed of. Warm and homey, it sprawled from a functional cooking center to a family area complete with round oak table and a used-brick fireplace with a raised hearth. Floor-to-ceiling bookcases were piled haphazardly with books and magazines. The pillow-ticking sofa peeked out from beneath assorted scattered clutter, mostly of the farm and ranch variety. Tractor parts catalogs were spread across the table, a half-braided rope lay on the back of the sofa, and a stack of *Stockman's Journal* magazines slumped on the braid rug.

"Dan's not much of a housekeeper," Lily apologized. She crossed the room and poured Madeleine a cup of coffee. "Neither am I, I'm afraid. Milk or sugar?"

"Black is fine. Is Dan your husband?"

Lily shook her head. "My brother. This is his ranch. I'm just stopping for a few days."

"Where do you live?"

Lily nodded toward the yard. "In that other truck mostly."

"In the truck? You're in rodeo, too?"

Lily nodded.

"So you're a . . ." Madeleine frowned, trying to remember what rodeo events women participated in. She'd read a book about rodeo just before she'd come, for all the good it seemed to be doing her." . . . barrel racer?" She managed at last.

"I used to be." Lily perched on the edge of the counter and sipped her coffee. "Now I'm a bull fighter."

Madeleine's jaw dropped. She didn't think Lily meant the sort with the sword and the cape. "You mean you're one of the . . . clowns?"

A misnomer if there ever was one. Madeleine knew very well that, for all their greasepaint and crazy clothes, theirs was a very serious business.

"I'm one of the clowns," Lily agreed. "I'm the one in the barrel mostly."

"Isn't that—" Madeleine swallowed "—still sort of dangerous?"

Lily got a faraway look in her eyes for a moment, then nodded. "Yes." Then she lifted her chin and met Madeleine's gaze squarely. "But that doesn't mean a woman can't do it."

"Of course not," Madeleine said quickly, sensing that Lily had had this discussion before. "Does your husband fight bulls, too?"

The faraway look again. Then Lily's lips pressed together. "He did." She paused. A second or two. No more. But enough.

Madeleine knew what was coming, felt it in her gut even before she heard the words.

"John's dead. He was a bull fighter, too. He died two years ago. At the rodeo in Reno."

Their eyes locked. Madeleine could see Lily's pain written across her face. It was stark, terrifying. But Madeleine didn't blink or look away. She just nodded slowly. "I understand why you do it then," she said quietly.

Lily blinked, then looked at Madeleine closely. "You do?"

Madeleine nodded, but knew that Lily wouldn't really believe her unless she could explain. "My mother is an anthropologist. She and my father worked together in remote, primitive places until he died. Afterward people said she should quit fieldwork, that she should get a teaching job and take me back to the States where it was safe. Instead we stayed in Bali. Then we went to Siberia. Then for a couple of years we did come back to the States, but we lived on a reservation, then we went to China. It wasn't until four years ago that she actually settled down."

Lily's lips curved into a slow smile. "You do understand, then," she said.

"Yes. I'm sure it hurts. I'm sorry."

Lily shook her head. "I'm the one who should be sorry, laying it on you like that. But I knew somebody would tell you sooner or later. Somebody always does—" she grimaced "—to protect me."

"They don't want someone saying something that might remind you, make you hurt?"

"Believe me," Lily said fiercely, "inadvertent comments don't come close to hurting me as much as having John die hurt me. If I can survive that, I can survive anything!" Lily shook her head and blushed furiously. "Listen to me, ranting on and on like some fussy old lady. I don't know what's the matter with me."

Madeleine knew. She knew Lily missed John desperately and hadn't yet come to terms with life without him. She remembered how it had been for her mother. Even at six and a half, she had known.

And it had taken time—a long time—before either she or Antonia had been really ready to live fully again.

She supposed she could count herself lucky that she had never felt that way about anyone. She'd wanted to feel that way about Scott. Maybe it was just as well he hadn't let her.

"Thank you for telling me yourself," she said gently now.

"Thank you for listening," Lily replied. She looked a little self-conscious. "I don't usually blather on like that. You should have shut me up. You're easy to talk to."

Madeleine smiled. "Maybe it's because I'm not a part of the rodeo scene."

"Maybe. But maybe it's just because you're a good listener. You'll be good for Chan."

Madeleine laughed. "Don't tell him that."

"If you say so," Lily agreed. "Now, how about that breakfast? Eggs? Ham? Bacon? Hash browns? Toast? All of the above?"

"Just toast. I'm not a big eater."

"Something else not to tell Chan. He'll clean your plate for you."

"They all ate pretty well last night," Madeleine said.

"Most of them do. Growing boys." Lily grinned. "You had dinner with 'em? Who've you met?"

"Mmm, let's see. Gil Trabert, Tom Holden...Devlin Gray."

Lily's smile faded. She turned away and put the toast in the toaster. Then she turned back and smiled. "Well," she said briskly, "you're lucky you got a bite with those four."

"You know them?"

"Oh, yes. I know them." Lily's voice was toneless. She got out the butter and jam and set them on the counter. "Chan should be back before long."

Madeleine wondered what had made Lily's smile vanish and the subject change so quickly, but she didn't ask. "Where is Chan?"

"He went out to Frank Parker's. A cattle ranch about twenty miles north. Chan promised his dad that he'd go up and take a look at a bull Frank might be willing to sell."

"For rodeos?"

Lily shook her head. "No. Breeding."

"I didn't know Chan was involved in that."

"Oh, yes. When he isn't on the road, Chan works on the ranch. He owns a lot of the stock, and they're always on the lookout for good new blood. Chan's real smart about it, too. He probably knows as much as both his parents put together."

"Julia has a Ph.D. in genetics."

"And she's taught Chan everything she knows," Lily said. "So has his dad. Dan was talking to Rick last week, says he's all excited about getting this bull, but it's up to Chan. Chan will know if he's right. Chan has a good eye." She handed Madeleine a plate of toast.

If Chan Richardson ever started a fan club, Madeleine was willing to bet Lily would join. She wondered if, when Lily finally got over John's death, she might start thinking Chan Richardson was a good catch. Good luck, she thought.

"When will he be back?"

"Before noon, he said. Want more coffee?"

"No, thanks. I was wondering, though, how I can get to town."

"Take the camper. Chan won't care. He's got Dan's truck."

"I can't." And at Lily's perplexed look, Madeleine explained. "I need to get a learner's permit. I don't have a license."

Lily looked almost as poleaxed as Chan had, but she recovered more quickly. "Finish your toast," she said, "I'll take you."

Dan's ranch was about seven miles out of town. Lily did the grocery shopping while Madeleine went to the DMV to get a copy of the vehicle code. She studied it while Lily went to the feed store and the hardware store. Then she went back and took the test for her permit.

"Good thing I'm a quick study," she said when she came back out.

"You got it?"

Madeleine nodded. "And I live here now, too. I had to have a local address. I hope you don't mind."

"Nope," Lily said cheerfully as they crossed the street to get in the truck. "It fits."

"What do you mean?"

Lily grinned. "Rodeo people are always *from* somewhere. They're never there. It's a fact of life."

"Sort of like anthropologists," Madeleine murmured as she got into the truck. "We never had a home, either. I always wanted one."

Lily put the truck in gear, looked over her shoulder and backed out of the parking place. "Places are nice, but they're not the most important. I never felt like I needed a home as long as I had John."

WHEN CHAN CAME BACK from Parkers' early that afternoon he expected to find Madeleine tapping away on her computer. Or chewing a pencil and staring off into space. Or sitting under a tree with her nose in a book.

In a million years he never expected to find her where he found her.

Inside a barrel.

He took one look, jumped out of Dan's truck and almost ran across the gravel toward the corral. There was a black Brangus bull at the far end of the corral regarding them curiously.

"What in hell are you doing?" he yelled at Madeleine.

"What does it look like?" she yelled back. She was grinning, and the sun touched her cheeks and the wind lofted her shiny dark hair. She looked beautiful and desirable and it made him mad as hell.

He gritted his teeth, then turned his glare on Lily. "Are you nuts?" He was so mad he forgot to treat her with kid gloves the way he usually did.

Lily stood stiff as her broom behind the barrel. "I don't think so, no."

"She doesn't belong out here! She'll get herself killed, for God's sake. Then what am I going to tell her mother?"

"That it wasn't your fault, she's a grown woman?" Lily suggested so gently that Chan, knowing he had overreacted, flushed deep red. It came from lack of sleep, he told himself. God knew he hadn't had much, driving all night. And then when he did go to bed he was acutely aware of Madeleine Decker sleeping like a baby practically right over his head. A couple of times he'd even got up and looked at her.

"Fine," he muttered. "Just fine. Do whatever the hell you want. It's no skin off my nose." And, turning on his heel, he stalked away.

"Chan!" Madeleine came after him, waddling in the barrel, with Lily and the broom bringing up the rear. They looked ridiculous. He wanted to laugh. He wouldn't. He waited, irritated. "What do you want?"

Madeleine reached the fence and climbed out of the barrel and onto the top rung, then jumped lightly down on the other side. "Don't get mad at Lily. It was my idea." She looked up at him with bright, hopeful eyes.

He pressed his lips together. "I'm not surprised." He turned away and started walking again.

She followed him. "Well, you can't expect me to tag along, as you put it, for two months and not want to know how to do the things I see, can you?"

He rounded on her. "I frankly don't know what the hell I can expect from you, Decker. But there's a hell of a lot safer things you can learn to do before you start baiting bulls."

"Such as?"

"You could muck out the barn for starters."

"We already did."

He masked his surprise, but he looked at Lily who nodded.

"We did," she said.

"Then you could learn to saddle a horse."

Madeleine nodded. "I will."

He scuffed his toe on the grass. "You could try roping a calf."

"I'd love to."

"But you better learn to drive first," he muttered. "Come on. We'll go get your permit."

"I went. Lily took me." Madeleine dug into her wallet and pulled out a permit, waving it under his nose. "How about this?"

She looked so pleased, he had to smother a smile. "Showing off, Decker?"

"Just trying to impress you." She gave him a cheeky grin. "Am I?"

More than he wanted to admit. "Come on," he said gruffly. "Let's get this show on the road."

"I THOUGHT you said you were patient?" Madeleine shut the ignition off and glared at the man sitting next to her in the cab of Dan's truck.

"So I lied. Start again."

"I've been driving for two hours."

"You should've been driving for ten years. Come on. Let's go."

Madeleine sighed and started the engine again. "You're making me nervous."

"You're scaring me to death. So I figure we're even. Take it halfway up that hill. Stop it and start again."

"I don't think I'm ready for hills. Won't we roll backward?"

"Not if you do it right."

"Why do I have to learn on a stick shift, anyway? Your truck isn't a stick."

"But you never know when you might have to drive one."

"Like when you're standing in the road and I want to run you down?"

"You got it. Now drive."

She did. They stalled. They rolled backward. She licked her lips and tried again. And again. Chan's knuckles went white and his mouth drew down at the corners, but he didn't say a word. Still, when they slid backward into the ditch, Madeleine wasn't sorry that he was the one who hit his head.

"Damn it!"

"Sorry. Are you all right?" Frankly she wished he were dead.

Chan grunted, rubbing the back of his head. "Terrific. Are you?" He sounded only remotely more sincere.

"Fine," Madeleine said shortly. Or as fine as anyone could be, sitting tipped at a forty-five-degree angle and faced with the prospect of having to drive back out.

Wearily she turned the key in the ignition.

"Forget it. I'll do it."

She ignored him.

"I said, I'll do it."

"No." She was determined now. She eased up on the clutch pedal slowly, pressed down on the gas. The truck jerked, shimmied, stalled, slid.

Once more Chan hit his head. He jerked open the door and got out. He came around to the driver's side and opened that door. "Move over."

"You wanted me to drive."

"And now I don't."

"And we always do what you want, is that it?" She felt like crying. Damn it, she was trying to do it right.

"You're not going to be able to get the truck out." He sounded reasonable, patient, long-suffering.

"And you are?" she said, knowing she was ungraciousness personified.

"Well, I stand a damn sight better chance than you do."

"Fine, Mr. Wonderful." Abruptly she slid over, shoved open the passenger door and went right on out the other side. "Go to it." Turning on her heel, she climbed up the side of the ditch and struck out along the road.

"Hey! Decker!"

She didn't even turn around.

"Where're you going?"

"Back to the ranch."

She half expected him to yell at her to come back, to come after her and demand it. The one time she'd walked out on Scott, he'd grabbed her and hauled her back.

Chan didn't say a word. She never turned around to look. When she got to the top of the hill she saw another truck coming her way. It drew to a stop as it came abreast of her.

Two cowboys she recognized grinned at her.

"Hey, Madeleine," said Dev. "What's up? Where's Chan?"

Madeleine smiled at him. "Hi, Dev. Gil." She nodded her head in the direction from which she'd come. "He's over there. In Dan's truck."

Dev cocked his head. "You running away already?"

"More or less. He was giving me a driving lesson. How to start on a hill. I rolled into the ditch."

"You can't drive?" Gil goggled.

"Chan's teaching you?" Dev said.

"*Chan?*" they both chorused.

Then Gil shook his head. "Will wonders never cease? So what happened? You roll over him?"

"I wish."

Dev grinned. "Like that, is it? Get in. We'll take you back to the ranch."

Madeleine hesitated. But it wasn't as if Chan was going to have trouble finding his way home if she took Dev's offer. In fact, she wouldn't be surprised if he got the truck out of the ditch and drove right past her. She got in the truck and Gil slid over to the middle.

"I didn't know you'd be here," she said to them.

"Lots of guys hit the same rodeos or most of 'em. We're riding in Santa Maria on Thursday, too. We'd sorta figured we'd hang around Vegas till then, but neither of us won a damn thing ridin', and we weren't having any more luck at the tables," Gil said.

"So we figured we'd better get out while we still had gas money." Dev grinned. "And Dan never minds if we drop by for a day or so. You've met Dan?"

Madeleine shook her head. "But I've met his sister."

"Lily's here?" Dev demanded.

"She was showing me how she works with the barrel."

Dev's mouth pressed into a thin line. "Damn fool woman," he muttered almost to himself.

"She says she doesn't take unnecessary risks," Madeleine said.

"Just bein' out there's a risk."

"But bull riders need—"

"I know what bull riders need," Dev said sharply. "I am one." His jaw tightened and Madeleine saw him swallow hard. She had the feeling he was stopping himself from saying more. The silence stretched awkwardly.

Finally Gil asked, "Chan go see that bull of Frank Parker's?"

"Yes." Parker's bull provided the topic for discussion until they reached the ranch. Lily's brother, Dan, was at the barn when they arrived. Dev introduced them. Dan was a tall, silvery blond, masculine version of his sister with a shy grin and a pronounced limp.

He shook her hand. "So you're Chan's girl."

"Not really," Madeleine said quickly.

"They're talking about marriage." Gil grinned and she shot him a hard look.

"We're traveling together. Doing research," Madeleine said.

Dan lifted one brow. "That what they're callin' it these days?"

Madeleine's cheeks went beet red. "Not that kind of research," she said hastily.

Dan gave her a broad grin and a wink. "Just kidding." Then he sobered. "Wish I'd done that with Laura. My wife. Ex-wife," he amended with a rueful grimace. "If I had, maybe I'da known it wouldn't work. She didn't understand the life-style before she got into it. And when she did, she hated it. You'll know before you marry Chan."

"I'm not marrying Chan."

Dan looked at Dev and Gil. They looked back at him. All three of them looked at Madeleine and shook their heads.

THE MEAL Lily put on the table would have fed the starving of Calcutta for years to come. At least that was the impression Madeleine had of the quantity of meat and potatoes and corn and salad that filled the men's plates and, in short order, their stomachs.

She volunteered to help bring things to the table from the stove, but Lily shook her head. "You just protect your plate and mine. I'll be along in a moment."

So Madeleine sat. Lily had put her next to Chan, who hadn't spoken to her since he'd come back.

She'd said, "Did you get the truck out all right?" And he'd given a one jerk nod of his head, and that was that.

She supposed he was mad at her for not learning everything she had to know in one day. Well, too bad, she thought. She'd done the best she could.

No one seemed to notice that they weren't speaking to each other. Dan talked to Chan. Chan talked to him and to Lily and Dev and Gil. They talked about Dan's crops and Frank Parker's bull. Then they talked about the stock they'd drawn for Thursday's rodeo. Madeleine listened.

Lily got up and went to get more corn from the kettle on the stove.

"I drew me Living Daylights," Gil said, then grinned. "Hope to hell he don't kick 'em right outta me."

"You stay on, you got a good chance of money," Chan said. "Better'n I do on Miser."

Gil and Dan made sympathetic noises.

Chan turned to Dev. "Who'd you draw? Dev," he said more loudly, "which bull'd you draw?"

Dev, who'd been staring off toward the stove where Lily was taking more corn out of the pot, looked around and blinked.

"Oh, uh, Shadow Boxer, I think." He frowned a minute, then nodded. "Yeah, Shadow Boxer."

Chan made a face. "Both of you are gonna wipe the floor with me."

"Vickers brings good stock," Lily said, coming over with more corn. She sat down across from Dev. "You'll all do fine. And I'll be there to save you if you don't."

There was a sudden jolt as Dev's corn skewer slipped. His elbow knocked his baked potato off his plate and into his cup of coffee. It slopped across the table.

There was an instant's stunned silence.

"Nice shot," Gil said.

"Reckon we'll put you in the barn next time," Dan added easily, tossing him a napkin.

Lily got up quickly. "I'll get a rag."

Madeleine passed Dev her napkin. "Can I help?"

He shook his head. He mopped with the napkins until Lily returned with the rag. Then he took it without comment. Lily stood waiting. She held out her hand to take it when he was finished.

He shoved his chair back. "I'm done." And he brushed past her, dumped the napkins in the trash and the rag in the sink and went right on out the back door.

It banged after him.

Lily stood staring, then came and sat down again and picked up her fork. Dan started talking loudly and determinedly about the price of feed. He was investing far more enthusiasm in the topic than Madeleine thought it warranted, but apparently she was wrong, for Chan and Gil chipped in with equal fervor.

Chapter Seven

It was almost eleven when the camper door opened and Chan came in. He seemed almost surprised to see Madeleine still up and sitting at the table, typing. He opened his mouth, then closed it again.

Madeleine didn't say anything either.

There didn't seem to be a whole lot to say.

She'd left almost immediately after they'd finished dinner. Lily had said that Dan and Gil would do the dishes. Dan and Gil looked surprised, but they didn't argue. Neither did Madeleine. She had taken it as an opportunity to escape.

"I have work to do," she'd said. It was only the truth. But the greater truth, the one she didn't say, was that she didn't want to spend any more time with Chan. The tension between them had grown all day. Madeleine wasn't sure what was causing it. Her driving skill—or lack of it—probably. She didn't know. She gathered he felt the same way.

Certainly he hadn't joined Lily and Dan and Gil in urging her to stick around after the dishes were finished to play cards.

"Come on. The more the merrier," Dan urged, and Gil and Lily had agreed.

Chan hadn't said a word. Madeleine figured she was doing them both a favor when she declined and left.

She'd spotted Dev over by the barn and watched him for a moment, curious about his reaction to Lily's pronouncement. He stood with his back to her, shoulders hunched, leaning against the corral fence staring off into the distance.

She didn't know what he was looking at, but she doubted it was anything she'd be able to see.

Did everyone else know? Probably.

Certainly Lily knew what was bothering him. But Madeleine knew instinctively she couldn't ask Lily, either. All those years spent traipsing after her mother had taught her that there was a time to ask questions. She knew this wasn't it.

"Lily says you can sleep in the house," Chan said now. They were the first words he'd spoken to her all evening.

She looked up at him. "Why?"

"I . . . well, I just thought you'd prefer it."

"You thought? Not Lily?" she ventured.

"We both thought, all right?" He shifted irritably. "I mean, this place isn't exactly the Hilton."

"I know." She paused. "But I don't mind it. I slept well last night."

"Lucky you," he muttered.

Madeleine smiled. "I suppose that means you didn't. Will you sleep better if I'm not here, Richardson?"

"God, I hope so."

And she would, too, she was sure. "Fine. I'll go." She put away her computer, gathered up her nightgown, toothbrush and soap. He stood watching her every move until she started out the back door of the camper.

"Decker?" He was standing in the lighted doorway looking down at her when she glanced back.

"What?"

"I'm sorry about today."

CHAN STARED AT LILY, who was sitting placidly in the kitchen nursing a cup of coffee. "What do you mean, she isn't here? We were supposed to go driving this morning."

"She went. Dev took her."

"Dev?"

Lily shrugged negligently as she got up and went to the refrigerator. "Why not? No law says you had to do it, is there? Do you want some eggs?"

"Yeah. No. I don't know." Chan shook his head. "Why'd she go with Dev?" He was unaccountably annoyed. "I was gonna do it."

"I got the feeling she didn't want to bother you."

"I apologized!"

Lily stared. "For what?"

"Never mind." Chan raked fingers through his hair. "It isn't easy teaching somebody to drive, you know."

"I know. I remember Dan and Dad yelling at me. Did you yell?"

"A little." He gave a brief shrug. "But I was polite, too."

Lily grinned. "I'll bet." Then her grin faded and she said abruptly, "Anyway, she went with Dev."

"How long ago?"

"Couple of hours."

"They should be back soon, then."

But they weren't.

SHE CERTAINLY hadn't planned to ask Dev. It was fate—what else?—that brought her out to the kitchen to find him there with Lily. She was standing at the stove with her back to him, stirring some hash browns. Dev was standing with his hands on the table staring at Lily's back. He'd obviously just finished saying something when Madeleine came in. The tension fairly crackled in the air.

"Uh, good morning," she said into the silence, wondering if she shouldn't be backing out instead of walking in.

Lily and Dev both turned.

Lily beamed. "Hi, there! How'd you sleep? Want some coffee?"

"Fine, thanks. Love some." She took a mug Lily handed her. "How are you?" she asked Dev.

"All right." His handsome face looked drawn. He pressed his lips together in a thin line. "You driving this morning?"

Madeleine grimaced. "Undoubtedly. Chan hasn't come in yet?"

Lily shook her head.

Dev offered, "I'll take you."

Both women turned to look at him. He gave Lily a look that Madeleine couldn't quite interpret before he turned his gaze on her. He smiled. "Or do you want to wait for Chan?"

She didn't even have to think. "No, thanks. I'd be delighted. After breakfast?"

"Sure. Take your time. I'll be outside." He turned and walked out the door.

Lily stared after him, letting the hash browns burn.

"Do you mind?" Madeleine asked hesitantly.

Lily jerked around, realized the potatoes were starting to burn and scraped them around in the pan. "Mind?" she repeated.

"If I go with Dev?"

Lily snorted. "Why should I care?"

Madeleine didn't know the answer to that.

She left with Dev half an hour later. He took her up in the hills to drive. He was quieter and calmer than Chan. He didn't wince when she jerked the truck. He didn't cringe when she came too close to the shoulder.

At first she just concentrated on her driving and they passed the time in silence, except when Dev gave her directions or made a comment. But then her confidence grew and she started asking him questions.

He told her about growing up in Omaha with just a hint of the West in the air, about how he'd always wanted more, about how he spent summers on his uncle's small ranch in Colorado and fell in love with horses and rodeo. He told her that he'd wanted to leave right after high school and join the circuit, but his doctor father had insisted he get a degree before he did. So he got one. And someday he might go back and become a doctor. But that wasn't where he was now. It wasn't what he wanted. What he wanted was to rodeo. He smiled as he spoke about driving for hours and riding mere seconds. And he smiled when he told her about winning buckles and breaking ribs.

She didn't imagine Chan would be that open with her if she traveled with him for a hundred years. Now if her mother and Dev had plotted to fix them up, she might consider it!

But there was something else Dev wasn't telling her. Something that haunted him, that caused him to stop mid-sentence and stare off into space.

Something about Lily? Madeleine wondered. Something that made the air thick between them. Whatever it was, Dev didn't talk about that.

After they'd been driving for a couple of hours, Madeleine said, "Are you ready to go back?"

"What do I have to get back for?" he said, and a sad, almost despairing look passed over his face. Then he shook himself out of it and smiled. "Let's drive into town. Get you around a little traffic."

"Traffic?" Madeleine said doubtfully.

"Gotta try it sometime."

So she drove to town. They passed fairly close to the house on their way to the highway, and she glanced over as they went by, wondering where Chan was. Wherever he was, she thought, he was probably vastly relieved not to be with her.

And she was glad not to be with him, too. She'd have felt more sure of herself if he hadn't apologized. She wasn't quite sure what to say to him since he had.

She couldn't remember any man ever apologizing to her in all her twenty-six years. Malcolm and Douglas never had, even when they'd been wrong. And Scott? Her mouth lifted in a wry smile. Scott had never been wrong. Just ask him.

"What's funny?" Dev said.

She shook her head. "Just thinking about a man I know who never did a thing to apologize for."

"That's funny?"

"No. It's stupid."

"That's what I thought."

Dev was silent a moment, staring out the window at the brown, rolling hills. Then he said, "Sometimes apologies don't do any good."

Madeleine waited for him to amplify. He never did.

Driving on the highway was a little nerve-racking. But in some ways it was easier since she didn't have to constantly shift.

"You're doing great," Dev said. "Have you seen the ocean from up this way? You want to?"

She nodded. They went. She drove them over winding, hilly roads, then out onto the freeway, then all the way down to Santa Barbara and parked near the harbor.

"Hungry?" Dev asked her.

"Oh, yes."

They bought take-out fish-and-chips from a little shop on lower State, then walked back toward the harbor. The sun beat warm against her back, but the breeze was cool even in mid-afternoon. They walked out to look at the boats tied up at the docks. Fancy boats. Splashy boats. Incredibly expensive boats.

"Did you ever wish you had a boat like that?" Madeleine asked him as they sat on the dock and dangled their legs over.

Dev shook his head. "Just as well, too. I'd never be able to afford it on what I make riding bulls."

"But someday, if you're a doctor..."

"I won't be doing it for the money."

And somehow she knew he wouldn't. "Will you specialize?"

He shrugged. "Maybe. Reckon I'll try to stay in the West. Work around rodeo if I can. They can use it."

"I imagine. When I saw Chan get kicked in the head—" She shuddered even now at the thought.

"It can be bad," Dev agreed. "Most of the time it isn't. Most of the time you just get a scare. But..." He swallowed and stared off toward the horizon. "Did Chan tell you about John?"

"Lily did." Madeleine pulled her knees up against her chest and wrapped her arms around them. "She said he died in the rodeo at Reno two years ago."

"It was one of those freak things. John was one of the best. He thought like a bull, you know? Always knew what they were gonna do next. And he was quick as lightning.

You always felt safer when John was out there for you."
He chewed on his lower lip.

Madeleine waited, not saying anything.

"He was out there all week at Reno," Dev said in a low
voice. "Then on Thursday he twisted his knee gettin' out
of the way once. No big deal, he said. Hell, gettin' wracked
up is part of the job. He went back out on Friday. No
problem. Until the last." His voice roughened slightly.
"The last rider made the buzzer, but when he tried to jump
clear, his hand got hung up in his rope. John and the other
clown were tryin' to get him free." He paused and ran his
tongue over his lips.

Madeleine waited. She watched a seagull strut past.

"John slipped. His knee gave out, I guess. That's what
the doc thought, anyway. On the videos you could see it
buckle. When he fell, the bull caught him from behind."

Dev leaned back, propping himself up with his hands
braced behind him, his face lifted toward the sky. He
swallowed again. "He just...just nailed John with his
horn. And that was it. He bled to death before we got him
out of the arena."

"Dear God," Madeleine whispered.

"The bull rider who got hung up..." Dev said. "It was
me."

By NOON Chan was pacing around the kitchen, pouring
himself coffee, gulping it, dumping the rest down the sink,
pouring more.

By one he was going out on the porch and scanning the
road as far as he could see.

By two Lily said, "Why don't you drive out and look for
them if you're so worried. I told you I saw them go past an
hour or so ago."

"Headed which way?" Chan demanded.

"Toward town."

He grumbled. But he didn't go look for them.

By three he was considering it. He needed to do something. Anything. He didn't like standing around, worrying, waiting.

Were they in a ditch somewhere? In a head-on? Dead?

All terrible possibilities.

But another possibility occurred to him too, one that he found he didn't like much better. Maybe she was interested in Dev.

It sure as hell looked like it at six o'clock that evening when they finally drove into the yard. Dev wasn't sitting clear over next to the passenger door of Dan's truck. And Madeleine was laughing at something he was saying.

Chan stood on the porch watching them, grinding his teeth and trying to think of something cool and polite and detached to say.

He said, "Where the hell have you been?"

"CAN YOU pass it?"

"I hope so."

"Because if you can't you're history."

"I know that."

"Well, good, because I would have taken you out driving yesterday, if you and Dev had ever come back."

"Which is exactly why we didn't come back," Madeleine said. They were sitting in Dan's truck across from the driver's license bureau. She was wedged against the passenger door. He was as far left as it was possible to be. "I didn't want to come back," she said. "You would have yelled at me."

"I never yelled at you." He paused. "Much. Besides I apologized."

"And then you yelled at me again yesterday evening when Dev and I came back."

"Because you'd been gone the whole damned day! I thought you were dead."

"So you yelled? I would have thought you'd rejoice."

"Maybe I should have," he said tightly. He yanked the keys out of the ignition and slapped them in her hand. "Go to it." and he got out and walked toward the café down the street.

Madeleine watched him go, confused. She weighed the truck keys in her hand and considered flunking the test.

She might, anyway, though Dev had really done a good job with her yesterday. She didn't jerk when she started now. She shifted smoothly. She used her mirrors. She could even, after a fashion, parallel park.

Unless the testing official asked her to do something she hadn't even thought of, or unless she had a complete blackout, she thought she stood a good chance of passing.

But maybe it would be better if she didn't. Maybe it would be best if she just ran over a curb or hit a stop sign, and went back to New York.

Certainly Chan would prefer it. He might have apologized the night before last. But as she'd just pointed out, he'd snapped at her plenty after that. He'd practically jumped down her throat when she'd come back with Dev.

He'd wanted to know what she'd done and where she'd been every minute.

"You're not my keeper, Richardson," she'd told him finally.

"Yeah, well, you need one!"

She'd lifted her chin. "Then maybe I'll ask Dev."

"Suit yourself!" he'd told her and stalked off toward the barn without looking back.

When he'd driven her into town this morning, he'd barely said anything else. She glanced over at the café now as he went in the door. Through the glass she could see him take a seat at a booth by the window.

So he could watch, no doubt.

She stared at him. He stared back.

There was some very strong, strange emotion arcing between them. Some connection. Some challenge.

"Probably induced by meddling mothers," Madeleine muttered to herself.

She didn't understand it in the least. Would she ever? Did it matter?

When she was first starting to write her dissertation, she had gone to talk to her adviser, taking with her a reading list of books she'd thought were pertinent to her topic.

Venable had scanned it, then said, "But where's so and so?"

And Madeleine had replied, "I didn't think it was relevant. It's not exactly in my field."

Venable had looked at her over steepled fingers. "How do you know what's in your field until you read it?"

Odd she should remember that now.

CHAN WAS A MAN of split-second reflexes, a whiz at the instinctive response. But when he had to juggle complete thoughts, weigh alternatives, consider options, he felt as if the sea was closing over his head.

Like now, for example. He sat in the café and watched as Madeleine went into the office. He sipped his cup of coffee and thought about what he wished would happen.

And the oddest thing was, he didn't know.

It would be easiest, he told himself as he watched her and the bureau official come back out of the office and get in the truck, if she flat-out flunked. She'd be gone, out of his life.

Dev and Gil would be happy to drive with him, and before long the leg Wiley had broken in Clovis last month would be healed and he'd come back.

Things would be normal again. Just like they used to be.

He could drive and ride and flirt and sleep.

And be bored.

Bored? He frowned at the thought. But it was true. The hours in the truck got long. Neither Gil nor Wiley was much of a conversationalist, and Dev spent long hours just reading.

Madeleine promised more. With Madeleine along, life wasn't going to be just drive and ride and flirt and sleep, he could almost guarantee it.

She'd bicker with him, argue, lift that stubborn chin of hers, then grin, then taunt.

And he'd taunt back.

And then . . .

And then she'd go off with Dev.

Well, why not?

His fingers tightened around the coffee mug. She'd been with him all day yesterday.

"Driving," she'd said. But when they got out of the car there'd been something between them that went beyond driving. Even a fundamentally unaware person like Chan Richardson could see that.

Then last night, when the rest of them played cards, she and Dev had gone out.

"For a walk," they'd said.

Hell of a walk. They hadn't come back until almost eleven-thirty. Chan had lost two steak dinners and his entire box of Royals 1970 baseball cards before he heard her come in and go upstairs. Only Lily played worse. And she wasn't much of a poker player, anyway.

He ought to be glad if Madeleine did like Dev, he told himself. Make his life easier.

Had she had sex with Dev?

Damn it, where had that come from?

If he was going to think like that, it'd be better if she was gone. He slapped the mug down with such force that the coffee slopped on the table.

"Get you some more, honey?" the waitress asked him.

But just then the truck came back around the corner.

Chan shook his head and got to his feet. He handed her some money and went out the door.

By the time he came across the street, Madeleine was standing by the truck listening intently to whatever the official was saying. He was gesturing, waving his arms. She was nodding, listening, then nodding some more.

Chan walked more slowly, watching all the while. The official said something, then marked something on a paper, then handed it back to her. He saw her nod and reply. The official said something else, then held out his hand. Madeleine took it. They shook hands. All very formal. Neither smiled.

The official turned and walked back inside.

Madeleine looked up. Her gaze met Chan's, wide and direct. "Do you want the good news or the bad news?"

He shook his head, swallowed.

"I passed."

He couldn't believe his relief.

"MADELEINE CALLED," Antonia announced without preamble. "She got a driver's license."

Julia thought she sounded astonished, but it might have been just the transpacific interference between Wyoming and Bali. Julia was astonished herself.

"I didn't realize she didn't have one." She felt fleetingly sorry for Chan, then brightened. "They must have had to spend a fair amount of time together while Chan was teaching her."

"Apparently Chan didn't," Antonia said. "Madeleine says he yells."

"Yells? I'll have you know that Chan is extremely mild mannered."

"Like his mother?"

Julia opened her mouth to tell Antonia exactly what she could do with her insinuations when she realized she wasn't going to yell, she was going to shout. She laughed. "Yes. Exactly like his mother."

"Oh, dear. You know, this could be difficult," Antonia said slowly. "I wonder, Julia, maybe they really aren't suited for each other."

"Nonsense," Julia said briskly. "You saw my research."

"Well, yes, but—"

"They're suited. Who could possibly be better for Madeleine?"

"I don't know," Antonia said slowly. "What do you know about a man named Dev?"

HE COULDN'T FIGURE her out. All Thursday afternoon she got weirder and weirder, popping in and out of the house, chewing her fingernails, making a bird's nest out of her hair.

"What's the matter with you?" he asked her. She'd said she was going to hole up in the camper and work on her dissertation. Instead she'd been wearing a path back and forth to the house.

She appeared in the doorway once again. "Are you sure you should do this?" she demanded.

"Do what?" He was sitting on the pillow-ticking sofa braiding a bull rope. He had been there all afternoon. He didn't know what the hell she was talking about.

"Ride tonight," Madeleine said. "Should you ride tonight? Are you sure?"

He looked up at her. Her dark hair looked like she'd attacked it with a rake, her green eyes were almost wild. "Of course I'm sure," he said.

"But—" Her eyes got wilder. Then she waved her fingers in the air and turned and left. Ten minutes later she was back.

"This bull. Miser? What do you know about him?"

Chan shrugged. "He's five years old. Brahma. Spins to the left comin' out of the gate."

"Can he kill you?" She pressed her hand over her mouth. "Oh, God. I didn't mean that."

Chan stretched his feet out in front of him and crossed them at the ankle. He gave her a slow smile. "Why, Decker? Are you hoping?"

The green eyes shot flames at him. "You are such an ass, Richardson!" She spun and stalked off, the screen door slamming behind her.

He tossed the rope aside and went after her. "Decker! Hey, Decker! Madeleine!"

She didn't stop. He had to run to catch her. And when he did grab her arm, she tried to pull away and would have done so if he hadn't dug his fingers into her arms and held her fast.

"Sorry," he said, dropping his hands when she stopped struggling. His mouth quirked slightly. "It's gallows humor. We all do it."

"Because it can happen." Her voice was a little rough, a lot worried. She was looking at him with those incredible wide eyes.

He nodded. "It can. Chances are it won't," he added more forcefully. "Look, Decker. You don't have to come, you know. I can pick you up here on the way back."

"I'm coming."

"It isn't necessary."

"I'm coming." The mule look was back.

They stared at each other. Finally Chan nodded briefly. "Suit yourself."

"I will." She rubbed her arm where his fingers had bitten in. He made an apologetic grimace. She gave him a faint smile in return. Then she turned and walked back toward the camper.

"You actually care, don't you, Decker?" he said after a moment.

She glanced back at him. "What do you think?"

He thought she was the strangest woman he'd ever met.

UNTIL Madison Square Garden Madeleine had never been to a rodeo. And even then she hadn't really seen it; she'd arrived halfway through, blasé to the point of being indifferent. It had seemed little more than a swirl of color, fun and recklessness, until Chan had got kicked in the head.

This time it was different. This time she was expecting the worst. Chan told her again when they got to the grounds that she didn't have to watch.

"Write your dissertation. Read a book."

"I have free will," Madeleine told him. "I'm watching."

And she would, even if she threw up.

She didn't understand how he could be so cool about it. Not knowing he could be dead within the hour. But he stood around during the bronc riding, laughing with Gil and a rookie he called Kevin. He didn't even glance back at where the bulls were penned. He talked to Lily during the calf roping as if he didn't have a care in the world.

Madeleine was a wreck. She'd asked around and found out which bull was his as soon as she got there. From where she was seated next to Dan in the stands she could see it in the catch pen. It didn't look anything like Charlie, that black marshmallow of a bull Lily had let her in the corral with.

Miser was huge and with narrow eyes and a huge hump. He looked like he could—and did—eat cowboys for breakfast. Madeleine felt sick.

Surely Chan wouldn't do anything so stupid as get on a two-thousand-pound bull's back.

She said as much to Dan. He laughed.

"It's his job. Look," he said. "There's Lily. And Pete."

Someone else to worry about. Lily and the other clown, Pete Somebody, appeared now, rolling out the barrel and setting up the dummy. And Madeleine leaned forward with her elbows on her knees and her fingers knotted in front of her mouth.

She watched Lily, then turned to watch the cowboys as they put the rigging on the bulls. She picked out Chan's bright blue shirt, noted briefly Gil's gray-and-red stripe and Dev's bold geometric print. Her eyes flicked from one to the other, worrying about all of them, but always coming back to Chan.

He sat on the top of the chute and worked his bull rope into the right place and pulled it up. The bull lunged and kicked. The chute clanged. She could feel the reverberations clear up in the stands.

She shut her eyes.

The announcer gave Gil's name and hometown, the chute gate opened, and the bull lunged and twisted coming out. Madeleine sat watching, her heart in her mouth as Gil clung on.

At the Garden she'd been so far away the men had looked like toys. Here she could see the hard set of Gil's jaw, the grim determination on his face.

Dan yelled encouragement. Madeleine sat mute, her hands twisting furiously. Only when the whistle blew and Gil flung himself off, scrambling for the fence while Pete and Lily distracted the bull, did Madeleine breathe again.

But only for a moment, for almost as soon as Gil's bull had departed and he'd been awarded a 77, the announcer gave Dev's name.

The gate swung open, the bull exploded out of the chute, spun, twisted and flung Dev against the fence.

It was over in two seconds. Maybe less. Madeleine gasped, horrified. Then Pete was distracting the bull and Dev was scrambling to his feet and over the fence.

The next rider was no luckier than Dev scorewise, but he didn't hit the fence. The one after that got a 78 and very nearly a hoof in the ribs. Lily's quick action saved him from that.

And then it was Chan's turn.

Madeleine saw him tug his hat down hard and settle in on the bull. She saw him say something to Dev who had come to lean over the chute and give the bull rope one last pull. She saw him run his tongue along his upper lip, then set his jaw, tuck in his chin and nod his head.

The chute gate opened. Miser spun out, twisted, ducked his head, then snapped it up again. Chan clung.

It was amazing. Madeline watched the whole ride as if it were in slow motion. She'd heard the expression "poetry in motion" countless times in her life. She never really understood it until now.

Chan and Miser were not opposing forces. They were complementary. Chan's body didn't fight Miser's. Instead he moved with the bull, his own strength growing almost organically out of the bull's might. Every moment Miser made was echoed by his rider. The bull snapped and spun, twisted and turned. And whichever way he went, Chan went with him.

It was a terrible beauty, a deadly ballet, and it drew Madeleine in, captured her, awed her. She'd never felt the combination of fear and exhilaration before that she felt in those few seconds.

"Whoooo-eee!" Dan yelled when the buzzer went. He and the rest of the crowd yelled and hooted and stood and stamped their feet.

And Madeleine rose with them, standing without knowing how she got there, yelling without realizing what she was doing.

She saw Chan loosen his grip. And as the bull ducked his head and threw his hind feet high in the air, Chan leapt away from him, landing on his feet to raise his arms in the air and grin.

"Give that man a hand, ladies and gentlemen!" the announcer bellowed. "The judges scored Chan Richardson an 87!"

But Madeleine barely heard him. She was scrambling down out of the stands and heading for the area behind the chutes.

HE WAS SWEATY and dusty, and he had a mouthful of beer when he saw her coming.

She was hurrying toward the catch pen, craning her neck, looking, he guessed, for him.

He held his breath, unsure what to expect, remembering her fussing, imagining the worst, especially after his showboat landing.

"You were wonderful!" Madeleine exulted, and damned if she didn't throw her arms around his neck.

Chapter Eight

His arms went around her, locking her in his embrace. He might have fallen over if he hadn't. He gave a wary look. "I was?"

"Oh, gracious, yes." She was smiling all over her face, her hair like an ebony halo, her cheeks bright rose. "You were beautiful! Both of you. I've never seen anything like it. Pure poetry."

"Poetry, Decker?" He shook his head, a laugh beginning to form somewhere inside him.

"Poetry! I couldn't believe it! When you're not getting kicked in the head, Richardson, you're really something."

"You liked it." It wasn't a question, and yet a part of him was still asking. He looked at her dazed.

Maybe, in fact, he'd got tossed off. Maybe he hadn't ridden as well as he thought. Maybe he was dreaming this. Maybe he was hallucinating after having been kicked in the head.

Two cowboys came past and slapped him on the back. "Nice ride, Chan. Way to go."

He nodded his thanks. Either he was awake or other people were having the same hallucination.

"Amazing," Madeleine said, shaking her head. "Truly amazing."

It was, Chan thought, taking a deep breath and letting it out slowly. And no one was more amazed than him.

SHE DIDN'T KNOW how long she slept. She couldn't quite tell if she'd even gone to sleep, she'd been so keyed up after Chan's ride and their steak and lobster dinner with Lily and Dan and Gil and Dev.

But it was past ten when they got on the road, and Chan said he'd drive first.

"But you'll call me?" Madeleine had insisted, still not sure that he trusted her driving.

"I'll call you. Believe me, I'm not going to drive all the way to Fort Smith."

But so far he hadn't. Still, they were a long way from Fort Smith.

"Fort Smith, *Arkansas?*" She hadn't been able to believe her ears when he'd told her. She'd thought there must be a Fort Smith, California. Or at worst Arizona. Maybe there was, but she and Chan weren't going to it.

"Now you know why you needed a license."

"That's a thousand miles from here."

"Closer to two. But you're not gonna back out, are you, Decker?" he challenged her.

And she'd grinned and shaken her head. She was still grinning when she fell asleep, and she smiled again now as she rolled over in the above-the-cab bunk.

The truck was stopped. That must have been why she'd awakened; the steady thrum of the tires on the road no longer lulling her to sleep. She rolled to the edge of the bunk and hung her head over to look around, but Chan was nowhere to be seen.

She pushed aside the curtain and peered out into the darkness. They seemed to be at a rest stop. There were a couple of semis parked a ways off and three cars lined up near their truck.

Just then the back door opened and Chan appeared.

Madeleine sat up. "Where are we?"

"Middle of nowhere." He yawned and flexed his shoulders, then rubbed the back of his neck as he looked up at her. "Did I wake you?"

"I think I woke when you stopped."

"I just needed a break to walk around a little."

"What time is it?"

"Close to three."

"I'll drive."

He hesitated. "Wouldn't you rather wait till it's light?"

"Would you rather I did?"

He tugged at his ear. "Well, I—" He shrugged.

"I suppose you won't sleep if I do."

He yawned. "I think I would sleep if you drove us right over Hoover Dam." He raised his arms over his head and leaned from side to side. His shirt pulled up and Madeleine could see a narrow expanse of midriff. She jerked her gaze back to his face.

"Are we close?" she asked with a smile.

Chan smiled a sleepy smile in return. "Not close enough." He fished the keys out of his front jeans pocket, juggled them in his palm, then tossed them to her. "You want to drive? Be my guest."

Madeleine looked from Chan to the keys and back again. "You're sure?"

"Aren't you?" One brow lifted in challenge.

Her fingers closed over the keys. She smiled. "Of course."

The keys were warm from being close to his body, and Madeleine was quite ridiculously aware of just exactly where they had been. She didn't ever remember being aware of anything so silly in all her life.

She clambered down out of the bunk, then realized that she was wearing a sheer cotton gown.

"Er," she said, suddenly extremely aware of his dark eyes on her, "I'd better get dressed."

She expected him to make some lewd remark. He swallowed. "Yeah," he said hoarsely. "You'd better get dressed."

When she came back out of the bathroom, suitably covered in jeans and a T-shirt, only moments later, Chan was sprawled face-up on the lower bunk fast asleep.

His lips were parted slightly, whistling a little with each breath he took. His lashes, longer than hers by far, lay in perfect half-moons against his lean cheeks. The only other man she'd ever seen asleep was Scott. She remembered thinking how angelic he looked with his blond curls and slightly full lips. There was nothing angelic about Chan Richardson even in sleep.

But she liked the way he looked.

It would never do, however, to have him wake up and find her looking at him. He'd wonder what on earth she was doing.

She wondered herself.

This truck was different from Dan's. Bigger. Boxier. But an automatic. And it didn't take Madeleine long to figure it out. She took a few seconds to find the lights, then put it in reverse and, sending a prayer winging to whichever saint protected novice drivers, backed out of the stall. She sent another prayer, of thanksgiving this time, for Chan's willingness to trust her, to just hand over the keys and go to sleep. She hadn't expected that much faith. It warmed her.

The highway, wide and almost empty, spun out like a silver thread across the California desert into northern Arizona. Madeleine drove steadily through the rest of the night noting the changes as desert gave way to stark hills and eventually trees and mountains.

They passed through few towns. Those they did were fast asleep. And as the morning dawned, everywhere she looked there was space and stillness.

She'd forgotten such stillness even existed. So consumed was she normally by the city and its demands and its millions of people that she hadn't remembered until now the quiet she had grown up in.

She reveled in it.

She rolled down the window and let the morning breeze blow through her hair. Later it would be much too hot for open windows, and they would have to use the air-conditioning, but now, for just a while, she could savor the wind against her cheeks and in her hair.

She thought about stopping in Williams, but rejected it. Somehow the idea of stretching her legs in a convenience store parking lot or gas station didn't appeal. She didn't want to cope with civilization, didn't want to look at name-brand junk food, didn't want to speak or break the mood.

So she waited until she was on the open road to pull over to ease the kinks in her back and the stiffening muscles of her legs, but mostly to bask in the quiet, to breathe in the clear, high mountain air.

She opened the door and got out quietly so she wouldn't wake Chan. Then she came around the truck to stand silently facing the sun.

It wasn't really dawn anymore, but it was far closer than she'd ever come to it in New York. Manhattan didn't have a horizon, at least not where she lived in the middle of the Upper West Side.

"Beautiful, isn't it?"

Madeleine spun round.

Chan was standing sleepy-eyed in the door of the camper, his shirt unbuttoned, the top of his jeans unsnapped, his feet bare. He stood there silently for a moment, looked from her to the horizon. Then he stepped down onto the ground.

Beautiful?

Yes. He was.

She took a step back, startled at the intensity of her reaction. "You'll hurt your feet," she warned inanely.

Chan looked down, then shook his head. "Naw." He padded toward her across the gravel, then squinted again at the sun as he stood next to her.

She saw him take a deep breath, then let it out slowly. He turned to her and smiled. "This is what makes it all worthwhile."

Madeleine looked at him, surprised.

He gave a sheepish shrug. "Well, winning's nice, too, of course. And all the cheering and hootin' and hollerin'. Makes you feel like you accomplished something. Makes you want to go on. But you spend more time blowin' and goin' than you do ridin' bulls. A hell of a lot more. You sit for hours and hours, drive for hours and hours. Through heat and dust and traffic jams. But—" he paused and took another deep breath "—you also get times like this."

Madeleine looked at him, blinked at the smile on his face, then smiled back. She couldn't help it.

"Pretty philosophical, Richardson," she said after a moment.

He grinned. "Yeah, isn't it?"

"All that profundity in a man who goes looking for kicks in the head kind of boggles the mind."

"Hey, you thought it was poetry, remember?"

She laughed. "So I did."

Their gazes caught, locked. She swallowed. So did he. He looked at her lips. She looked at his.

And then she said, "Sometimes you surprise me."

He opened his mouth as if he were going to say something, then closed it again. He looked at her for a long moment, then he nodded.

"Ditto," he said. Then he tucked his hands into his pockets and turned and walked away, heading toward a small stand of trees.

Madeleine watched him go and thought how much he seemed to fit into the landscape, his ruggedness blending well with the forest and the meadows and the rough San Francisco peaks in the distance. But like them, the hardness of his features was gentled by the low-angled sun, which at a distance seemed to dust with gold the stubble on his chin and cheeks.

He turned and looked at her, then headed back toward her. He was smiling as he came, and she found herself once more looking at his mouth. He had a strong mouth, firm and wide and uncompromisingly male.

She wondered how he kissed.

Her whole body jerked. Then she blinked, hauling herself out of her reverie, annoyed at the direction of her thoughts. She beat a hasty retreat back to the camper.

"Something wrong, Decker?" Chan called after her.

"Not a thing," she said quickly. "I'm just ready to go!"

Chan stood where he was for a moment, then gave a small shrug, then followed. "I'll drive."

Madeleine tossed him the keys.

He slid into the driver's seat and started the engine. She went to work.

It might be only five in the morning, but she had no intention of trying to go back to sleep.

She didn't even climb back into the bunk; she knew what she would do if she did.

She would lie there and think about Chan Richardson's mouth.

CHAN SPENT THE DAY thinking about Madeleine Decker's mouth.

Mile upon mile of Arizona and New Mexico desert slipped past unnoticed. With one conscious part of him he kept alert, his eyes on the white line and the traffic. In his mind's eye he saw Madeleine Decker's mouth.

He touched it, tasted it, savored her lips with his own.

Second by second, move by move, he saw, he tasted, he felt their kiss unfold. He saw himself take her in his arms and hold her, saw himself smooth her hair back, stroke her cheeks, then tilt her face and touch his lips to her.

He did it all in his mind.

Preparing himself. Just like when he was getting ready to ride a bull.

He laughed.

Behind him Madeleine stopped typing. "What's funny?"

He shook his head. "Nothing." Madeleine Decker might be improving, but he couldn't see her appreciating that. "How's the dissertation going?"

She groaned. "Drivel. Pure drivel." She had been working all day. She'd even made him stop once so she could call her adviser. She wanted to get his opinion on something. She got it, but it didn't seem to be making her happy.

She came back to the camper more out of sorts than when she'd left. And since then there'd been an awful lot of fuming and muttering coming from the table where she sat.

She sighed and stood up. "I'm having a problem in chapter four. Venable doesn't think it works."

"Want me to read it?"

There was a pause. He glanced over his shoulder to see her standing in the aisle staring at him.

"I can read, Decker," he said a little irritably.

"I'm sure you can, Richardson. I'm just surprised you offered."

He shrugged, turning back to his driving. "Think of it as a compatibility test."

Madeleine considered that. "Fair enough."

OTHER PEOPLE had read parts of her dissertation. Malcolm had read it. So had Douglas. Alfie's cousin Sarah, who was a post-doctoral fellow at Columbia had read and critiqued the part on Kant.

Madeleine had awaited all their comments with equanimity and confidence. She didn't know why she was so nervous about Chan. She didn't even know why she was letting him read it. What did he know about philosophy?

She flicked a glance over her shoulder. He didn't look up. She chewed on her thumbnail for another five miles, then looked again. This time the truck swerved.

"Watch it, Decker. You're too new at this to be driving, looking over your shoulder."

"Just read, Richardson."

He read.

Finally when they stopped to eat at a rest stop somewhere in west Texas, he handed it back to her.

"So what's his problem?" he wanted to know.

"His problem?"

Chan shrugged. "What doesn't he like? I think it sounds fine. Impressed the hell out of me."

Madeleine smiled faintly. "He says I've given it the wrong emphasis."

Chan scratched his head. "The wrong emphasis?" His mouth lifted at the corner. "What's that mean?"

Madeleine grimaced. "I think it means that I'm not seeing this topic the way he sees it."

Chan frowned. "Whose dissertation is it, yours or his?"

"Well, mine, but—"

"Then you pick the emphasis."

"That's not precisely the way it works," Madeleine said.

"It ought to be."

SHE WAS STILL SMILING about that when they got to Fort Smith. Everyone else who had read her dissertation had told her what she should do. Everyone had had advice, suggestions, comments, criticism.

Chan said it was hers, she should do what she wanted.

Then he'd shrugged in the face of her open-mouthed stare. "Well, hell," he'd said. And she thought she'd even seen a faint reddish hue along his cheekbones. "It seems simple enough to me."

Madeleine didn't know if it was really any simpler or simply refreshing. But it made her smile every time she thought about it.

And when Chan was heading off to ride the bull in Fort Smith, it made her reach out and grab him as he tried to slip past her in the camper. It made her smile right into his stunned blue eyes. It made her whisper, "Good luck."

It made her kiss his cheek.

IT TOOK CHAN thirty hours to drive to Fort Smith to ride a black Brahma bull with the unlikely name of Mr. Bo-Peep. It took Mr. BoPeep 3.2 seconds to dump Chan on his butt in the dust.

He shouldn't have been surprised.

He broke the cardinal rule of bull riding: he let himself get distracted.

But who the hell wouldn't have been distracted, thinking about the touch of Madeleine Decker's mouth on his cheek?

What in the hell had possessed her to kiss him?

Christ, he could still feel it now as he stumbled back to the camper. He could feel that soft touch more than he could feel the throb of his elbow where he'd hit it on the fence or the smarting where his rear end had hit the dirt.

He touched his cheek, amazed, dazed.

Then he looked up and saw her waiting, her eyes wide and worried.

"No poetry this time," he said, his mouth twisting as she came up to him.

"Are you all right?"

"Of course." He brushed past her, climbing into the camper. "Let's get moving."

"We're going? We just got here."

Which was true enough, but he didn't see the point. "Why not? Something you got to stay around for?"

"No. You mean—" she looked at him, aghast "—that's it? Don't you get another chance? Don't you get to ride a bull?"

"Yeah. Tomorrow. In Strong City." He sat down and pulled off his boots.

"No, tonight. You fell off tonight."

He stuffed his riding boots back into his rigging bag and rubbed his elbow. "No joke."

Madeleine frowned, touching his arm. "You're sure you're all right?"

"I'm all right!"

"Okay, okay. But then, don't they let you—"

He stood up. "No, Decker, they damned well don't let you."

"But—"

He held up a finger. "One bull. One ride. Those are the rules."

"You mean we drove all the way to Fort Smith, Arkansas, for you to fall off a bull?"

He shrugged, undoing his shirt and trying to ease out of it without brushing his elbow. "Win a few, lose a few."

"But—" But apparently she couldn't think of an argument. At least not one that would do any good. She took ahold of his shirt and helped ease it off for him, wincing when she saw his elbow. "You're going to have a terrible bruise."

"I'll live," he said shortly.

"I'm sure you will." Her tone was just as sharp. "To ride again another day." She sounded almost mocking. It set his teeth on edge.

"It's your fault," he said, his voice gruff.

"Mine?"

"You kissed me!"

Her jaw dropped. She stared at him, disbelieving. Then her cheeks turned bright red. "Well, may the saints strike me dead for my sin," she said sarcastically. "I had no idea my kisses could wreak such havoc, Richardson. Please forgive me."

At the moment that was beyond him. "Shut up, Decker," he said and shut himself in the shower.

THEY DIDN'T TALK all the way to Strong City, Kansas. The silence was rigid and complete, neither even meeting the other's gaze until they got there just in time for Chan to ride the next afternoon.

Only when he was heading out the camper door with his rigging bag, still silent, did Madeleine finally muster her determination and speak up.

"I'm sorry," she said stiffly. "I shouldn't have kissed you. I should never have overstepped the bounds. It was a mistake. Put it down to propinquity."

"What?"

"The nearness of you," she said.

"I know what the word means, Decker."

"Good." She wiped her palms down the sides of her jeans. "Then you know it was nothing special about you. I'm sorry that you were distracted."

He just looked at her, dazed. "Yeah," he said. And then he walked out.

Madeleine watched him go. She didn't go watch him ride. She sat staring at her computer screen, telling herself to stop thinking about damnable Channing Richardson and concentrate instead on free will, which was what really mattered.

Her mind, it seemed, had a will of its own. And it freely chose to think about Chan no matter what she said.

So what else is new? Madeleine thought grumpily, and her mind dragged her along to spend another hour replaying the infamous kiss.

She was stunned when he'd yelled at her about it.

Was it really so awful? She didn't suppose a normal woman would feel this way. A normal woman probably never had doubts. But then she hadn't been normal since Scott. Or maybe even before, she thought wearily.

Probably she shouldn't be let around men at all. She didn't seem to know what to do with them. She would just have to try to be aloof.

She stared at the screen again. Resolute. Determined.

Then the door opened and Chan came in. He had a smudge of dirt on his cheek and a grin on his face and all that propinquity came rushing back.

"An 80." He grinned. "Good enough to win."

"Because I didn't kiss you, I suppose," Madeleine said.

He grinned. "I've been thinking about that."

"What do you mean?"

"Propinquity. I've got an idea." He was stripping off his boots and his shirt even as he spoke. Madeleine thought she was spending an awful lot of time watching him get undressed.

She looked at him warily. "What idea?"

"You should do it again. A lot."

"What?"

"Get it out of your system."

"But I thought you hated it."

He stared at her as if she'd lost her mind.

"You fell off the bull," she reminded him.

He shrugged. "Yeah. Because it surprised the hell out of me. I was thinking about the kiss not the bull. Hell—" he rubbed a hand against the back of his neck "—I liked it, Decker. A lot."

"You did?" She tested the notion, then swallowed the smile that touched her lips. She felt funny all of a sudden, silly, breathless. She looked around to see if the sun had just come out.

"So," he went on, "I was thinking it wouldn't be quite so distracting if you did it more often." He grinned.

Madeleine narrowed her eyes and looked at him. "Richardson," she warned.

His grin widened. "Hey, why not? Desensitize me, too."

"I've heard some lines in my time, Richardson—"

"You have?" He gave her such a look of wide-eyed innocence that she laughed.

"You're a shark, Richardson. A predator."

"Not me. I'm just a normal, red-blooded American boy."

There wasn't anything boyish about him except, perhaps, his grin. "Sure," Madeleine said.

He laughed. "Come on, Decker. I've ridden my bull for the day. It's safe. I promise I won't fall on my, er, rear end."

"If I thought it would knock you on your, er, rear end," Madeleine said, "I might do it."

"Well?" He waited, blue eyes bright and challenging.

She looked at him, felt something warm and willing inside her begin to emerge. God, it was tempting. She fought the temptation. She might be a graduate student in philosophy, but she had a classical education. She knew all about Pandora and her box.

"I don't know, Richardson. I'll have to think about it."

I DON'T KNOW wasn't no.

It wasn't yes, either. Yet.

But it would happen. Chan was ever an optimist. Things were looking up.

And thank God for that, too, he thought now as he drove into Gladewater, because she was right on about that propinquity bit.

He'd always had an eye for the ladies—smiling with them, talking with them, flirting with them, even occasionally going to bed with them.

But when they weren't around, he had no trouble thinking about other things to do. Trouble was, Madeleine was always around. He was getting to be a wreck.

But she was still thinking, when he got thrown off his bull in Gladewater and again the following day in Wichita Falls.

Dev won there.

Madeleine kissed him. He came away from the pay window and swept her into his arms, and damned if she didn't kiss him! Chan was outraged.

"You kissed Dev!" he accused her when they got back to the camper. He kicked the door shut and slung his rigging bag under the table and slapped his hat down on the bunk.

"So? What's the matter with that?" She looked wholly unconcerned.

"You won't kiss me!"

"I did kiss you. Once. Now I'm thinking about doing it again."

"And in the meantime you'll just kiss Dev for practice," he grumbled.

She shrugged. "Why not? He threw his arms around me." She turned, opened the refrigerator and got out the bottle of iced tea and poured herself a glass. "Want one?"

"No, damn it, I do not want one!"

"I just asked," she said mildly. She tipped her head back and took a long swallow. He watched her—watched her Adam's apple move, watched her lips on the glass.

She finished drinking and looked at him. "Are you going to take a shower or not?"

"Why? Want to join me?"

She gave a long-suffering sigh. "No, thank you, Richardson. But I am getting hungry. Dev and Gil said they'd meet us for dinner."

"We've got to go to Oregon."

"For dinner?"

"Hell, no. But we've got to be there by Saturday."

"Does that mean no dinner?"

"No, Decker." He expelled a deep breath, conceding defeat. "We can have dinner."

She kissed Dev again after dinner.

They were standing by Gil's truck, getting ready to leave. He and Gil were talking about a new stock contractor, and out of the corner of his eye he was watching Madeleine and Dev talking in low tones a few feet away.

He saw Dev nod, then nod again, then grimace wryly. He saw Madeleine put her hand on his arm. He saw Dev smile at her and her smile at him.

And then, once more, she kissed him.

"It isn't propinquity that's getting you to kiss Dev," he said tightly the next morning.

He'd fumed about it for hours, all night, in fact, while Madeleine slept. But now she was driving and he was supposed to be sleeping. He hadn't drifted off yet.

He kept seeing Madeleine kissing Dev.

She glanced back, giving him a startled look. Then she laughed. "No, it isn't that."

"You got the hots for him, have you?" He lay back on the bunk, folded his arms under his head and, with determined indifference, stared out the window at the telephone wires as they passed.

Madeleine glanced back at him, and he arched his back and tipped his head back so he could look at her upside down. She was smiling.

"No, Richardson," she said, still smiling, "I do not have the hots for him."

"Yeah, right." He sagged back onto the mattress.

Another hundred or so telephone poles passed. Then she asked, "Would you care if I did?"

"Hell, no."

"Well, then..."

"You're supposed to be testing your compatibility with me," he reminded her. He sounded like he was whining. He'd better shut up.

"Are you...jealous, Richardson?" Her voice floated back to him, amused.

He rolled over, his head snapping around so he could glare at the back of hers. "No, Decker, I'm damned well not."

"You're just horny."

"I'm what?"

"Horny, Richardson," she said cheerfully. "If you understand a word like *'propinquity,'* I should think you'd understand that."

"I understand the term, Decker."

There was a smile in her voice as she said, "I thought you might."

OF COURSE, she was right. But he didn't have time to do more than think about it over the next three days. He had no time to advance his campaign for kisses or anything else. They had to get to Sisters, Oregon, by Saturday afternoon, so they spent virtually all of the time driving.

They drove in shifts, four hours on, four hours off. When they weren't driving, Madeleine was typing or sleeping, Chan was stretching or exercising or sleeping. They only stopped briefly, now and again. They pulled in at one overlook in the Rockies to stand and stare at the majestic mountains all around them, to appreciate, to savor, to breathe in pure mountain air.

They stopped another time to get gas, and there was a stream right behind the gas station. When Chan finished filling the tank and went looking for Madeleine, he found her wading.

She waved and grinned. "Come on in," she said. "The water's fine."

He shook his head, but in the end he allowed himself a few minutes of icy water running over his feet and ankles. And he had to admit it felt good.

"Like being massaged with ice," Madeleine said.

Chan tried not to think about massages at all.

He was punchy and sleepy and—she was right—horny and trying to get his head on straight as he headed into Oregon.

He needed to think about the bull he was coming up against. It wasn't working.

They were almost there when Madeleine loomed behind him to ask, "What do you do when you prepare to ride a bull?"

He glanced back at her. She was putting her computer away, shuffling some notes into her briefcase. Her long hair obscured her face from his glance—all but her lips.

He turned back to the road, focusing determinedly. "What do you mean?"

She shrugged, coming up to sit beside him in the front. "You said I distracted you, so I was wondering what you were thinking, what I distracted you from."

He shrugged. "Thinking my way through the ride, I guess. Seeing myself doing it. Concentrating." She was distracting him again right now.

"On each individual bull? I mean, do you see it different each time?"

"If I know the bull."

"Do you know this one?"

He nodded. "Tough little sucker called BeBop."

"What's different about him?"

"Temperament, I suppose. I've ridden him a couple of times. He's not big. Lots of guys think the little ones are easy. Well, some of 'em are. Not him. It's like he's the smallest kid in the class, you know? Got to be aggressive to make up for it. Probably got picked on in the catch pen when he was a boy." He grinned.

"So how do you deal with him?"

"You can't give him any room to maneuver. He's small enough you can get a good grip with your legs. That's the trick. But he doesn't like it much. He's got this wiggle. There aren't many bulls that wiggle."

He went on and verbally rode the bull for her, explaining, answering her questions. And she listened. And asked more questions. And he answered those, too.

And before he knew it, they were there. And he was focused. He was prepared.

He got a 92.

"Is that an A?" Madeleine asked him when it was over and he was grinning his head off.

"That's an A!" He grinned and slung his arm around her as they walked together back to the camper, their hips brushing, their strides matching. "But was it poetry, Decker?"

Madeleine smiled up at him. "It was poetry, Richardson," she said.

And then, at last, she kissed him.

SHE COULDN'T HELP herself. But with him yammering about it all the time, misinterpreting it, misinterpreting *her*, she hadn't dared. Probably she shouldn't have dared this time, but she didn't think; she just did.

Like an athletic shoe commercial, she mocked herself. But she couldn't mock herself too long because Chan dropped his rigging bag, slipped his arms around her and kissed her back.

Madeleine had been kissed before. By Malcolm, by Douglas. By Scott.

But never like this.

Malcolm had given her dry little pecks that reminded her of a chicken rearranging straw. Douglas's kisses had been wet, sloppy events from which Madeleine always escaped wishing it didn't look so rude to wipe her mouth. And Scott?

Well, Scott kissed the way he did everything else—with a goal in mind.

Channing Richardson kissed for the moment.

He kissed hungrily and thoroughly, his lips moving over hers eagerly, taking what she gave and asking for more. And Madeleine gave it to him. And what she got back was sweet, tender, warm, and just a little wild.

It made her shiver. It made her hum. It made her tighten her arms around his neck and touch his lips with her tongue.

He groaned, hauling her hard against him and meeting her tentative touch with a more practiced thrust of his own. And Madeleine opened her mouth for him, let him taste her, tease her, shuddering wildly at the possessiveness of his touch.

She'd never been kissed like this.

It was heavenly.

It was dangerous.

She wanted more. She knew she'd already had too much.

Reluctantly, yet determinedly, she pulled back, gathered her wits as best she could and finally opened her eyes to meet his stunned blue gaze.

"Goodness, Richardson," she said as lightly as she could when at last she dared to trust her voice. "What do you suppose our mothers would say about that?"

Chapter Nine

He didn't intend to ask.

He never would have brought it up himself. God knew he didn't go around talking about kissing girls with his mother.

But he ran into Kevin Skates again at Livermore. Kevin had passed through the ranch on his way from his sister's wedding in Rapid City. He said Chan's father wanted to talk to him about Frank Parker's bull that he'd had shipped from California.

His mother wanted to talk to him about Madeleine.

Kevin didn't tell him that.

"Ma, I don't have time to talk now."

"Nonsense, you just spent twenty minutes talking about the bull with your father."

"It was important."

"And Madeleine's not? You like her, don't you?"

"Sure. She's fine," Chan said dismissively. "Really, Ma, I gotta go. I'm riding soon."

"Channing, I am not a green girl. I have been to a few rodeos in my time. Bull riding is always last."

"But it's—" he glanced at his watch "—damn near three and—"

"It's two where you are. They can't be close to the bull riding yet. Does she like you?"

He sighed. "Of course she likes me, Ma. What's not to like?"

"Not a thing, darling. I'm so pleased."

"Don't be. And don't go getting any ideas," he warned her, "just because we haven't killed each other yet."

"You know me, Chan, I always get ideas. I'm glad you haven't killed her. Have you kissed her?"

"Ma!"

"Well, have you?"

"Ma, I'm not gonna tell you about my love life."

"Ah. Then it is a love life." Her tone was cheerfully smug.

"It's not a love life," Chan said through clenched teeth.

"Then you haven't kissed her?" When did his mother get so good at expressing maternal disappointment with just the tone of her voice? "I always knew you weren't as fast a worker as Mark or Gard, Chan, but—"

"I've kissed her, damn it."

Julia sighed her relief. "I thought so."

"You're a very sneaky woman."

"Not at all. I've always been very up-front with you," Julia insisted. "And so I will be now. I think you should kiss her a lot."

"I don't," Chan said flatly.

"Why? Didn't you like it?"

"Ma!"

"I was only asking," Julia said in her most wounded tone. "I mean, I could certainly understand if you didn't. Was she cold and unresponsive?"

"I don't believe this." Chan's fingers strangled the receiver.

"It's a simple question, Channing."

"Ma, I gotta go."

"It might have been a fluke the first time," she went right on. "You could try it again. Maybe she was nervous. Maybe next time she'll respond. I can't believe she's really indifferent to you, Channing. Try kissing her every day. I'm sure things will improve. Would you like to talk to your father again? He's a wonderful kisser. Maybe he could give you some advice."

"Bye, Ma." And Chan hung up.

"So how's it going?" Lily asked. She was taking off her greasepaint in front of the mirror in Chan's camper. The Livermore rodeo had been over for half an hour. Chan and Gil and Dev and Dan had gone out for a beer. Lily and Madeleine had declined.

"It's going fine," Madeleine said now. "A little tiring. He did two rodeos yesterday. Sisters and then Roseburg. We just barely got there for that one. They had to hold his bull for him. Then overnight we drove down here."

Lily nodded, swiping with a tissue at her cheek. "It starts getting like that this time of year. Wait till around the Fourth of July. It's crazy."

"Yes."

Lily looked at her curiously. "But you don't hate it?"

"No. Not at all."

"Lots of people hate it. All the traveling, the running, the being on the road all the time."

"I don't." Oh, she'd have preferred more time, more sleep, fewer hours on the road. Who wouldn't? But she liked the change, the variety, and yet at the same time, the sense of community that existed wherever they went.

Not all the same people went to every rodeo. But their paths crossed often enough that she was beginning to recognize faces, to collect names, to know who to expect.

She looked for Gil and Dev to show up at many of the same places they did. Sometimes she saw Tom Holden. There were others, rough stock riders mostly, since they didn't have to bring their own animals, who hit a lot of the same places. She hadn't seen Lily since Santa Maria. Chan had told her that Lily worked mostly in the far western states. But they were seeing her now. They'd see her again in Reno. Wherever they went, Madeleine had a sense not of being a stranger, but of belonging.

It was very different from being an anthropologist, always on the outside, spectating, objectifying, taking notes.

"I like it," she said to Lily now.

Lily grinned. "What about Chan? Do you like him?"

Madeleine shrugged. "Sure."

"Sure?" Lily's eyes caught hers in the mirror. "Have you kissed him?"

"Lily!"

"Well, have you? You have, haven't you? While you were 'compiling evidence'?" Lily was laughing, her own grin almost as wide as the painted one she was wiping off from ear to ear. "Come on, Mad, tell the truth. Did you?"

Madeleine made a face. "So, all right. I kissed him."

"Was it good?"

"What do you think?" she answered crossly.

"I think you liked it. A lot."

"So? He's a very good kisser." Madeleine lifted her chin, defying Lily to find her reaction strange. "I'm sure I'm not alone in saying so."

"I'm sure you're not," Lily agreed readily, and Madeleine was surprised to find that that nettled.

"He probably has girls all over," she said gruffly.

"They like him, all right," Lily said. "Heck, what's not to like? He's gorgeous. Sweet. Fun. Just a little bit wicked."

"What do you know about him being wicked?" Madeleine wanted to know.

"Nothing," Lily said quickly. "But, heavens, you've only got to look at him. I bet he kisses pretty wicked, doesn't he?"

"Mmm," said Madeleine.

"I thought so." Lily finished removing all the grease-paint, then ran water in the sink and rubbed up a lather on her hands. She began rubbing it onto her face. "So have you changed your mind?"

"Changed my mind? About what?"

"Marrying him. Or rather, not marrying him."

"No."

"Haven't even thought about it?" Lily pressed.

Madeleine shook her head adamantly. "Nope."

"You just like kissing him?"

"Hardly the same thing."

"It could lead there," Lily pointed out.

"There are many more important things in marriage than kissing."

Lily nodded slowly. "I know that." She had that far-away look in her eyes again, and Madeleine knew she was remembering John.

"Lily?"

"What?"

"Do you ever think you might...marry again some-day?"

"Hey," Lily said lightly after a moment, "don't try to palm him off on me now."

"No. Not Chan. Just...married."

"No."

"Never?"

"Why? You have someone in mind?" Lily looked at her sharply.

Madeleine traced a pattern on the countertop. She ran her tongue over her lips and wondered at the wisdom of this. She hardly knew Lily. And yet somehow right from the start they'd connected. She glanced at Lily out of the corner of her eye. "I don't know."

Lily's eyes narrowed. "Who?"

Madeleine hesitated. She hated to say it, knew she was taking a chance.

"Who?" Lily demanded again.

"Dev." She looked up to see Lily's reaction when she said his name.

Lily's jaws came together with a snap. "Dev? *Devlin Gray?*" She flung the washcloth into the sink. She stepped out of the room, started toward the door, stopped, came back. "Don't even think it. You know—you know he was the one who—who—" She broke off, unable to finish.

"I know he was the one who was riding when John got killed, yes," Madeleine said quietly.

"Then how can you suggest—" Lily's voice was anguished.

"Was it his fault?"

"Of course it wasn't his fault! These things happen. It's part of rodeo. It's part of life. God, don't you think I, of all people, know that?"

"But you've never forgiven him." She'd listened to Dev talk about the guilt he felt almost every time she'd seen him. She knew he would rather have died himself than consider himself responsible for another man's death. She knew—as he did—that he hadn't caused it. But it didn't help. Not when Lily risked her life weekend after weekend. Not when she turned her back on him. Not when she could scarcely bring herself to speak to him.

Lily stopped. She stared at Madeleine, her eyes wide and haunted. The color seemed to drain from her face.

"I told you," she said desperately. "It wasn't his fault. He wasn't to blame. No one was. It just . . . happened."

"He needs you to tell him that, Lily. He needs you to talk to him."

Lily just shook her head. "No. No, I—I can't." She turned away, her head bent over the sink, her fingers locking around the edge of the countertop so tightly that her knuckles went white.

Madeleine got up and came to stand behind her. "He cares about you, Lily."

"Well, he doesn't need to bother! I'm fine."

"Are you?" Madeleine asked softly and was totally unprepared when Lily whirled around to face her.

"All right, you want to hear me say it? No, damn it, I'm not! I'm never going to be fine, ever again, because John is gone, and he's never coming back!" Tears welled in her eyes, spilled down her cheeks. And Madeleine put her arms around her and held her shaking body and cursed her stupidity for having meddled.

"Shh, Lil. I'm sorry. I'm so sorry."

Lily sobbed and hiccuped and shuddered, her shoulders heaving as she fought for control. Minutes passed before she achieved it. Finally, though, she raised her head and swiped at her eyes. Madeleine passed her a tissue. She rubbed them again, then shuddered and sniffed and wiped her nose.

"I'm sorry," Madeleine said again. "I had no right. I'm a fool. Forgive me, please."

Lily shook her head. "No." She blinked rapidly and rubbed at her eyes again, then met Madeleine's stricken gaze. "No, you are right."

"I'm an idiot. A meddler. I think I can solve the problems of the world. I can't even solve my own!"

But Lily was still shaking her head. "You're right. You're right," she said. She was breathing shallowly, and now she slowed and took a deeper breath, holding it, then letting it out gradually. "It hurts," she whispered. "It still hurts so much."

"I'm sorry."

"But . . . I know it hurts Dev, too. I know that! I can see it every time I look at him. And I want to go to him. I want to tell him...talk to him...and I...I don't know how. I'm afraid I'll..." She shook her head and buried her face in her hands once again.

Madeleine rubbed her shoulder, stroked her arm, tried in the only way she knew to say that she was there, that she cared, that she'd do whatever she could possibly do. "I'm sorry, Lil," she murmured again and again. "What can I do?"

Lily sniffed. She swallowed. She rubbed her fist against her eyes making them even blotchier. She gave Madeleine a pained smile. "You already did it," she said. Her voice was hoarse.

"Swell," Madeleine muttered.

Lily smiled faintly. "It isn't swell," Lily said. "But you are right. I need . . . I need to talk to Dev . . . to tell him . . ."

Madeleine worried her lower lip. "I might be wrong," she said. "I could be." Maybe she was backpedaling, but all she could envision was more hurt, more pain for both of them. And her being the cause of it.

"Do you really think so?" Lily asked her. Her lips trembled slightly. Madeleine saw her make tight fists of her hands and wrap her arms across her breasts.

Do you really think so?

Did she really think she was wrong? Did she really think that Dev wasn't hurting, didn't care, didn't need a word, a touch—something—from Lily.

Slowly, because even if she was wrong, she had to be honest, Madeleine shook her head. "No."

THERE WAS SOMETHING the matter with Decker.

At first Chan thought it was just that she was tired. God knew that wouldn't be surprising.

They'd driven from Wichita Falls to Oregon in less than thirty-six hours, then had kept right on going to Livermore. Then they'd turned around and headed the other way, up to Manitoba, and she'd driven first.

But she'd slept, and then he'd slept, and then finally when they were up at the same time, still driving, he spoke to her, but it seemed like she wasn't there.

Hours and miles passed. They took more turns driving and sleeping. Chan talked about the bull he'd ridden in Livermore, about the one he was going to ride in Brandon, then in Innisfail after that. He tried to get her to talk about her dissertation and her moron of an adviser. Maybe that was the problem. But she didn't reply. Eventually he talked about the sun and the moon and the stars and everything else he could think of.

He didn't think she heard a word.

He rode well at Brandon. He told her he got an A. She blinked as if she didn't know what he was talking about.

He got thrown at Innisfail. Maybe it was because he didn't have the rope secure enough or maybe it was because the bull went down when Chan was expecting him to go up. Or maybe it was because he was worrying about her.

She sat in front of her computer and stared at the screen hour after hour. If she typed anything, he never heard. Or she gazed out the window, but when he pointed out antelope at dawn one morning and a scraggly herd of buffalo on a South Dakota ranch as they headed south again to

North Platte, she murmured but she didn't even turn her head.

He told himself she wasn't his problem, that she wasn't his business, that what Madeleine Decker did or didn't do, said or didn't say, had nothing to do with him.

He'd given himself that speech before, over other women. And generally he had no trouble believing himself. Generally he could put right out of his mind whatever woman was on the verge of causing him grief.

Not Madeleine Decker.

She was under his skin.

"Thanks, Ma," he muttered now. He said it audibly. Madeleine was sitting right behind him at the table, staring at the computer while he drove.

She didn't even look up.

He was afraid it was the kiss.

Her distraction had begun not long after it. She'd kissed him after he'd won at Sisters. Then it had been a mad scramble to get to Roseburg that night so he could ride there. And then from there they'd driven right on through the night to Livermore.

Worse, she'd driven. Which had probably given her hours and hours to regret it.

Was that it? Did she regret it?

He faced the possibility. Probably she did, knowing her. Perverse woman that she was.

She sure as hell hadn't kissed him as though she was regretting it. He'd never had a kiss quite like that. Chan had kissed a fair number of women in his life. Lots of them had been enthusiastic as hell.

He knew about enthusiasm. He knew about lust and hunger and all those basic biological drives. He knew those good genes had a will of their own, didn't he? He was, after all, his mother's son.

He'd felt those things in Decker's kiss. But he'd felt something more. Some need. Some connection. He shook his head, not quite able to put a name to it. Only able to wish they could do it again.

And she was walking around like a zombie. Hardly an encouraging response. He ought to be glad, he told himself. It meant she wasn't going to throw herself at him. It was a matter of his own perverse nature, he decided, that he wasn't.

"Are you coming to watch tonight, Decker?" he asked. He raised his voice louder than it needed to be because she always acted like she was hearing him—when she heard him at all—from a long way off.

"What?" she said vaguely. Then, "Oh, I suppose."

"Newness wearing off, is it? Well," he muttered almost to himself, "maybe seeing Dev will cheer you up."

"Dev's going to be there?" She straightened and there was a spark in her voice suddenly, as if she'd just landed back on the same planet.

Chan's jaw clenched. "Said he was when I was talking to him in Livermore," he told her tightly.

"Oh." He heard her take a deep breath. Then, "Oh, God." She sounded as if she'd swallowed her computer.

"What's the matter with you, Decker?"

"N-nothing." But there was life in the back of the camper now, movement. She didn't sound as if she was sleepwalking anymore.

Chan felt something akin to irritation snake through him. "Does Dev kiss that much better?"

"What?" The shuffling stopped.

His fingers tightened on the steering wheel. "Nothing." He'd been an idiot to ask that. He clamped his teeth together and put his foot down on the accelerator. Then he remembered the last time he'd done that and eased off. He didn't need another speeding ticket on top of everything else.

SHE DIDN'T KNOW what to say to Dev. Didn't know if she should say anything at all. She'd worried about what had happened with Lily for days, regretting her words, regretting her involvement, wishing she could take it all back.

Not for her the enthusiastic meddling her mother seemed to thrive on, Madeleine thought. She doubted if Antonia ever once questioned what she did. Madeleine was a wreck.

And she couldn't talk about it. She could just imagine what Chan would say.

But now she was going to have to face Dev. Had Lily seen him? Talked to him? Were things better or worse? She felt a little sick.

She debated holing up in the camper while the rodeo was going on. If she did, maybe she could avoid Dev altogether. A good cowardly solution. But she didn't think she could live with not knowing what had happened, either. Knowing he was mad at her would be better than not knowing how he felt.

So in the end she went.

She didn't see him to talk to until after the rodeo. And when she did, having waited in trepidation near the camper, not daring to venture back near the chutes, he came out with Chan and Gil and greeted her like a long-lost friend.

"Maddy!" He gave her a hug and a kiss and asked how she was surviving her travels with Chan. Then he asked about her dissertation. She answered him with vague, babbly sorts of answers, all the while trying to look beyond his smiles.

The four of them had dinner together and nothing was said. He didn't know, she decided. While she and Chan had gone to Canada, he and Gil had gone to Utah and then Grand Junction, Colorado. From what he said, she knew he hadn't seen Lily since the performance at Livermore.

She wondered if she ought to tell him what she'd done. She picked at her food, crumbled her roll and shoved it around her plate. She glanced at him, then poked at her potato.

"Something wrong with the food?" Chan asked.

"No. It—it's fine."

He gave her a hard look. The waitress came back to re-fill their coffee cups and batted her eyes at Chan.

He teased and flirted right back. Madeleine's teeth were on edge.

She was glad when the meal finally ended and they all walked out into the parking lot.

"See you in Reno," Gil said.

"Is that next?" Madeleine asked.

"Thursday," Chan told her.

Lily would be in Reno. Reno where it all began. "Can I talk to you a minute, Dev?"

Leaving Chan and Gil standing there staring after them, she took his arm and dragged him off toward the far end of the parking lot.

"Something wrong?" he asked. "Chan giving you problems?"

"No. It's not Chan. Or me." She hesitated. "Well, no that's not exactly true. It's me. Or rather, it was me." She was babbling and she knew it. "I talked to Lily, Dev."

He stared at her. "What do you mean, talked to Lily?" His eyes were glittering, intense.

"At Livermore. She was talking to me about Chan. About marriage. And I asked her about . . . about whether she'd marry again."

"Mad—" He looked stricken.

"I know. I know. I shouldn't have. I should have kept my big mouth shut. But I didn't."

"She's not ready to get married again."

"No, but someday she may be."

"Don't count on it," Dev said flatly.

"No, I don't believe that."

"So you told her she ought to?"

"Not exactly."

"Good."

She chewed on her lip. She swallowed, her throat feeling incredibly dry. "The thing is, Dev, I...I sort of... mentioned your name."

"My name! Hell, Mad—" He kicked at some pebbles with the toe of his boot, then lifted his gaze to glare at her. "You know how she feels about me!"

Madeleine looked down at her own toes peeking out of her sandals. "She's wrong!"

"You didn't tell her that!"

She didn't say anything. She didn't have to.

"Oh, Christ," Dev murmured.

"I—" She looked up to meet his anguished gaze. "I'm sorry, Dev," she whispered. "It...just happened. I didn't do it to make things worse!"

"I know that! But for God's sake, Mad—" He grimaced and shook his head, despairing.

She put out her hand to touch his arm, then drew back. She couldn't. How could she offer comfort when she'd been the one to make things worse? He stared at the ground. She saw a muscle ticking in his jaw.

Then finally he lifted his gaze. "What'd she say?"

There was no way Madeleine was going to tell him that. Not all of it. "She said . . . she'd talk to you."

"She already has talked to me." His jaw tightened and his eyes flickered with remembered pain. "Or looked right through me. I don't need that again."

"She was hurting, too, Dev. A lot. Maybe—" Madeleine stopped, then started again. "Maybe this time it won't... be that way."

Dev just looked at her.

A family, laughing and talking, came out of the restaurant and walked past them. Chan and Gil still stood by the camper. They didn't seem to be saying anything.

"Do you really think so?" Dev's tone was fatalistic, not hopeful at all, and Madeleine heard in it the echo of Lily's.

She sighed. She shrugged and gave her head a little shake of desperation. "I don't know, Dev. I don't know."

THEY DROVE as far as a campground somewhere between Cheyenne and Laramie.

"No reason to drive all night when we don't have to get there till Thursday," Chan said. "Suit you?"

"Fine," Madeleine said, her tone remote.

So what else was new? he thought irritably.

Well, her little one-on-one with Dev in the parking lot, for one thing. That was new. He couldn't believe it when she'd just taken Dev's arm and walked off, leaving him and Gil standing there.

He'd tried to ignore it, to go on talking to Gil about some cattle Gil was thinking of buying, but his gaze had kept drifting over to Madeleine and Dev at the end of the parking lot, their heads close together as they talked.

They looked like lovers, totally wrapped up in their own universe. And not happy lovers at that. And they'd both looked miserable when they'd finally come back.

They hadn't kissed goodbye, either. Chan had taken a certain amount of grim satisfaction in that.

He'd got damned little satisfaction from anything else. The drive to the campground had taken a little less than five hours. In that whole time she'd stared out the window and hadn't said a word. Of course, he hadn't, either. He didn't know what to say to her.

He heard her shifting around in the bunk above him. The bed creaked, then creaked again. He folded his arms under his head and stared out the window into the moonless night. She was as restless and sleepless as he was.

Probably wanting Dev.

She shifted again. Rolled over.

"Richardson?" Her voice, when it came so soft and tentative, startled him.

He glanced up. In the darkness he could just make out her eyes peering down at him from the upper bunk. "What?"

"I think maybe I'd better go back to New York." There was a hollowness in her voice he hadn't heard before.

"What brought that on?" he asked gruffly after a moment.

He heard her roll over again and guessed she was lying on her back now. He couldn't see her anymore.

"I don't belong here."

He didn't say anything for a mon.ent. Then he admitted something he didn't think he'd ever admit. "You haven't done too bad."

"I've made a mess."

He sat up and turned to look up toward the bunk, but she was lying down and he still couldn't see her. "What's that supposed to mean?"

She didn't say anything for a moment. The covers moved as if she was plucking at them with her fingers. "Oh, nothing," she muttered at last.

"Did you—" he took a deep breath, not sure he wanted to know this, but knowing he was incapable of not asking "—did you screw things up with Dev?"

She sat up and looked down at him in the darkness. "How did you know?"

"Well . . . he didn't kiss you goodbye."

Madeleine made a small sound in the back of her throat. "I can hardly blame him. He thinks I may have screwed up his life." She lay back down again. "And I may have," she said after a moment. "I talked to Lily."

"What's Lily got to do with it?"

"He loves her."

"*What?* Dev loves Lily?"

Madeleine's head appeared over the edge of the bunk again. "You don't have to sound so surprised," she said mildly.

"I *am* surprised." Stunned was more like it. "That doesn't make sense. He's the one in the arena, the one who—"

"He was on the bull," Madeleine cut in sharply. "He did not kill John."

"I know that!"

"Everyone knows that. Even Lily knows it, I think, deep down where it counts. And even deeper down, I think she may feel something for Dev. The same something he feels for her. But right now that only makes it worse."

Chan's mind was reeling. He couldn't take it in. "All this stuff with Dev? It's about . . . Lily?" He felt like he'd just got a metaphorical kick in the head.

"Of course," Madeleine said matter-of-factly. "What'd you think?"

"I thought—well, hell, Decker, he's been kissing you!"

Madeleine stared at him. Even in the moonless night he could see the whites of her eyes.

"You're very hung up on kissing, aren't you, Richardson?" She swung around so that she was sitting cross-legged, her head bent beneath the roof of the camper.

"I never used to be," Chan muttered under his breath.

"What?"

He met her gaze frankly. "I said, I think I'm losing my mind."

Which was, perhaps, putting it mildly. She wasn't hung up on Dev? None of this sighing around for the past few days had anything to do with her and Dev—or not in a man-woman sense anyway.

It had to do with Dev and *Lily?*

Chan did his best to get a grip on it. He'd always known that understanding relationships wasn't his strong point, but he couldn't remember ever having been so messed up as to have got the participants wrong before.

"So you're not sighing after ol' Dev, huh?" he said after a moment. He felt just a little bit better.

"You thought I was?" Madeleine sounded amused.

"You acted like you were."

"I acted like he was my friend."

"Those were friendly kisses?"

"Honest to God, Richardson, what is it with those kisses? You weren't... You aren't—" she gave a small gasp, then giggled "—*jealous,* are you?"

"Of course I'm not jealous! Why the hell would I be jealous?"

"Well, I don't know." Madeleine pulled her knees up to her chest and wrapped her arms around them. "I don't really know a lot about men. I guess I figured you could be territorial, you know. Like resenting him because you think I'm yours just because I'm staying in your camper."

"You're not mine, Decker."

"You'd better believe I'm not," she replied with just as much force.

Neither of them said anything for a long moment. Chan supposed Madeleine was doing some sort of silent boundary building.

He was trying to reassess exactly where things stood. He wasn't very good at that, either. It would be nice, he thought, since guys were expected to know how to deal with women, if somebody would give you a game book. He sighed and stretched out on his back and stared up at the ceiling.

"Richardson?"

"Huh?"

"Would you have slept with that waitress if I hadn't been along?"

He sat up with a jerk. "Where the hell did that come from?"

"You were flirting with her. Would you have—"

"No, I damn well wouldn't have. Honest to God, Decker, what's the matter with you? Do you think I go to bed with every female who smiles at me from coast to coast?"

So maybe there was a bit more righteous indignation in his tone than he had a right to, but, damn it, she didn't have to ask questions like that!

"I just wondered," Madeleine said. "I mean I know you haven't been getting any... er, well, I mean, I don't *think* you've been getting any... er..."

"Rest assured, Decker, you're absolutely right. I haven't been getting any... er, well," Chan said sarcastically.

"That's another reason I've been thinking I ought to go back to New York."

"So I can have sex?" He was incredulous.

"Well, you must miss it," she said reasonably. "And you keep talking about kisses."

"So sorry."

"Are you?" She turned suddenly serious. "Sorry you kissed me, I mean?"

I give up, he thought desperately. He stared at her. "Hell, Decker, what do you think? Did I act like I was sorry?"

"Well, I don't think so," she said, her tone almost diffident. "But I really haven't kissed a lot of...I mean, I've hardly ever—"

"And don't give me any crap about inexperience! I won't believe it. You weren't kissing me with any lack of experience!"

There was an instant's pause. Then, "I wasn't?"

"If that was inexperience, believe me, kiddo, you're a natural."

"I *am?* I mean, I am." She giggled again. "Of course I am!" The giggles positively bubbled out now. She got on her knees and leaned over the bunk so her head hung down toward his. "Richardson?"

"What?"

"Kiss me."

Chapter Ten

She didn't have to ask him twice.

He kissed her.

It might have been the stupidest thing he'd ever done, but...

He kissed her.

He'd wanted it for so long, had done it in his mind so many times, had hung on to the memory of that last kiss so tightly that he couldn't imagine doing anything else.

He kissed her.

He stood up slowly, not answering her, not speaking at all. Just stood and came to her so that his face and hers were on a level, their eyes probing each other's in the darkness, their breaths mingling as he closed the distance between them.

And then he touched his lips to hers. A light touch. A feathering. The barest hint of pressure. And then release. Touch. And go. Touch. And go. Touch. And...

And then he didn't go. He stayed, lingered, savored. And felt the heat rise within him, felt the fires, banked so long, now flame to life. And he raised his hands and took her face between them, held her gently. He let his thumbs graze her cheekbones, his fingers trace the line of her ears, as all the while, slowly and sweetly his lips melded with hers.

Melded . . . melted. Either. Both.

He didn't know where he left off and she began. He didn't know which breath was his and which was hers.

And kissing wasn't going to be enough before long. He wanted more, needed more, ached for more. More touching, more savoring, more tasting, more mingling of his and hers.

He shifted his weight to push himself up, to haul himself onto the back of the bench, to bring them closer, to slide his body onto the bunk next to her.

She put her hands on his shoulders and held him where he was. She drew her mouth slowly away from his. He could hear her heart hammering. Or was it his?

"Decker?"

She bowed her head. "My mistake, Richardson."

"Mistake?"

"Leading you on. I told you I wasn't very experienced." She lifted her gaze and looked at him ruefully. "What you said . . . it went to my head. I wanted to try it again. But I can't . . . I can't . . ."

He sucked in a sharp breath. "Yeah," he said gruffly. He sank down onto his bunk and hunched over, shutting his eyes, trying to will his aroused body into a calmer state. It wasn't easy. Especially when she didn't move, just hung there watching him.

"I'm sorry, Richardson," she said softly.

He gave a half laugh. "So'm I."

"Do you hate me?"

"Yes."

She gasped. "You do?"

He turned a rueful glance on her. "Mostly, Decker, I hate my mother."

"Is there anything I can do? I mean—" he knew if he could see her she'd be blushing "—besides...besides that."

"Go to sleep, Decker."

"You're sure?"

He rolled himself onto the bed and briefly buried his face in the pillow. "I'm sure."

He heard her shift, heard the bunk creak, then settle. Far off he heard the sound of a semi downshift, coming down the pass. Closer by there came the soft hoot of an owl.

"Richardson?"

He gave serious thought to pretending he was asleep. Then he heard her roll over and knew she was looking down at him.

"What?" he said.

"You kiss very well."

WELL, HE DID. So she said so.

It was important to be honest.

Sort of. As honest as she dared, anyway. She was in over her head on this trip with Chan Richardson, and she knew it. The wisest thing—the sanest thing—would be to say she couldn't swim.

She wasn't quite honest enough for that.

Why not?

Because...because she wanted to find out what would happen next.

She felt like a child given the end of a string and told to follow it into an enchanted forest. Every step into this new world brought her new knowledge, new friends, new insights into herself. And now...even though she sensed she was losing her bearings, she couldn't find it in herself to head back.

The one rational bit of her left had surfaced last night when she'd suggested going back to New York.

But was she getting on a plane today in Salt Lake City? Was she doing the sensible thing and calling it quits?

No.

Why?

Because she wanted to know what happened between Lily and Dev. Because she wanted to see Reno and Calgary and Prescott and Window Rock and the dozens of other places in between. Because she liked this new person she was becoming, this one who got involved in people's lives, who knew how to drive, who dared to kiss Chan Richardson, who dared—she smiled at this—to ask him to kiss her.

That, she admitted because she was being honest with herself, was the main reason she was staying.

Because of Chan Richardson.

Not that she thought she was going to marry him. Not that he'd suddenly become her perfect man. Heaven forbid.

But he was an interesting man, a tantalizing man, a man she liked being around, whom she wanted to know better.

"All knowledge is useful," Antonia always said.

Madeleine was willing to admit she'd learned some things from Chan. She touched her lips, then smiled. She suspected he might have a few more things to teach her.

She would have to be careful, though, she knew that. Not just for herself, but for his sake, too. She couldn't play games the way she'd played them the night before. She might not know a lot about men, but she knew better than to tease one. Chan Richardson was a good man, a surprisingly tolerant man, but even a good man could be pushed too far.

Madeleine didn't want to go too far. But if they set out the ground rules beforehand . . .

"SO," SAID A FAINT, far-off voice that Julia recognized immediately despite the long-distance echo and crackle, "what have you heard?"

"Nothing."

"Nothing?" The voice was suddenly stronger, though whether it was due to improved phone transmission or concern on the part of the caller, Julia wasn't sure. "Not a word?"

"Not a word."

"But they've been gone weeks!"

"Almost a month," Julia agreed cheerfully.

"Do you think that's a . . . good sign?" Antonia was clearly doubtful.

"Well, you know what they say, 'No news is good news.'"

"Honestly, Julia, you'd think a woman of your education wouldn't stoop to clichés."

"Well, fine. What do you think happened?"

"He might have killed her."

"What?"

"Oh, not literally," Antonia said hastily. "It's just that Madeleine can be, well, exasperating at times."

"So can Chan," Julia admitted.

"So you think they're just happily exasperating each other?"

"I'd say it's a good bet. They've kissed, you know."

"Well, I should hope," Antonia said. "Madeleine might be exasperating, but she's not slow."

Julia laughed. "Do you think you might want to re-phrase that?"

"You know what I mean," Antonia grumbled.

"Yes. I'm sure she's all that's proper. That's one of the reasons I think she'll make a good match for Channing. He needs a woman like that. A challenge and all."

"Madeleine's a challenge," Antonia said. "I can guarantee that." She paused. "So, you think we can breathe easy for the moment, do you?"

"I think so. I hope so," Julia said. "I'm sure they're still together, anyway. I feel quite confident that Chan would call and berate me if anything disastrous had happened. He always does."

"Why is it," Antonia wondered, "that children are always so ready to blame their mothers?"

"I can't imagine," Julia said. "I've finished my part of the guest list. Have you finished yours?"

RENO, NEVADA. The biggest little city in the West. Or that's what they called it, anyway. And as far as Chan was concerned, they were right. It was certainly more city than he was used to spending time in. After a month of small-town rodeos and all-night driving, it was not only an oasis in the desert, it was an oasis in the rodeo schedule that was his life.

Every year he looked forward to it—to the neon and the nightclubs, to the cowboy golf tournament and the black-jack games, to wandering down Virginia Street just soaking things up, checking things out. He looked forward to a little dancing, a little playing, a little drinking with his buddies. All the performances were in the daytime. He could—he had—stayed up all night.

This year, with Madeleine in tow, he anticipated there would be a slight crimp in his plans.

Some dancing, yeah, if he was lucky and she knew how; although, after the driver's license business he had learned not to take things for granted. There'd be a little less playing and a little less drinking. Of that he had no doubt. He wasn't sure yet about the staying up all night—living with Madeleine was more unpredictable than riding any bull he'd ever known—but a guy could hope.

He could plan. He could dream. He could anticipate.

How could he have guessed he'd have to spend four days in a hotel room with an ice pack between his legs?

He couldn't even blame it on Madeleine. Not directly at least. And even indirectly he had to stretch the truth pretty far to attribute it to her. She was in the stands when it happened. He wasn't even thinking about her. He'd made a beauty of his first ride. It was on a tough son-of-a-gun bull, and he was bailing out when it happened. His foot slipped in the dust and he skidded, almost doing the splits.

He got, pure and simple, a groin pull.

The groin pull was the major occupational hazard of bull riders—less notorious than getting gored or being stepped on—but still painful as hell. And you didn't get much sympathy, either. You got smiles and snickers from those to whom it hadn't ever happened. You got "Sure as hell sorry, fella. Glad it's not me," from the ones who knew firsthand what you were going through.

Chan knew it well. He'd done it before. He felt the snap and pull even as it happened. It was all he could do to haul himself to his feet and limp to the fence while Lily distracted the bull.

Climbing the fence would have made him see stars, but he used arm leverage to haul himself up. Once over it he slumped down on the ground back behind the chutes and wished the pain would go away.

He was still sitting there when nearly everyone else had left and Madeleine came looking for him. She was gawking around until she saw him. Then she came on a run, dark hair flying.

"What's wrong?"

He grimaced. "No big deal. I just landed wrong."

"When you got off? I saw you do the splits. Does it hurt?"

"You could say that."

She knelt down beside him. "Where?"

"Think about it, Decker. I'm sure you'll guess." He winced, trying to haul himself to his feet and was even grateful when she leapt up and offered her outstretched hand to pull him the rest of the way, then steadied him when he got there.

"Can you talk or should I see if I can bring the truck closer?"

"Naw." He tugged his hat down on his head and picked up his gear bag. "It's okay. I can walk." But he moved slowly and it hurt like hell when he did so.

"Stay here," she said finally. "I'll be right back."

It was a measure of how much he was hurting that he did what he was told. He stood leaning against the side of one of the cars and waited until she brought the truck around. Then he climbed in. Even those few steps hurt.

So did the long trek through the lobby to the elevator and the walk down the hall to their room. And it was a little like running a gauntlet. He kept running into well-wishers, fans, cowboys and other people he knew.

"Great ride, Chan!"

"Nice goin'!"

"Be rootin' for you in the finals!"

"Playin' golf tomorrow?"

"Wanta go out on the town tonight?"

He smiled and nodded at all of them, though he didn't think he'd make it out on the town tonight or be playing golf tomorrow. He thought he'd be lucky if he wanted to move.

He was lying on the bed, still wearing his dirty riding pants and his shirt with the paper number on the back when Madeleine, who'd gone to put the truck in the lot, came in.

"Shall I call a doctor?"

He shook his head. "Nothing a doc can do. It just happens."

"So what do you do about it?"

"Ice it. Wait. Eventually it heals."

"By Sunday?" That's when the finals were. The finals he had qualified for with his ride this afternoon. The finals that would pay off to the tune of $14,000. The finals that would improve greatly his chances of going to the NFR.

"Let's hope," he said. He sighed and shut his eyes.

"Let's do more than hope," Madeleine said. "Take your pants off."

Chan's eyes snapped open. He stared at her. He didn't even move. She bustled over and grabbed the bucket off the dresser and headed for the door.

Then she turned back. "What's the matter with you, Richardson? Can't you move?"

"Er," he said.

Madeleine rolled her eyes. "I'm going to ice you, not arouse you. Come on. Move it." She set down the bucket and took hold of his boots one at a time, pulling them off and dropping them on the floor. "There. Do you want me to take your jeans off, too?" She gave him a stern look, the sort his mother often gave him, then left the room.

Chan, fumbling, took them off. But he knew damned well that Madeleine Decker bore no resemblance at all to his mother, and though she might only intend to ice him, there wasn't a doubt in the world but that she was going to arouse him, too.

IT WASN'T AS IF he was naked, Madeleine told herself. And even if he were, she was sure she could handle the situation. After all, she had a more extensive background of male nakedness than many women her age—many women, that is, with her relatively limited sexual experience.

She had lived during her formative years among peoples who had different standards regarding appropriate dress than middle-class Americans, hadn't she? Thus her knowledge of the nude masculine form had not been limited, as so many young girls' was, to well-thumbed issues of *National Geographic*.

And then, as well, she'd had Scott.

But somehow even seeing Scott naked had never evoked quite the same reaction in her as the sight of Chan Richardson did in nothing but his shorts.

They were not leopard-spotted shorts or tiger-striped or paisley silk or anything of the sort. They were plain white cotton briefs.

"Tidy whiteys," Alfie once called them, giggling disparagingly about the underwear wardrobe of her current hot date.

Well, to each her own, Madeleine thought. In her opinion they were the sexiest shorts on earth.

Of course it could have been the man wearing them, propped up against the headboard of the bed, his lean, muscular body bared for her delectation, except for what was covered by those white cotton shorts.

Or not.

Hers was not to reason why. Hers was simply to trek to the ice machine, bring back buckets of ice, crush the ice and put it in plastic bags, then hand it to him and watch with considerable interest as he lodged it between his legs.

"Do you need any help?" she asked him in a hopeful tone as she sat down on the bed beside him.

He gave her a look halfway between a grimace and a grin. "Don't make me laugh, Decker."

"It only hurts when you laugh?"

"And when I stand and when I walk and when I move."

"And nothing helps?"

"Nothing but ice and rest."

She sighed and propped herself against the headboard next to him and folded her hands in her lap. "Then I guess I won't offer to kiss it and make it better."

"Decker!" he groaned.

THERE WERE, Chan discovered, certain advantages to a groin pull.

Not that he would necessarily want to have another one anytime soon. Not that he wouldn't prefer to be the recipient of those advantages for reasons other than that he couldn't move. But having Madeleine Decker hovering over him, granting his every wish—well, maybe not his every wish, but close—was something he could get used to.

She made his enforced captivity tolerable. Even though she spent a fair amount of time typing her dissertation, she still found time to watch television movies with him and read magazines with him. She went down to the specialty shops and brought him back grisly, fast-paced thrillers and blood-and-guts Westerns to read. She supplemented their room-service menu with treks to the grocery store for bananas and graham crackers and tortilla chips and three kinds of salsa, and she didn't yell at him when he ate them in bed.

After all, as she pointed out, it wasn't her bed.

That was the one wish she hadn't granted.

And damn he wished she would.

He liked all this time she was spending with him. But at the same time she was tempting as hell. And that made him cranky and irritable. She thought it was because he hurt. Just as well.

"Can I get you anything else?" she asked him.

It was late Saturday afternoon. So far they'd spent virtually forty-eight hours in their hotel-room cocoon, except for a trek to the whirlpool this morning.

Chan, not used to being cooped up in anything unless it moved, knew he would have gone out of his mind if it hadn't been for Madeleine. At the same time he was going out of his mind because of her, too.

He wanted her. He had wanted her since he couldn't remember when. But the urgency was growing by the minute. And even a pain in the groin didn't seem to be enough to take his mind off it.

Madeleine seemed oblivious. Oh, she joked with him at times. She even stole or let him steal the occasional teasing kiss when she was bringing him a new ice bag or helping him out of the whirlpool.

But starting something that would finish with both of them naked in bed was something else entirely different and he knew it. It was driving him wild.

"Nothing," he said shortly now, which wasn't exactly true. She wouldn't. So he turned his attention back to a baseball game on television. Or tried to.

"Why don't you go for a swim or something? Aren't you tired of hanging around here?"

She had just brought him another bag of chips and some salsa and was now spreading her notes on the table to sort through them. Nothing she was doing was particularly enticing, still her very presence was all he needed to start his thoughts going in directions she wouldn't approve of.

She looked up at him, startled. "Excuse me?"

"I said why don't you go for a swim?"

"Trying to get rid of me?" Madeleine said, but she was smiling and her voice was light.

"Yeah." And if she knew what he was thinking, she'd be glad he was trying to chase her away.

She looked at him for a long time, as if she was trying to figure out what was going through his head. He hoped she wasn't a mind reader. He met her gaze with as much defiance as possible.

She began putting her note cards away. "Maybe you're right. Maybe too much togetherness is a bad idea."

He wanted to tell her that wasn't the point, but he never knew where these verbal chess matches would go with Madeleine. He kept his mouth shut.

She went into the bathroom and got her bathing suit. "Can I get you anything before I go?"

He shook his head without looking away from the television.

"I'll see you later."

"Don't hurry," he made himself say. Then he stared at the screen and counted the minutes until she came back.

"So, ANYWAY," Madeleine said, "Gil came for a swim after the performance, and I told him I'd have dinner with them. Gil and Dev and some of the others. I didn't think you'd mind," she added almost hesitantly.

"Why should I?" he said. Just because she'd been gone almost three hours and he'd damned near called the pool to see if there was a lifeguard on duty didn't mean he cared if she was gone again this evening.

"Exactly," Madeleine said in a tone that proclaimed, *I can be testy, too.*

"He said he might take me dancing after. Or to play a little blackjack."

"Swell," Chan managed before his teeth snapped together.

"I wonder if I have a decent dress to wear," she mused, studying the contents of the closet, considering the meager wardrobe she had brought. "I saw a really sharp-looking red dress in one of the shops downstairs."

"Buy it. You'll blend right in with the wallpaper," Chan said sourly.

Madeleine nodded. "You're right. I didn't think of that. But I don't have anything suitable."

"Jeans are suitable," Chan said.

But Madeleine shook her head. "No, they're not. I don't have to leave for an hour. I'll just run down and see what I can find." She started for the door.

"Hey, Decker? See if you can find me another Western, will you? I finished the Louis L'Amour."

"I don't have much ti—" she stopped, looked at him lying there, then nodded. "If I can."

She did. She found him two. And she found a skimpy backless sparkly dress in a deep royal blue. She held it up so he could see it.

"*That?* You're going to wear *that?* Is he going to bring a gun to keep the wolves off you?"

Madeleine laughed. "You're so good for my ego, Richardson."

"Ego, hell. You'll get attacked in that." And if she didn't while she was gone, when she got back, he'd see what he could do.

She obviously didn't take his warning seriously. She went into the bathroom humming and emerged a few minutes later in the dress. She had pulled her hair up into a knot on the top of her head, and only a few curling tendrils escaped down her cheeks. The upswept style accentuated her slender neck and delicate features. The dress hugged every single curve, especially those breasts she'd been camouflaging beneath XL T-shirts.

"So," she said, pirouetting in front of him so that the dress flared out to treat him to a brief glimpse of long tanned legs. "What do you think?"

She looked stunningly sophisticated and breathtakingly beautiful. Chan felt his groin tighten and knew it had nothing to do with the muscle pull. He suspected Gil and Dev and every other cowboy in Reno would feel the same way.

"I don't think you ought—" he started, when there was a knock on the door.

Madeleine opened it to Gil and Dev and Kevin Skates all dressed up in their cowboy best. One glance at Madeleine and they all looked poleaxed, exactly the way Chan thought they would.

"Wow," Gil said unnecessarily.

Kevin and Dev just smiled.

"Sure sorry you can't come, Chan," Gil said cheerfully as he took Madeleine's arm.

"I'll bet."

"Can I get you anything before we leave?" Madeleine asked him.

Chan couldn't think of a thing that would change the way he felt.

GIL HAD MADE the finals. Dev had not. Madeleine supposed that might be the reason for Dev's reticence during the meal. She had no chance to talk to him privately. She didn't know how things were between him and Lily. She wasn't sure she wanted to know. She still felt guilty for having spoken, but still felt that it was something she had to do.

She'd been almost grateful for Chan's injury, though of course she never told him that. It kept her out of circulation for most of the time they were in Reno, so she didn't have to face whatever she had set in motion. Maybe, she thought, she hadn't set anything in motion. She dared hope.

The hope, she realized, was in vain, halfway through their meal when Kevin looked over and said, "Hey, here comes Lily and Peyton."

Madeleine turned to see Lily coming through the dining room, looking stunning in an Indian-inspired dress of pale blue with white leather fringe and trim. At her elbow was a tall, broad-shouldered cowboy as blond as she was.

"Who is that?" she asked Gil.

"Michael Peyton. Steer wrestler from Oklahoma. Won the world twice a few years ago."

"Hey, Mike, how ya doin'?" Kevin greeted him. "Lily."

Michael nodded, smiled, got introduced to Madeleine. Lily smiled, then looked away. Dev didn't say anything. But when they went on to their own table and Kevin was saying what a knockout Lily was, Madeleine saw the white of Dev's knuckles as he held his fork.

"She oughta wear that dress when she's in the arena," Kevin said. "Bulls would never notice a cowboy in the dirt."

"Cowboys wouldn't get many bulls ridden, either," Gil said. "She does fine just the way she is."

"She doesn't do fine," Dev said suddenly, making them all look up. "Didn't you see her this afternoon after Kevin rode. She damn near got gored."

"It happens," Gil said. "You know that."

"Is she all right?" Madeleine asked.

"She's fine," Gil and Kevin said in unison.

"She's a damn fool," Dev said angrily. "And we all know it. Question is, how much longer till she gets killed?"

"She won't get killed," Gil said quickly.

"Course she won't," Kevin put in.

"And it's her business, anyway." Gil aimed his fork at Dev. "Not yours. You can't stop her."

"Hell, you're the last person can stop her!" Kevin said emphatically.

"Haven't you heard? I've been forgiven."

"She talked to you?" Madeleine asked, concerned at the flicker of pain in his eyes.

"You could say that. I was waiting to ride at the end of the steer wrestling yesterday, and she came up to me back of the chutes. Said, 'I hear you feel I've been avoiding you. I'm sorry. I just want you to know I don't blame you.' Then she gave me this tight little smile, said, 'Good luck today,' and walked away. Right out into the arena."

"Oh, Dev."

"I'm lucky I lasted a second and a half. After, I tried to find her, to talk to her. She skipped out. I rang her room. Left a message. No answer. And today she's been sticking to Peyton." He shrugged and slumped back in his chair. "Ain't life grand?"

"Did we miss something?" Gil wanted to know. He and Kevin were looking distinctly out of their depth.

"I'll talk to her if you want," Madeleine said.

"No."

"You're right," Madeleine said miserably. "I've said enough."

And she probably would have left it alone, if later that night she hadn't run into Lily in the ladies' room. Lily gave her a bright smile.

"How's Chan? I heard he got hurt."

"He's getting better," Madeleine said. She hesitated, wondering if she dared, then had the decision taken from her when Lily spoke.

"By the way, I took your advice and told Dev I didn't blame him."

"I'll bet you made his day, didn't you, Lily?" Madeleine said.

She saw a flash of anguish in Lily's eyes before the other woman quickly looked away.

"I need to go," she said. "Michael's waiting." And she hurried out.

Madeleine stood looking after her, sighed, then shook her head.

IT WAS EASY enough to see what Lily and Dev should do—or at least try. What was not so easy was to see what she should do about Chan. On the surface everything between them looked fine.

They weren't bickering...much. They weren't sniping at each other...or only a little. They could almost consider themselves friends...of a sort. That was a surprise in and of itself. And Madeleine knew she should be grateful things had turned out as well as they had.

Still, there was a problem.

There was, there had been since Las Vegas, in fact—propinquity. And the most salient thing about propinquity, Madeleine was beginning to discover, was that it wouldn't go away. Not unless she did...or he did. And neither one of them had.

In fact, they were together more than ever.

She'd thought that getting a hotel room in Reno would ease things up a little, give them more space, more room to avoid each other. She should have opted for two rooms. But at the time it seemed somehow silly. Hadn't they been sharing a camper no bigger than this hotel room's bathroom for the past few weeks? Why spend the extra money for two, when even a single hotel room would feel palatial?

Or would have if Chan had ever left her alone in it. Since they had been effectively together twenty-four hours a day, it, too, had become cereal-box size.

And increasingly there was between them what Madeleine had come to think of as "the physical thing."

She was an educated woman. She understood about physical urges. She knew that proximity and time spent in each other's company only made it worse. But having him there virtually naked half the time wasn't helping, either. Especially since it was all too clear that he wanted her, too.

It was why he'd practically thrown her out this afternoon, and she knew it. When she thought about it, she'd been glad to go. And had been even happier when Gil proffered his dinner invitation.

She was glad the evening lasted as long as it did, glad that Gil and Dev really had taken her dancing. It was nice to get away, let her hair down, metaphorically at least.

And when she put her key in the lock at one-thirty in the morning, she hoped to heaven he was asleep.

He was wide awake and glaring at her. He looked at his watch, then at her and lifted an eyebrow. He didn't say a word.

"I don't need a father, thank you," Madeleine said.

He muttered something under his breath. "I don't suppose I have to ask if you had a good time." He took in her flushed cheeks and loose hair. She saw his teeth clench.

"I had a good time," she said. "We danced. Some very drunk lady bumped into me and knocked one of my hairpins loose. Hence—" she shrugged, then lifted her hair with the backs of her hands.

"Did I ask?" Chan said brusquely.

"Fine. I won't tell you." She stepped out of her shoes and wiggled her toes. "Ahh." She breathed a sigh of relief, went into the bathroom and changed out of her dress and into the elongated T-shirt she wore to sleep in. She brushed her teeth and washed her face and tried to will herself into a state of calm before she went back into the bedroom. She needed to sleep, not lie awake all night tossing and turning.

But the dancing had got her blood running hot. And the sight of Chan on the bed hadn't cooled it any. She patted her cheeks with a cold, wet washcloth, then went back into the bedroom.

Chan was still lying in his bed, hands folded behind his head. The covers were thrown back, giving her a clear view of his almost-bare body, his hair-roughened chest, the white shorts that seemed almost to accentuate his masculinity, his slightly spread legs with the ubiquitous ice pack wedged there.

"Are you going to be ready to ride tomorrow?"

"I hope so." He was looking at her from beneath hooded lids. There was a look about him that she had always associated with the aroused male. A sort of urgent, hungry look. She didn't think she'd ever seen a man look more inviting in her life.

She looked away and cleared her throat. "Can I get you some more ice before I go to bed?"

He shook his head. He reached down to remove the pack and handed it to her. She looked at him questioningly. "No more ice."

"But—"

"I think I need a little heat right about now."

"It's two in the morning. The whirlpool's closed."

"Yes." There was a reddish flush along his cheek-bones. He shifted his legs, and her gaze moved in that direction. Yes, he was clearly aroused. And so was she.

She drew her tongue along her lips. "Do you want to try sitting in the bathtub," she asked after a moment. She thought her voice sounded funny, sort of hollow, a little faint. Would he wear his shorts in the bathtub? she wondered.

"I'd never get out again."

"Do you want me to get you a hot, wet washcloth?"

"It'd soak the sheets."

"Well, then, what? I mean, this is a hotel room, Richardson. We only have access to certain amenities. And a heating pad isn't one of them."

"I was thinking more in terms of 98.6."

"Huh?"

"Body heat." His lids lifted and deep blue eyes met hers. "How about it, Decker? For the sake of the cause?"

Her cheeks burned. "You want me to—" She licked her lips again. She took a deep, steadying breath.

"Just . . . help me do a little stretching. Then warm me, Decker."

Warm him? "H-how?"

"Come here. I'll show you. Stretching first. Take hold of my foot and lift my leg. Slow. Careful." She hesitated, then because he was waiting, she reached for his foot and lifted it. Slowly, carefully.

"Yeah, now flex my foot. Uh-huh. Like that."

She held his ankle in one hand, bent his foot with her other. His leg was heavy. The hair-dusted skin was slightly rough against her fingers. She wanted to run those fingers on up his calf to feel the scratch of the hair there, to learn the contour of the muscles.

"Yeah." He made a tiny sound in the back of his throat. He closed his eyes, an expression of bliss mingling with pain on his face. "Again."

She did it again. And again. Holding him as he stretched, bearing the weight as again and again he worked the muscle. Finally he said, "Enough. Now come here. Kneel on the end of the bed."

Obediently she knelt.

"Put your hand under my thigh and lift it. Bend my leg back toward my chest."

"Under your thigh," Madeleine repeated in a faint facsimile of her normal voice. But her hands did what he said. One slipped under his thigh to lift, the other bent his leg back toward his chest.

She lifted. She bent. He moved, stretched, tested. His skin where the ice had touched it was cool against her hand. Everywhere else he was burning. Burning almost as badly as she was herself. She dragged in a deep draught of air.

"'Nuff," Chan said at last, sagging back against the pillows. "Thanks. Helped."

"You're welcome." Madeleine began to straighten away from him.

He caught her hand. "Now the rubdown."

"Chan," she warned, though whether she was warning him or herself was questionable.

"You can't quit now, Decker. It's just skin on skin."

"Sure it is."

He grinned. It was a sultry, sexy grin. "A rubdown is what you make it."

"That's what I'm afraid of."

"You're a cruel woman, Decker. You know you want to touch me. Are you chicken?" he taunted softly.

Her teeth came together with a snap. "Just tell me what to do."

"Rub me. Here." He showed her where.

"There?"

"It hurts all the way up to—"

"You asked for it, Richardson. Let me get some body lotion."

His flesh was still cool to begin with, firm and resilient beneath her touch. She stroked him gently at first, smoothing, rubbing back and forth. He shut his eyes. She saw his chest rise and fall slowly, then as she began to knead his thigh, his breathing quickened.

He shifted restlessly beneath her touch. His left leg splayed wide, and she moved up and leaned against it, getting a better angle on the right. He let out a soft moan.

"Does it hurt?" she asked quickly.

"Yes. No. Keep going."

She kept going. Her fingers soothing and smoothing. Her own emotions and physical reactions weren't soothing at all.

Neither, from what she could see outlined in his shorts, were his. He shifted again and her elbow brushed against the fly of his shorts.

"Better?" she asked him finally, a little breathlessly.

"Yesssss." It was halfway between a whimper and a hiss. His hips lifted as her hand moved up the inside of his thigh. His back began to arch.

Suddenly his hand reached down and grasped hers, holding it still and so tight against his thigh that she could feel the blood pounding in his pulse there.

"Point of no return, Decker," he said hoarsely. His lids flicked open. Blue eyes met hers.

"Point of—?"

"You know what I mean. Make up your mind."

"Me? Why is it always the woman who has to decide?" she protested.

"Because men know what they want." His fingers tightened over hers. "Well?"

Oh, hell. Oh, damn. She wanted it, too. She did. Biological urges were biological urges whether you wanted them or not. But if she had sex with him, if she shared that last intimacy with him...

She gave a little tug. He clung for an instant, then reluctantly loosed his grip. Her hand slid away, brushing his thigh one last lingering time.

"Night, Richardson," she murmured.

She padded across the room and turned out the light. He heard her come back and get into her own bed, then roll away from him so she was facing the wall.

He lay there and listened to his galloping heart, to the blood surging through his veins, pulsing, quickening, wanting....

Night? he thought. Yep. And it was going to be a hell of a long one, he'd give her that.

Chapter Eleven

If there was ever a way to effectively take your mind off a case of terminal sexual frustration, it was probably to ride a bull when you had a groin pull.

At least Chan found it was something else to think about as he climbed over the chute and contemplated Ground Zero, the broad-backed Brahma who was stamping and nudging and hooking at the chute gate, the same Brahma that he was going to have to spread his legs over in a very few minutes.

The thought sent a cold chill right down his back. It was a good thing he'd ridden with pain before. He knew how to look past it, focus on the goal, on getting to the other side. He wished it would work as well with the frustration he was feeling with Madeleine Decker.

Trouble was, with Decker he didn't know what the other side was.

Dev moved around to pass the rope up to him. "You ready?"

"As I'll ever be," Chan muttered. He eased himself down over the bull. He felt his groin muscle stretch, protest, then stretch a little more. *Easy does it. Easy. Easy.* He settled down, pulled the rope, wrapped it around his hand. He glanced over toward the stands, to where he knew

Madeleine was sitting. He'd seen her there on Thursday. He looked for her now, as if she was some sort of talisman.

Hell of a notion, he told himself. He'd got this damn thing showing off when he bailed out. Still, he checked to see she was there. Then and only then did he grit his teeth and move forward. He tucked his chin, tightened his hand, nodded his head.

It was poetry again, once he got going. Poetry, he and Ground Zero, shifting and switching, bucking and twisting, right from the start. Eight seconds of style.

Lucky poets. They never had to dismount.

He hung on well after the buzzer sounded, considering his options. Showing off wasn't one of them. He wasn't taking any chances on his leg going out from under him and doing it again. And the fence was too far to make a leap for that.

Well, hell, there was no help for it. It might not look pretty, but it was a damn sight safer. And he wasn't getting scored on it, anyhow, he thought as he tucked and rolled and did his best imitation of a parachutist coming down.

"Do you know what time it is?" Julia said, squinting at the clock on the bureau.

"Five-thirty in the afternoon," Antonia replied promptly.

"Not here," Julia said heavily, rolling over in bed, trying not to wake her slumbering husband. "And no, they haven't called."

"Madeleine called me," Antonia said loftily.

"In Bali?" Julia sat up, then lay back down again, as sitting pulled all the covers off Rick. "Why? What happened?"

"They were in Reno. Chan rode in the finals today. He was wonderful, Madeleine said. He took second. But the best news is, he had a groin pull."

Julia knew she was sleepy, but she didn't think that, even completely comatose, she'd misheard that.

"That's the best news? Antonia, groin pulls are painful."

"Amen," Rick mumbled and rolled over.

"I know," Antonia said eagerly.

"So why'd she call *you?*"

"I'm getting to that," Antonia said. "Be patient. It seems that the groin pull slowed Channing down a bit. Tied him to the bed more or less. And Madeleine got to fuss over him and bring him ice and help him stretch and such. You know where that sort of thing can lead."

Julia did indeed. "You mean . . ." She sat up straight. "Do you think they've actually . . . I mean, groin pulls permit you considerable intimacy," she added hopefully. "I remember Rick's."

"For God's sake, Julia," muttered her husband. "Is nothing sacred?"

Julia leaned over and kissed him. "Go back to sleep, dear." She snuggled against him, the receiver next to her ear. "Do you think so, Antonia?"

"Well, actually no. Not yet. But—" Antonia's voice became dramatic "—I think they're close. *Very* close. Madeleine wants to quit!"

"*What?*" The covers flew off again as Julia sat up. "She said so?"

"Not in so many words. But she asked about the validity of studies of four weeks' duration." Antonia paused to let the significance of that sink in.

It did. Julia sank back into the pillows. Rick tugged the covers around them and held her there.

"I told her they were always suspect," Antonia went on. "Highly unreliable. I told her that in any good, significant, in-depth study the researcher always reaches a plateau, a point at which she always feels she can't dig any deeper, where she always feels she's got all she's going to get. I told her that the important thing was to dig deeper. Hang on."

"Persevere," Julia said.

"Exactly. I told her it was of utmost importance to do the full two months, to wait out the plateaus until at last you break through to a new level of confidence. To really understand, I told her, you need to forge ahead to that new level of intimacy with your subject, a deeper level of knowledge. Only then are your conclusions reliable."

There was a pause, then Julia said, amazed, "And she bought it?"

MADELEINE DIDN'T imagine she'd have any trouble getting Chan to agree to a "new level of intimacy." It seemed to be exactly what he had in mind.

She just wished she was sure it was the right thing to do.

What, after all, she asked herself, had that level of intimacy accomplished with Scott?

She wasn't positive, of course, but somehow she thought that their increased intimacy might have been the shove that had sent their relationship downhill.

Well, she asked herself, what's wrong with that?

A little disenchantment with Channing Richardson was exactly what she needed. She was too interested in him as it was. The best defense against such preoccupation was to know him well. Extremely well. When there were no more mysteries, there would be no more daydreams.

Such an increased level of intimacy would answer all her most pressing questions, like—for example—what exactly was he like beneath those white shorts?

Then, too, there was the probability that Chan would become disenchanted with her. That was somehow not quite so cheering to contemplate, reminding her as it did of her experience with Scott.

But it would serve the same purpose. It would satisfy their mutual curiosity. She didn't want him to declare his undying love, after all.

All in all, Madeleine decided, it seemed like the best thing to do.

But making up her mind was one thing. Broaching the subject with Chan was something else.

She supposed she could simply say, "Remember when I was giving you that rubdown and you said to choose. Well, I'm changing my mind."

She didn't imagine he would object. But somehow she wanted a little time and privacy.

Time and privacy, however, turned out to be the two things they had very little of.

When she drove the truck around to pick him up after the finals at Reno, he wasn't waiting alone. Kevin Skates was with him.

"Gee, hope you don't mind me taggin' along," Kevin said as he clambered into the truck and stowed his gear bag alongside Chan's. "I reckon I got me a shot at the finals if I take a run at it, and Chan said you wouldn't mind if I rode with you as far as Calgary."

Madeleine looked at Chan. *"Calgary?"*

He looked right back. "Under the circumstances..." he said and let his voice trail off significantly.

Kevin, of course, thought he was referring to Kevin's wonderful potential NFR contention.

Madeleine knew what he really meant.

HE DIDN'T KNOW what she looked so unhappy about. It wasn't like having Kevin along was going to cramp their style. They didn't have a style! Madeleine had a dissertation and Chan had a pain in his crotch. And that was that.

Well, maybe that was putting too harsh a spin on it, but he didn't know what else to think. If she didn't go to bed with him when he was riding high, and she wouldn't go to bed with him when he was at his most vulnerable, she wasn't going to go to bed with him at all. Fine, so be it.

So they might as well bring Kevin with them.

Besides, they were never in one place for more than the space of a rodeo, between June 27 and July 12.

They called it "the cowboy's Christmas," that period around the Fourth of July when every town from the Pacific to the Mississippi seemed to have a rodeo. Chan had spent a fair amount of time figuring out which ones to hit, and he'd picked a dozen they could drive to. When he spelled it out for Madeleine, she looked at him like he was crazy.

She said, "Do they give frequent-driver miles as well?"

"You don't have to come," he said. "What's the point?"

But Madeleine resolutely shook her head. "I'm coming. There's a point."

"Oh?"

"I've changed my mind."

"What?"

"We need to dig deeper."

"Into what?"

"You'll see. We're at a plateau," she told him. "I've been thinking, and I think I might have been mistaken."

"Mistaken about what?" God, she was infuriating.

But she just smiled, looked archly at Kevin, who was driving, then back at Chan.

Mistaken? About what? Changed her mind? About what?

He asked her then, he asked her later. He asked her one day, he asked the next.

She just gave him coy little looks, speculative looks, and then she'd start typing again. She also gave him rubdowns at night that set him on fire, though he was sure she didn't intend them that way. If she wanted to drive him nuts, she'd sure hit on a terrific method.

They drove from Greeley, Colorado to Pecos, Texas to Prescott, Arizona and then Window Rock, Arizona, then St. Paul, Oregon to Williams Lake, British Columbia, hitting six rodeos in six days. It gave him plenty of time for wondering and driving and stretching . . . and aching. She helped lift his foot and bend his knee. She smiled at him. Still she didn't say.

They had thirty-six hours to drive from British Columbia to Folsom, California, then a whole two days to get to Utah, then another down to Sante Fe. They had two full days to get to Wolf Point, Montana and another two to cruise leisurely on up to Calgary. And all the while, she didn't say.

She lifted and flexed and bent for him. She kneaded his muscles, and her fingers lingered until he moaned, and Kevin said, "It's weird, you know, I almost wish I had a groin pull, too."

"No, you don't," Chan said sharply. Because he wasn't sharing Madeleine's fingers with anyone. Besides Kevin didn't realize that it was torture, too.

He couldn't believe she'd changed her mind about making love with him. He couldn't think of any rational reason why she should. And with Madeleine he knew there would have to be some rationalization.

Still he wasn't sorry when they got to Calgary very late Sunday evening, and Kevin bounded off to find the friends he was sharing a room with, and he and Madeleine were left facing each other and a hotel room together in Calgary.

From the way she was looking, all eyes and hair and pale, pale skin, he was certain that she hadn't changed her mind about making love with him. In fact, he was beginning to get another idea that made a lot more sense.

They went into the lobby and up to the desk together and Chan began to get an inkling of what was in store when she said, "I'll arrange things."

Why hadn't he thought of it before? "I suppose you want separate rooms this time," he said.

"On the contrary," Madeleine said and walked up to the reservations clerk. "We'd like a room with one bed."

"IT'S *WHAT?*"

"Research," Madeleine said calmly, leaning back against the door of their hotel room and watching as he flung his duffel bag next to the dresser and turned to glare at her.

"The hell you say! Research!" The very thought made him want to explode.

"Well, if you don't want to make love with me..."

"Of course I want to, Decker! You know that. But I'm damned if you're going to be taking notes!"

"I wasn't—"

"And *you'll* be damned if I catch you writing it up for our mothers!"

"I would never—"

He shook his head. "I don't believe this!"

Separate rooms would have been better! He did a furious limping lap of the room—not easy, as he had to avoid the king-size bed that Madeleine had requested for them.

"I don't know why you're so offended," Madeleine said reasonably. "It's like I told Gil and Dev back in Vegas— just more compiling of evidence. Once you would have agreed."

Which was true. Early on he'd suggested compiling a bit of that sort of evidence himself. Sex was sex, he'd always thought. At least, so far it had been. He didn't know, though, now that he thought about it.

Everything in his life seemed to change when Madeleine touched it. Why should sex be any different? Still, he couldn't see how. She'd have to show him.

He turned and faced her. "Fine," he said. "I'm yours. Ravish me."

Her jaw dropped. "Richardson!"

He shrugged. "Go ahead. Think of me as a guinea pig. Do your clinical, philosophical worst. Or best, Decker. Whichever."

"Richardson!"

"I'm waiting." He spread his arms out slightly from his body and lifted his chin, daring her.

Madeleine just looked at him. Her eyes moved slowly from his head down to his toes, then took a lingering local journey back up again. He began to feel just the slightest bit warm under her gaze.

"Fine," she said in a soft sultry voice he'd never heard her use before.

And she started toward him.

He stood his ground. Just. One part of him wanted to take off running from this intent, determined woman coming toward him. Another part, the braver part, was curious as all get-out about just what Madeleine Decker had in mind. He stayed right where he was.

She stopped just inches from him and lifted her hands to his chest. She smiled at him, her green eyes wide and luminous. He held himself rigid under her touch as her fingers slid beneath the opening of his shirt to pop the snaps one by one. Then she took each of his arms in turn and unsnapped the cuffs so they hung open. Tugging on the fabric, she pulled his shirt loose from the waistband of his jeans.

"Yes," she said softly as her hands came up again and brushed lightly down across his chest. Chan sucked in his breath. How many times had she given him rubdowns that had aroused the devil out of him? Twenty at least. But not one of them had sent shivers right through him the way her lightest touch did now.

"Here now," she said and eased the shirt back off his shoulders. It fell to the floor unheeded. Her hands moved to his belt.

"I'll do it," Chan said.

Madeleine shook her head. "This is my research."

So he let his hands fall to his sides. He shut his eyes. Her fingers fumbled with the clasp of his belt. It was a bull-riding-championship buckle from Salinas. The prettiest, most coveted buckle, next to the NFR gold, in the entire rodeo world. He just wished it were easier to get undone.

He never had any trouble with it! What was she taking so long for? He felt a soft brush against his chest and opened his eyes and glanced down. Madeleine's head was bent, her hair brushing against him as she concentrated and, finally, accomplished the task. She undid the snap, then eased down the zipper. The backs of her fingers grazed against his erection, which pressed against the soft cotton of his shorts. At first he thought it was accidental.

Then as his jeans slid down his hips, her fingers skimmed against him again.

He'd had enough of being a research object. He went into action. He put his hands on her waist to hold her right where she was, and then he kissed her. He kissed her full and hard and with every bit of the pent-up, unsatisfied hunger he'd been traveling with for weeks.

Her eyes widened, she tried to pull back, but he wouldn't let her. She'd said she wanted this, after all.

"Chan!" she gasped at last when he broke for a breath. "You can't. What about my research? What happened to your being a guinea pig?"

"Changed my mind," he said, kissing her again. "If you can change your mind, I can change mine."

"But—"

"This is a two-person deal we cooked up here, Decker. It isn't just you doin' research on me. It works both ways. Let's see you be factual and objective about this."

And then he fell back on the bed and pulled her with him. It was the craziest bout of lovemaking he'd ever been part of. It was sweet and silly and tough and tender and warm and wild by turns.

He kissed her until she stopped protesting and kissed him with a fervor equal to his own. He fumbled with her buttons and her buckle and took every bit as long as she did. Her sneakers, however, were considerably easier to remove than his boots, tangled as they were in his jeans. He didn't show all the finesse with which he was capable of removing a woman's clothes. But what he didn't display in finesse, he made up for in eagerness.

And Decker met him at least halfway.

Her hands were all over him, stroking and kneading, rubbing and teasing. Driving him wild. And he returned the favor with all his skill. He ran his hands over her body, reveling in the smoothness of her skin, in its milky white softness, in the way her breasts fit in his hands just the way he always knew they would.

He made her straddle him and he sat up and kissed them, cupping them in his hands as he tasted them, suckled on them, each in turn. And then he nuzzled between her breasts while his hands slipped down behind her and lifted her against him, his fingers brushing against the dampness between her legs.

"Chan!" It was a whimper, a moan, an eager pleading. And just hearing it almost made him lose control.

He pressed himself against her, bit down on his lower lip, recited to himself the genealogy of his father's favorite cow. And finally he dared breathe again, dared slide his fingers up once more to touch her wetness. "Yes," he said. "Yes, that's it. Yes. Are you ready, Decker?"

The only answer was another whimper. Her hips lifted, arching so that he could raise himself and probe against her center. "Like that, Decker?" He almost couldn't get the words out. He was trembling, his body beginning to shake. "Do you?"

"Yes, Chan! Come on. Yes!"

He liked it, too. A lot. Almost too much. He wanted to savor it, make it last. But the one ounce of rationality he had left reminded him that they would be here a week. They had time. They had a bed. They had each other.

He drew her down on him, brought the two of them firmly and finally together. It almost ended for him there, but he held on. Stopped. Then slowly, gently began moving, rocking, sharing.

Loving.

Loving Madeleine Decker?

He didn't consider the implications then. Then he didn't consider anything at all. He simply felt, surged, shouted his triumph, and savored the bliss of feeling her body contracting around him, of feeling the shudders that coursed through her, that caused her to collapse, trembling against him.

And finally he eased backward, still coupled with her, two made one, in the wide king-size bed.

She lay with her head tucked beneath his chin, her cheek against his chest. Her arms were wrapped around him, he could feel the individual press of her fingers against his back. Then she eased them out, stroked his sides, then, one hand still against his ribs, the other slid down to stroke his hip. Her breathing slowed, but still it stirred the curling hair on his perspiration-damp chest.

And even now he could feel that she was a part of him, that they were still joined, that he was a part of her.

Of Madeleine Decker?

The tiniest of warning signs began to go off in his head.

He reached one hand up and rested it on her hair. He lifted it and touched her ear. He'd never thought about Madeleine Decker's ears. They were small, delicate ears. His hand slipped down to brush against her shoulder. She had narrow, slender shoulders. He remembered her shoulders better than her ears. He'd seen them hunched over the computer often enough when she was working on her dissertation.

This was Madeleine Decker.

The Madeleine Decker his mother expected him to marry.

His hand stilled. His mouth got dry.

"This doesn't mean we're getting married," he said.

Madeleine's hand stilled on his hip. Her head jerked up. Stunned jade-colored eyes stared at him bare inches from his face. Then, a shuttered expression came over them.

Slowly, deliberately, she shoved herself away from him. The two were no longer one. They were separate.

"Of course it doesn't," she said and casually picked up her shirt.

Chan watched her. There was something about her movements, some deliberateness that made him think she hadn't heard him right. "I didn't marry any of the other women I've ever had sex with," he told her.

Madeleine, in the process of gathering up her jeans, stared at him. There was an odd spark of fire in her gaze. "Did they ask you?"

"Well, no, but—"

"And I'm not asking you, either!" she said, and her voice was suddenly as close to shrill as he'd ever heard it. She grabbed her duffel bag and stalked into the bathroom, slamming the door behind her.

Chan stared after her, equal parts confused and amazed.

"Women," he muttered, then decided that was too general and unfair to the species in general. "Decker!" he fumed. He shook his head, shut out the light, and crawled under the covers.

He wasn't certain when it dawned on him that she wasn't coming out. Maybe an hour after the water stopped running. Maybe when the light went off and the door stayed shut.

He frowned. Now what?

He staggered out of bed and went over to the door. "Decker?"

No answer.

He stared at the door. Jiggled the handle. It was locked. "Decker?"

Nothing.

"Decker! I know you're in there. You're too big to fit through the heating vent."

"Shut up and go away!"

"Well, at least you're awake."

"I'm trying not to be. Go away."

He rolled his eyes. "Decker, what in hell is going on? You can't sleep in the bathroom."

"Can't I." It wasn't a question.

"For God's sake!" He rubbed a hand through shaggy, uncombed hair. "What's the matter? You liked it. Damn it, Decker, I know you'd like it. We both did."

"Bully for us."

"So what are you mad about?"

"You figure it out."

Him figure it out? Ha. He wasn't a bloody mind reader. He was a man. And as such, he didn't have a prayer. Figure it out? How the hell could you figure out what went on in the head of a woman who made mad passionate love with you one minute and locked herself in the bathroom the next and yelled that she wouldn't ask you to marry her, either?

Hell, she hadn't even let him finish his sentence, he thought. He'd been going to say, "Well, no, but they wanted me to ask them."

Obviously Madeleine Decker didn't want him to ask her!

And a good thing, too, he thought, because he'd be damned if he would! He stalked away from the door and yanked on his jeans and shirt and boots and grabbed his hat off the dresser. He didn't need this grief. He needed a buddy and a beer—or maybe more than one. It had been a hell of a long while since he'd tied one on.

"So long, Decker," he yelled. "Hope you enjoyed your research. The bed's all yours."

HE WAS DAMNED if he was going to tell her he'd fallen for her. So what if he had?

He'd had crushes before. Miss Dickens, his eighth-grade math teacher. Lola Fargazer, the girl he took to the senior prom. That blond Cheyenne Dandy, what's her name. Well, hell, a guy couldn't be expected to remember every girl or woman he'd entertained serious thoughts about, especially when he was half a dozen beers down the road to self-pity.

Crushes were crushes. You had 'em. You got over 'em. You sure as the devil didn't marry 'em. God, just imagine what it would've been like being married to the Dandy. Or even Lola Fargazer. Miss Dickens would've been too old for him.

And Madeleine Decker?

Madeleine Decker was wrong. All wrong. Had been wrong from the very start.

Oh, she was nice enough. Damn nice. A good sport. Worked hard. Never complained. Even got her driver's license and had probably driven ten thousand miles. She was funny and cheerful and she knew exactly how to rub his leg so it wouldn't hurt quite so much. Pretty, too. He liked her hair all blowsy and tangled, he liked the way her eyes spit green fire at him. He liked the way her breasts just fit in his hands. And when they made love—well, hell, she damn near burned him down.

But she was Madeleine Decker, for God's sake. A Ph.D. candidate in philosophy. The daughter of a long line of distinguished scholars. The woman his mother had set him up with!

And even if Madeleine was the greatest woman on earth, he was damned if he was going to let Julia Richardson pick out his wife for him!

"I'm an adult, damn it," he snarled into his beer. "Aren't I?" he demanded of Dev and Gil and a half a dozen others who were seated with him at a table near the bar. "I can make my own decisions!"

Dev looked at him sideways. "Yeah."

Gil grinned. "Sure."

Kevin Skates nodded knowledgeably. "Maddy bossing you around is she?"

"Decker? Naw." Chan shook his head. "It's my mother."

"MA?"

"Channing? Are you all right?"

"No, damn it! 'M not all right."

"Has there been an accident? Are you hurt? Is Madeleine—"

"Damn Madeleine!"

There was a pause. Then a change in tone, no longer worried, now disapproving. "Channing, do you know what time it is?"

He fumbled to get his watch out from beneath his shirt-sleeve, then peered at it blearily. "A'most four-thirty."

"The question was rhetorical," his mother said. "What's the matter with you?"

"I'll tell you wha's the matter with me! *You!* You and your lousy ideas! 'Go see Madeleine.'" He mimicked her tone. "'She's perfect for you. You'll enjoy her. Think how enlightening it will be.'" He stopped long enough to draw a breath, then went right on. "It was enlight'ning all right. I learned a hell of a lot. And I wish I di'n't know any of it. Lemme tell you, Ma. Stick to bulls and mamma cows for your matchmaking from now on 'cause with people, your ideas stink!"

"Chan—"

He hung up on her.

IT WAS A reasonable hour, at least reasonable for her—Julia had stopped trying to find a reasonable hour in both Wyoming and Bali—when she called Antonia.

There was a bang and a crackle and several thumps before it was answered, as if the receiver had been dropped then fumbled for.

"Now what?" came a sleepy, somewhat cross voice.

"Awfully sorry to wake you, Tonia," Julia said cheerfully, "but I thought you'd want to know— I've heard from Channing. He was a wreck. Absolutely livid." She smiled with satisfaction. "We're almost there."

"I've just got off the phone with Madeleine, too. Yelled and ranted and carried on for half an hour or more. She sounded dreadful," Antonia said. "It was almost worth being awakened for. I think we ought to book the church."

Chapter Twelve

Of course it didn't mean they were going to get married!

Madeleine knew that. But he didn't have to pick that very moment to bring it up, did he?

What kind of a man made mad passionate love with you one minute and announced that he wasn't going to marry you the next? It wasn't as if she'd asked him to!

On the contrary, she'd been doing it to find reasons that she shouldn't.

The trouble was, she hadn't.

The trouble was, she'd loved it.

And the biggest trouble of all was . . . she loved him.

"I love Channing Richardson." She sat on the bed and said the words out loud. She felt sick in the pit of her stomach. This was never supposed to happen.

So much for new and deeper levels of intimacy. She would love to have told her mother what it had got her, but she didn't want her mother to know.

There was no way on earth she was going to tell her mother she'd fallen in love with Chan. Why should she? What good would it do?

Chan wasn't going to marry her. He'd already made that abundantly clear.

The whole mess was beginning to seem a lot like the fiasco with Scott who had happily made love with her and taken advantage of her and hadn't wanted to marry her, either.

And she had precipitated that lovemaking, too, she remembered with consternation. It was true what they said, being well educated didn't make you smart. God knew Madeleine would apparently never learn.

The question remained: what was she going to do now?

The smart thing—from an immediate self-preservation angle at least—would be to pack her computer, her duffel bags and what was left of her self-esteem and her heart and catch the next plane back to New York.

In the long run she knew it was smarter to hang on. If she left now, her mother would undoubtedly find out. She and Julia would put their heads together, speculate, connive. It didn't bear thinking about.

Of course she would have to face Chan, and that would be difficult. But they were adults, weren't they? Surely he wouldn't expect her to continue making love with him. She didn't imagine it would be in either of their best interests for her to try explaining that she didn't want to do it again because before, she hadn't actually been in love with him, but, heaven help her, she was now.

No, she couldn't see Chan understanding that.

She frankly wondered if Chan intended to come back. It was almost noon and she hadn't seen him yet. His one small duffel was still lying alongside the dresser, where he'd slung it last night. But she knew he didn't really need it. Most of his things were still in the camper. Which was probably where he was, too.

She knew he was riding this afternoon in the first go-round. She wondered if he'd come back to the room and pick her up. She waited, uncertain whether she ought to.

In the long run it didn't matter. He never came. And when she went out to look for the camper in the hotel parking lot, it was gone.

She debated whether to go to the rodeo or not.

She decided not.

She didn't owe him that. It wasn't part of their deal. She was used to going, but it wasn't something they'd ever agreed upon. It was time she started considering herself and not complying with her mother's notion of good research or Chan's obligations. It was time she started seeing to her own needs.

She typed right through the performance. She debated ordering room service, then thought she needed to get out. And she didn't want to be sitting there if he decided to come back. She had no intention of letting him think she was waiting for him.

So she went down to the lobby, but the hotel was filled with cowboys, some of whom she knew, though happily not Dev or Gil or Kevin. Still, she didn't want to eat there. She went out and wandered down the street.

She liked Calgary at once. The people were friendly. The city was clean. The air was pure. And she had a sense of having the best of three worlds—city and prairie and mountains right at her fingertips. She lost herself in the moment, following a group of tourists into a local Italian restaurant and ordering a panzerotti with ham and cheese that was the most wonderful thing she'd smelled and tasted in what seemed like forever.

She just wished she felt like eating it.

The waitress looked worriedly at her when she finally gave up and asked for the check. "You're not well?"

"I'm in love," Madeleine said, surprising herself.

The waitress smiled sympathetically. "That'll do it every time."

THE BLACK DUFFEL sat untouched Tuesday, Wednesday and Thursday. Madeleine saw neither hide nor hair of Chan. She overheard in the elevator that he'd got thrown from his first bull Monday.

"Ol' bull really plowed him down," the man said cheerfully.

It was all Madeleine could do not to demand whether he'd been hurt. It wasn't any of her business, she told herself sharply. But all the same, she wondered. And she was almost relieved to have Dev hail her in the lobby Thursday evening.

He swept her into a bear hug, then held her out at arm's length and said, "Hey, where you been?"

Madeleine gave him her best imitation of a smile. "Around. I've had work to do."

"Yeah. Chan said."

Madeleine nodded, wondering if that was all he'd said. Probably. Chan wasn't one to broadcast his troubles.

"You all right?" Dev asked. "You look like you been sick."

"Allergies," Madeleine lied.

"Too bad. But you guys'll be movin' on tomorrow, won't you? So you'll get away from whatever's bothering you."

Would that it were that simple, Madeleine thought. In fact, she'd be taking her trouble with her. If Chan even let her come. She hadn't heard they were leaving, and she didn't know how to ask without telling Dev she hadn't spoken to Chan.

"You got time for a drink?" he asked her. "I owe you one."

"You do?" Madeleine cocked her head. "Why?"

"Come with me and I'll tell you." He took her by the arm and steered her into the cocktail lounge right off the lobby. They got a small table in a secluded corner, and Dev said, "What'll you have?"

"Scotch," Madeleine said.

He looked at her a little strangely. "On the rocks?"

"No," she said. "I think I'll have it straight."

Dev gave the order, but when he looked back at her, his expression was one of alarm. "This some new allergy medication I don't know about?"

A corner of Madeleine's mouth lifted. "It desensitizes. Isn't that what they say?"

"Maybe," Dev allowed. "You want to talk about it?"

Madeleine shook her head. "Not now. I want to hear why you're buying me this scotch."

"Because Lily called me when I was in Prescott. She said she'd seen you, talked to you for a minute that night in Reno and you made her think. She told me that she really meant what she said about... about it not being my fault. She said there was nothing to forgive. She said she knew she should have said it a long time ago, but she couldn't. She was embarrassed because... because she cared, too, and it felt wrong. She said maybe if we started to talk, maybe it wouldn't feel quite so wrong anymore." He looked up at Madeleine and shook his head, amazed.

Madeleine smiled at him.

"And then we talked. For the first time. For hours." His voice grew softer as he spoke. And Madeleine saw a vulnerability in him still, but the pain was seeping away. There was a kind of quiet sheen of light in his eyes. The reflection of the chandelier? she wondered. Or tears?

Whichever, she was thrilled for him, for both of them. She reached out and took his hand. "Oh, Dev. I'm so glad."

He nodded. "Me, too. I called her the next night. We've talked quite a bit more since then. Really talked. About her. About John. About what happened. About the way I felt. It isn't easy."

She rubbed her fingers along the back of his hand. "I'm sure it isn't."

"I'm afraid to hope sometimes. I mean, when I think about John, it doesn't really seem fair."

"Don't talk yourself out of happiness, Dev."

He smiled at her. "I'll try not to."

"Good."

She didn't drink much of the scotch, after all. Mostly she used it to toast Dev and the happiness she hoped he would find someday with Lily. Partly she used it to try to melt the ice she felt growing deep down in her heart.

She thought about Scott. She thought about Chan. She thought about love and loss and hope and the courage to try again.

And she wondered if she would ever find it in her.

Finally, just as they were about to leave, she had to ask. "Dev, was Chan hurt on Monday?"

"Not much."

"How much?" Had she been sitting here for four days while he was in the hospital?

"Bruised some ribs is all. Why?" He looked at her closely. "Didn't he tell you?"

"I haven't seen him."

"Hell, Mad, what happened?"

"We made love." She couldn't tell him the rest of it. It hurt too much.

Dev shook his head slowly and gave her a squeeze around the shoulders. "I was afraid of that," he said.

HE EXPECTED she'd have checked out. But every day when he asked at the desk, no, Miss Decker was still there. And every day he thought about going back and then thought, to what?

So he stayed away.

Besides, he didn't need to go back to hear what he already knew. She didn't even come to the rodeo on Monday. He looked up in the general area she always tried to be in. She wasn't there.

And just as well, since he barely lasted five seconds and then got himself run over. She might've enjoyed it, he thought sourly. She'd run over him herself.

He didn't understand why she was still there. She couldn't be planning to honor the rest of their damned agreement, could she?

This is Decker, ol' buddy, he reminded himself. Enough said.

He stopped at the hotel Friday morning. Yes, she was still there, the hotel clerk said. So he went up to the room. He debated using his key. He knocked instead.

She opened the door at once, then looked shocked to see him there.

"You were expecting room service?" he asked.

"As a matter of fact, yes."

"I'm sure they'll be along in a few minutes. I just thought I'd tell you I'm pulling out today right after the performance. I didn't make the finals, as you've no doubt heard. Shall I take you to the airport, have you made your own arrangements or are you going to stick this ridiculous thing out?"

"I'm going to stick it out," she said, just as he had feared.

"Swell," he said and turned on his heel and left.

She was there when he rode that afternoon. At least he didn't get thrown in front of her. He didn't make any money, but at this point the money didn't matter as much as his pride. He made a point of not limping or acting like his ribs hurt.

She was waiting for him when he came out. He unlocked the camper and stood back to let her go in first. It wasn't so much politeness as it was another example of pride. He didn't want her seeing how awkward he was.

"Do you want to drive first or shall I?" he asked her.

"Suit yourself."

He tossed her the keys. "I'll take a shower."

"Is Kevin coming?"

"No," he said wearily. "It's just us."

It would have been easier if she weren't still so damned attractive. It would have been a piece of cake if she were shrewish or bitchy or she snubbed him. She was so much the same. So very... so very... *Decker.* Just more aloof.

It was like there was a wall of politeness between them. A "you first," "no, after you," sort of consideration and respect that was so unlike the way he and Decker had normally treated each other that drove him wild.

But it wasn't just her, he was doing it, too. So how could he complain?

They got to Salinas with no missteps. She typed. He drove. She drove. He stretched.

One evening while he was stretching and she made a rest stop, she came back into the camper from a brief walk in a small forest glade and said, "Do you want me to help you with that?"

He was lying on his back, lifting his leg, trying to press his knee toward his chest, then rotate it outward. It hurt. He could just barely do it bearing his own weight. She'd helped him before. He was torn. He wanted. He was afraid...

He said, "Yeah. Why not?"

The why not was relatively obvious to him just a few minutes later. Her hands on him still had the power to arouse him. Her touch made him burn. Yes, he could do the repetitions now. Yes, he could get more range of motion without the possibility of damage.

One kind of damage, anyway. Not another.

"That's enough," he said hoarsely and rolled away from her to the side, drawing both his knees toward his chest.

"Did I hurt you?" She actually sounded worried.

"I'm fine. You'd better start driving if we want to get down the mountains before we stop."

Madeleine was silent a moment. He heard her take a breath. It seemed almost to catch in her throat. Then she said, "Yes."

SHE SHOULDN'T HAVE touched him. She knew it. She was a fool. She knew that, too. But she'd thought she could do it, had thought she'd developed enough immunity. Had wanted to prove to herself that he didn't matter anymore.

The more fool she.

She got back behind the wheel and pulled out rapidly, setting off down the pass more quickly than she normally would. Everything in her now just wanted to be finished with this, with him.

"Hey, Decker. Is that a cop?"

"What? Where?" Her foot hit the brake even as she spoke.

"No cop," Chan said. "Just slow down."

"There wasn't a cop? You just said that?"

"You were driving like a bat out of hell!"

"You're a fine one to talk! You want to drive? Fine! Do it yourself." She pulled over onto the shoulder, shut off the engine and flung the keys at him.

"Hey, Decker, I only said—"

But she was already out of the driver's seat and climbing up into her bunk above it. "I heard what you said, Richardson. Go to hell."

IT WAS ALL downhill after that.

In Salinas they went out with Lily and Dev. There was no way either of them could gracefully decline without putting a damper on what was supposed to be a happy evening. And, in fact, Madeleine supposed that for Lily and Dev it was.

They were talking together, smiling at each other. They were so wrapped up in each other that she hoped they didn't even notice that she and Chan hardly said a word.

Oh, Chan talked about some stock he'd talked to a fellow about in Wolf Point. And Madeleine said yes, that her dissertation was doing well. But they never talked to each other. They never smiled at each other. They scarcely even looked at each other.

And when Lily and Dev walked off hand in hand, Chan went out for a beer with the boys and Madeleine went straight to bed.

The next day he might not have talked to her at all except that he was having trouble getting his ribs taped himself. He struggled with the prewrap, ending with it slipping and the sticky tape stuck to his chest. Every time he tried to redo it, he pulled off the tape, grimacing as it pulled off his chest hairs, then swearing when he messed up the tape.

Madeleine was typing and she tried not to look up. It wasn't easy. Finally she said, "Do you want me to do it?"

He looked at the tape, then looked at her. She could tell it was a hard decision.

"It won't break my heart if you don't," she told him.

He thrust the tape at her. "All right. Yes."

She taped him as snugly and securely as she knew how. It wasn't a professional job by any means, but he seemed satisfied. He muttered, "Thanks," then said thanks again when she helped him on with his shirt and handed him his hat.

He grabbed his gear bag and headed for the door of the camper, then stopped.

"You coming or not?" he asked.

Fool that she was, she went.

HE MADE SOME MONEY in Salinas which was just as well. There wasn't anything else worth calling home about.

Not that he was calling home these days. It would be a while before he could call Julia Richardson and talk cordially instead of wanting to punch his mother out.

There was nothing good to say about the trip to Salt Lake. They got caught in a thunderstorm in the Sierras. Madeleine needed computer disks in the middle of nowhere, and they had to backtrack to Reno. They got a flat tire somewhere just this side of Elko. And the ignition system went out fifty miles west of Salt Lake.

Chan could roll with the punches most times. He felt like he'd been punched and kicked and stepped on now. He said so and he said a few succinct four-letter words, too.

"Well, it's not my fault," Madeleine told him.

"Who needed computer disks?"

She rounded on him. "Who didn't have a pumped up spare?"

"Who didn't bother to tell me she was having trouble getting the truck to start?"

"Who— Oh, who cares!"

"I care, damn it!" Chan yelled. He kicked his rigging bag and sent it crashing against the wall of the camper.

"I'm going to miss my ride! And I drew Rock Shox. He's almost guaranteed to be in the money."

"He might be," Madeleine muttered. "What about you?"

By the time they got to Cheyenne on Monday of the last week in July, Madeleine thought they'd managed to blame each other for everything from the common cold to unrest in the Middle East.

"There's no sense going on with this, is there?" she said to Chan as they pulled up to the rodeo grounds in Frontier Park.

He shut off the engine and looked around at her. He looked as bleak as she felt. "No," he said tonelessly. "There's not."

"I think you could say we proved our point," Madeleine said. She tried to smile but it didn't work well, and even she thought her voice sounded husky and remote.

"Yeah." He looked away, staring out the window at the rows of campers and trailers beyond.

"So let's forget it, shall we? I'll go home."

He didn't say anything for a moment. It looked as though he was worrying the inside of his cheek. His fingers opened and tightened once, then twice, on the steering wheel. "Now?" he said finally, turning to look at her. "What happened to the two months business? How's it going to look?"

"Do you care how it looks?"

"Do you?"

They looked at each other. Neither said a word. There didn't seem to be any more to say.

Finally Madeleine said, "I got to Vegas on the 29th. I can leave on the 28th. That'll be two months exactly. Neither of our mothers should have the slightest quibble. All right?"

Chan shrugged. "Whatever you say."

SHE DIDN'T KNOW why she bothered. What was she doing, hoping against hope? Looking for a miracle? Holding out for the infinitesimal chance that he would declare his undying love and ask her to stay?

No.

Then what?

Aching. Yes. And looking. Yes. And storing up memories, filing away in her mind sights of Chan, sounds of Chan, even, when she taped him up that one last time, the feel of Chan beneath her hands.

She was doing, she realized, what she'd done countless times before in her life. Every time they'd been somewhere—in Bali or China, the reservation or Alaska, she'd stored up bits and pieces of that world and tucked them away. In an envelope, in a box, in a folder, in her mind and in her heart. And then she'd gone away.

She could never take them with her. She'd learned not to try. She'd thrown out her memories of Scott. They didn't matter anymore. They seemed shallow compared to the ones she had of Chan.

What a summer this would be to haul out and share with her future family someday.

Would there be a family? she asked herself. The question left her feeling hollow, despairing, bereft.

But she had to believe there would.

Someday there would be the right man, the suitable man, the perfect man. The man who could touch her soul and her heart and who, in turn, would bask in her love.

And if she dared, she would tell him about this cowboy whom, one crazy summer, she had so foolishly loved.

HE DIDN'T EXPECT to see her there in the stands. but it was a habit to look for her now. He rosined his bull rope; he fitted on his glove; he settled in on the bull; he wrapped the rope around and around his hand; he looked for Madeleine. He'd done it so long now it was part of the drill.

He did it Monday afternoon. He settled in and pulled up on the rope, got Dev to pull it tighter, took that one last wrap with his hand. He glanced over to his right and up, looking.

She was there, watching him. Intent. Serious. Beautiful.

He rode and even he knew it was poetry.

On Thursday he rosined, he settled, he fitted, he wrapped.

But he knew even before he looked: Madeleine Decker wasn't there.

Chapter Thirteen

Good, Chan told himself, focusing once more on the hump on the Brangus bull's back. It was over. Finished. Done. He was free at last.

Now he could concentrate.

He monkeyed himself a little farther up against his hand. He felt the pull in his leg arrowing up to his groin. He settled his spurs. He tucked his chin and centered himself. He nodded his head.

The chute gate opened and the bull, a wily young one named Howard's End by a stock contractor with apparent literary aspirations, spun out into the arena.

If Monday's ride was the bull rider's version of a Shakespearean sonnet, this one was pure bad verse. Chan got knocked sideways going out of the chute. It was all he could do to hook his leg around and make a desperate stab at recovery.

He made it. Barely. He might qualify for the finals if nobody did great on Friday or Saturday. If the wheel turned and he was lucky.

"Hey," Gil said to him after, "you want to come down to the Cheyenne Club tonight?"

"Sure," Chan said. "Why not?" Celebrate his freedom.

Cheyenne during Frontier Days was a happening town. For every authentic cowboy and cowgirl there were a dozen or more wannabes walking around in flashy new shirts and fine, new, sharp straw hats. It didn't matter to Chan. Cowgirls who didn't know which side to mount a horse from could flirt as well as the real ones.

Chan was ready for a little flirting. He was ready for a lot more than that. He teased and laughed and flirted with the best of them. He even bit his lip and tried a little dancing. There was a blonde from Arkansas who cozied up to him right away. There was a redhead from South Dakota who seemed almost attached to his arm. There were half a dozen others that he could have made a play for and probably succeeded.

But when he left it wasn't much past midnight. And he left alone.

His ribs hurt. He was tired. He couldn't do justice to them. He had plenty of reasons. Take your pick. He hitched a ride from an Alberta cowboy on his way back to the camping area.

"You wanta stop and have a beer with us?" the cowboy offered, nodding toward the camper he was sharing with friends.

"Thanks, no." Chan declined. "I'm beat. Reckon I'll just go to bed."

It wasn't the first night he'd spent in the camper alone in two months. There were those days in Calgary after they'd made love when he'd walked out and left Madeleine alone in the hotel. But those days he'd shared the camper with anger and a grudge the size of Howard's End.

Tonight the grudge was gone. So was the anger. So was Madeleine. He was alone.

He shucked his boots, stripped off his shirt and jeans, then carefully, so he wouldn't hurt his ribs, climbed up into the bunk above the cab. She wasn't there now, and it was his bunk, anyway. Always had been until she'd infiltrated his life. Now he could have it back.

He settled in. Tried to rest.

But Madeleine was all around him.

He rolled onto his side and buried his face against the pillow. He could smell the flowery scent of her in the linen. He rubbed his cheek against the cool percale, wallowing in it.

"Should've changed the sheets," he muttered to himself.

He would. Tomorrow.

Tonight—just one night—he needed this.

"I HATE NEW YORK."

"What?" Alfie stared at her as if she'd gone mad. "It's your favorite place on earth." She quoted Madeleine the sentiment she'd expressed more than once.

"I've changed my mind," Madeleine said, then winced, remembering where changing her mind last time had got her.

"Well, I don't think it's New York you should be hating," Alfie said. She was considering the menu, trying to decide what to have for brunch, and she glanced at Madeleine only briefly. The eggs Benedict looked better. "I think it's wherever you spent your summer vacation. I don't like to be depressing, Mad, but frankly you look like hell."

"Thank you very much."

"Well, you do." Alfie considered her dispassionately over the top of the menu. "You're pale and wan and you look half-dead. What did he do to you, make you ride bulls?"

Madeleine shook her head.

Alfie sighed. "You look like you did. You look like they trampled you."

"I'll recover," Madeleine said. "I'll just have toast," she said to the waitress.

Alfie looked at her, disgusted. "Bring her some fresh fruit, too. And a pot of coffee. You have to eat, Madeleine, if you're going to recover."

"Fine," Madeleine said wearily. She knew she would, but it was going to be hard.

She'd counted on walking off the plane and feeling the rush of enthusiasm she usually felt when she landed in New York. Instead she felt empty. She felt dead.

She'd counted on a good night's sleep refreshing her, a brisk walk in Central Park reviving her, a brunch with Alfie this morning making her feel bright and focused again. They did not.

"So your mother was wrong, I gather," Alfie said. "Since I see you didn't bring Roy Rogers home."

"Of course my mother was wrong," Madeleine said sharply. "That's why I went, didn't I? To prove it?"

Alfie shrugged. "I guess."

That was why she went; Madeleine had to keep reminding herself of that.

She poked at the cantaloupe the waitress set in front of her. "Do you think that people with advanced degrees are perhaps more stupid about life than the average person?" she asked.

"It's possible," Alfie said cheerfully. "They have a tendency to overanalyze, to make things too abstract. Simple is sometimes better."

"I was thinking that," Madeleine said. She stabbed another piece of cantaloupe thoughtfully.

"Sometimes," Alfie went on through a mouthful of Hollandaise, "I think people who are extremely well educated think they can control things they can't. Sometimes they need to learn to leave well enough alone."

IF SHE'D LEFT well enough alone she wouldn't be hurting like this. She wouldn't know about rodeos and roundups, about campers and cattle, about wide open spaces and cool desert mornings and prairies and mountains caressed by a big, big sky.

She wouldn't have fallen in love with Chan Richardson.

She wouldn't be walking around New York now, feeling like hell.

She might even be up for this meeting with Jordan Venable she was about to walk into, instead of wondering what she was going to say. She didn't suppose it mattered much. It was all pro forma at this point. Just a progress report, to let him know what she'd accomplished, to hear his view on what she'd already written.

Maybe, she thought a little desperately, something he would say would jar her loose from this fit of the dismals and set her back on the right track.

She lifted her chin as she walked up the steps to the building near Washington Square where he had his office. She squared her shoulders when she knocked on his door.

"Come in."

Venable was sitting behind his desk, leaning back in his antique oak, swivel office chair, puffing on his pipe. His feet were on his desk, crossed at the ankles. He was wearing rose-and-gray argyle socks. He smiled when Madeleine came in.

"Welcome back, traveler. Have a seat."

"Thank you." She sat down on the straight-back chair opposite him. He folded his hands behind his head and waited as she settled. Then he said, "What do you mean by free will?"

Madeleine, who had been comparing his gentle smile and patrician features to her memory of Chan's lean, hard-edged face, blinked and stared. "What?"

"I said, what do you mean by free will? I've read your chapters, and while I think you have all the philosophical speculation down pat, I don't see the practical application anywhere."

"I—" she stopped, floored. "But I thought the speculation, the exploration of the differences in attitude—I thought that's what you wanted, what we talked about."

He nodded slowly. "Yes. But just for the sake of the world at large, those who live but don't necessarily read philosophy—" he smiled "—give me a concrete example of free will."

"A concrete example?" She shook her head, confused.

"I'm just playing devil's advocate, Miss Decker. I think you've got the abstract notion spot on. I want to know where you'd go with it from there."

"But isn't that outside the scope of philosophy?"

Venable shrugged. "Maybe. Should it be?"

Madeleine opened her mouth to say yes. Then she remembered her brunch with Alfie just two hours before. She remembered Alfie talking about overanalyzing, about making things too abstract. "Maybe not," she said slowly.

"So then, for the sake of discussion. To apply this philosophy you've been writing about, give me an example, from your own life, if you wish, of free will. Where have you been free to make a choice, not constrained by fate or the will of others?"

The will of others?

"There's this cowboy," she said, "that my mother wanted me to marry."

Venable's brows looked like the Washington Square arch. "A cowboy your mother wants you to marry? But I thought your mother was Dr. Decker, the anthropologist."

"She is," Madeleine said. "But she's still a mother." And then she told him about Julia and Antonia, about their genetics and their anthropological studies. She told him about Chan, about the camper, about the rodeos, about the summer. Sometimes when she talked her throat tightened, and she felt she could hardly speak past the lump there. Sometimes her eyes got damp and her nose threatened to run, and she wondered if she was allergic to Venable's pipe smoke. She dabbed at them and went on.

"So you see," she said almost desperately, "that's an example of free will. I'm choosing not to marry him, not to even try to marry him, even though my mother wants me to."

Venable puffed for a moment, then let the smoke swirl curl into the room. "Possibly," he allowed.

Madeleine frowned. "What do you mean, possibly. It's quite clear. I'm not letting her dictate my life. I'm exercising my own free will."

There was a long silence. Then Venable smiled a gentle smile. "Are you, Miss Decker?" he said quietly. "I would have thought that particular question didn't have anything to do with your mother."

"Hi."

"Chan! How are you? How's everything? Are you in Cheyenne?" Julia's voice was cheerful, optimistic. All must be right in her world. Lucky her.

"Yeah, I'm in Cheyenne."

"Did you make the finals today?"

"Barely. But barely counts and I got a good chance. Got me a good bull. Red River."

"He is good," Julia agreed. "But isn't he the one who kicked you unconscious in . . . in New York?"

"He's the one," Chan said. He was trying not to think about that. He was trying to get focused, to see himself ride, not let last year's bad experience do him in.

"Well, he'll be a challenge, then, won't he?" Julia said with all the optimism she could muster. "Good luck."

"Thanks. I'll need it."

"You'll do fine, darling. I know you will." There was a pause, then she asked, "How's . . . Madeleine?"

"Fine, I suppose."

"You . . . suppose?"

"I don't know. She's gone."

For a good twenty seconds Julia didn't say anything. Then she simply echoed his word. "Gone, Chan?"

"Gone. Why not?" he said trying his best to sound nonchalant. "Her two months were up. She came the end of May. Now she's gone home to New York where she belongs."

"To New York?" Julia was having trouble speaking, all at once.

"To New York," Chan repeated firmly. "See, Ma," he said, determined to put an end to it, "you were wrong."

There was such a long silence he thought for a moment the connection was broken.

Then she said, "Was I, Chan? Was I really?" And this time she hung up on him.

"I DON'T KNOW," Julia said to Antonia moments later. She didn't care what time or even what day it was in Bali. This was an emergency. "I'm worried. Are you sure this is going to work?"

"It's got to," Antonia said. "Everything's in place. The caterer is set. He said just let him know the date. I wired the florist. She said the same. The printer can do invitations at the last minute. The rector said any day, any week, except Saturdays at St. James. All we need is a bride and groom."

"Well, the bride and groom are not cooperating," Julia said. "Chan called this morning. He's in Cheyenne. Madeleine's gone home."

"*Home?* To New York?"

"Apparently."

"Stay right where you are," Antonia said. "I'll call her and get back to you."

Julia sat by the phone for the rest of the morning. It was well past noon when the phone rang again.

"I called and called and called. I left messages on her machine until I used it up. She's not there," Antonia cried. "What shall we do?"

FOCUS.

Ride the bull in your mind.

Concentrate.

Anticipate all his moves.

Center yourself.

Have goals.

See yourself succeed.

Chan stood behind the chutes amidst the noise and bustle and confusion and tried to blot it all out. He knew what he had to do.

But as one rider after another went, while he was usually helping them and focusing on his own upcoming ride, this time he couldn't. He fished his bull rope around and started tightening it, then stared up at the grandstand again, distracted.

"You need some help?"

"Huh?" He looked around to see Dev alongside him on the chute. "No, I'll manage."

"You all right?"

"Fine." He tried to think what he had to do next. He didn't seem to be able to.

"What's the matter with you?"

"Nothin'." Chan pulled on the rope, tightening it.

"Watch it!" Dev said as the bull twisted in the chute, almost trapping Chan's leg.

Chan shook his head, trying to clear it. "Can't seem to get my head together," he muttered.

"Why? What's wrong?"

"I can't concentrate."

"Figures," Dev said.

Chan's head came around sharply. "What's that mean?"

"You're missing Madeleine."

"That's crazy."

"Is it?"

"Of course it is. I mean, it's not like I didn't know she was leaving. I always knew."

"Yeah, you knew. But did you want her to?"

Chan wasn't letting himself think about that. "It doesn't matter what I want," he said gruffly. He eased his leg over Red River's back and settled carefully down onto the bull.

Dev shrugged. "If you say so." He gave Chan's bull rope another pull.

"I say so," Chan insisted. "And anyway, I can't think about her now, damn it. I don't have time. I can't get distracted. I have to think about what's most important."

"Maybe she is."

The words were soft, barely audible, and yet they seemed to hit Chan like a two-by-four alongside his head.

Maybe she is.

He shoved them away, wrapping the bull rope around his hand, then sliding up against his hand, bracing his feet, centering himself.

Maybe she is.

Was she? Was his mother going to get her way after all? Or did his mother and what she wanted even matter?

Ever since he was a little boy he'd fought for his autonomy, fought to be the man he wanted to be and not the man he thought his parents wanted. Even when he was wrong and they were right, he'd held out for the sake of holding out, reacting instead of acting.

He'd done the same thing when his mother had mentioned Madeleine. He'd been determined to dislike her, to find fault with her, to walk away from her.

He'd fallen in love with her.

And he'd never said so. He'd let her go. To spite his mother. But whom was he hurting—besides himself?

"Do you reckon it's ever too late to grow up?" he asked now.

Dev blinked. "Huh?"

Chan shook his head. "Nothin'."

"You ready?"

As I'll ever be, he thought. He nodded.

The gate opened. The bull surged out, twisted, ducked, flung Chan around to the right. The grandstand was a blur before his eyes. It always was. He'd never cared before. It hadn't ever mattered.

Now it did.

He couldn't help it. He looked.

He forgot the bull, forgot his focus, forgot it all to take one brief glance up where Madeleine had been all summer, where he wished—oh God, how he wished—she was now.

And there—

No, it couldn't be. But he saw dark hair, tangled, windblown. He saw milky white skin and slender shoulders. He saw—Madeleine?

No. It wasn't possible.

She was gone. Back to New York.

The bull whipped left and Chan went with him, but he wasn't really paying attention. He was twisting back, trying to grab another look at the grandstand.

Somewhere it was written that you couldn't scan a crowd and ride a bull at the same time. Or maybe it wasn't written. It ought to have been self-evident enough that it didn't even need to be written down.

In any case, he didn't see her. He saw a blur, a spin . . . and then he saw stars.

He didn't even remember being carried to the medical trailer.

And when he came around at last, woozy and nauseated, he wasn't even sure he'd come around then. Maybe he was still out. Maybe he was dreaming, hallucinating, because wasn't that Decker, all eyes and hair, staring down into his face?

He had an awful sense of déjà vu. He shut his eyes and wondered desperately if maybe he wasn't destined to relive this particular loop of his life until he got it right.

"I've been thinking," Madeleine said, just as she had all those months ago in New York.

Chan groaned.

SHE COULDN'T SEEM to stop crying. She felt like an idiot, standing there sniveling and sniffling, with everyone looking at her. He wasn't dead.

He was concussed, the doctor told her. But unless the X rays showed something terrible, he would be fine. But still she couldn't stop crying, and he'd opened his eyes again and was looking at her as if she'd lost her mind.

Perhaps she had. God knew she was certainly acting out of character. Or maybe, she thought, she'd finally got in touch with her true self.

"What's the matter with you?" he asked her.

"You," she told him. "I saw you get—get—"

"You've seen me get kicked before," he reminded her.

"I didn't love you then."

There, she'd said it. Loud and clear and in front of God, seven cowboys and the Justin medical staff. They didn't seem to find anything amazing about it. Chan looked poleaxed.

"That's why I came back," she said, when he didn't say anything. She said the words quickly, almost defiantly. She glared at him as she spoke.

He stared to shake his head as if he didn't believe her, then winced and said instead, "Well, I'll be damned."

"Probably," Madeleine said tartly. "I wouldn't be the least surprised."

A grin spread slowly across his face. "Marry me," he said.

She stared at him. "What?"

"You heard me."

"Just, marry you? Just like that?"

"Why not? You love me. I love you. What could be simpler?"

Madeleine opened her mouth to argue, to ask him how he knew he loved her. He'd never told her that. Not until now. Then she remembered Alfie. She remembered simple.

Simple, Madeleine thought.

Still she had to ask, "Are you serious?"

"Never more."

"In spite of our mothers?"

"How'd you guess?"

HE WAS BRUISED and cracked and battered. His head hurt, his ribs ached, his groin had suffered another pull. The local paper wrote him up as a walking disaster. But Channing Richardson had news for them: he'd never felt better in his life.

She loved him. She'd come back to him.

He rolled over in bed—very carefully—and said again, "I still don't get it. Your dissertation director sent you back?"

"We discussed the true nature of free will. In the concrete rather than the abstract. I was telling him how I had come back to New York to prove to my mother that she didn't run my life. And he said— Well, I don't remember exactly what he said, but I suddenly realized that the question wasn't what she wanted me to do or didn't want me to do. The real question of free will was what I wanted."

She leaned toward him and kissed his nose, just about the only part of him that didn't hurt. "I wanted you," she said.

He smiled. He wrapped his arms around her and snuggled her close against his chest, and she came, careful of his ribs, kissing him softly, taking his kisses in return, until just kisses weren't enough anymore.

Then with infinite gentleness, she moved over him and he eased inside her. She smiled down at him.

"All my life I was looking for the perfect man, the perfect place, the perfect home," she told him. "Lily once told me that she didn't need any place as long as she had John, that when she was with him she was home. I know now what she meant. And I'll go with you wherever you go for as long as you want."

Chan blinked. His throat tightened. "You haul good, Decker," he said hoarsely. "I do love you." And then he began to move.

And Madeleine moved with him, rocked with him, soared with him, landed with him in the heaven of their embrace and whispered, "I love you, too."

"So you will marry me?" Chan asked, his lips against hers.

And Madeleine said, "I will."

The next day

"ONE MOMENT and I'll connect you."

"Ma?" Chan said.

"Mother?" said Madeleine.

"Chan!" said Julia, half hopeful.

"Madeleine, where have you been?" Antonia said, three quarters apprehension.

"Flying," Madeleine said. "I was in New York. Now I'm back in Cheyenne. With Chan."

Someone's breath caught. Julia's? Antonia's? Either. Both.

"You were right," Chan told his mother.

"You were right," Madeleine told hers.

"You mean it?"

"You're in love?"

The sighs could be heard halfway around the world.

"Wonderful," said Julia when she'd stopped sighing. "I told you so, if you'll recall."

"As did I," Antonia reminded them. "We know the perfect place for the wedding," she went on. They could almost hear her rubbing her hands together as she spoke.

"Oh, we're already married," Chan told them. "We did it this afternoon at the rodeo grounds."

"Married?! On the rodeo grounds!" A horrified duet screeched over the phone wires.

"That's right." Madeleine laughed and hugged the man at her side. "It was wonderful. Just right. It barely took eight seconds." She nibbled at his chin. "That's all the longer Chan can concentrate."

"Not so," he said, and Julia and Antonia took their solace where they could find it—from the distinct sound of very thorough kissing.

"In fact," Chan said, when at last they came up for air, "I reckon I'll be concentrating on Madeleine for the rest of my life."

HARLEQUIN®
AMERICAN ◆ ROMANCE®

You asked for it...and now you've got it. More MEN!

MORE THAN MEN

We're thrilled to bring you another special edition of the popular MORE THAN MEN series.

Like those who have come before him, Sean Seaward is more than tall, dark and handsome. All of these men have extraordinary powers that make them "more than men." But whether they are able to grant you three wishes or to live forever, make no mistake—their greatest, most extraordinary power is that of seduction.

So make a date next month with Sean Seaward in
#538 KISSED BY THE SEA
by Rebecca Flanders

SUPH5

American Romance is goin' to the chapel…with three soon–to–be–wed couples. Only thing is, saying "I do" is the farthest thing from their minds!

You're cordially invited to join us for three months of veils and vows. Don't miss any of the nuptials in

GTC

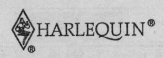

Harlequin Books requests the pleasure of your company this June in Eternity, Massachusetts, for WEDDINGS, INC.

For generations, couples have been coming to Eternity, Massachusetts, to exchange wedding vows. Legend has it that those married in Eternity's chapel are destined for a lifetime of happiness. And the residents are more than willing to give the legend a hand.

Beginning in June, you can experience the legend of Eternity. Watch for one title per month, across all of the Harlequin series.

HARLEQUIN BOOKS... NOT THE SAME OLD STORY!

WEDGEN

INDULGE A LITTLE 6947 SWEEPSTAKES
NO PURCHASE NECESSARY

HERE'S HOW THE SWEEPSTAKES WORKS:
The Harlequin Reader Service shipments for January, February and March 1994 will contain, respectively, coupons for entry into three prize drawings: a trip for two to San Francisco, an Alaskan cruise for two and a trip for two to Hawaii. To be eligible for any drawing using an Entry Coupon, simply complete and mail according to directions.

There is no obligation to continue as a Reader Service subscriber to enter and be eligible for any prize drawing. You may also enter any drawing by hand printing your name and address on a 3" x 5" card and the destination of the prize you wish that entry to be considered for (i.e., San Francisco trip, Alaskan cruise or Hawaiian trip). Send your 3" x 5" entries to: Indulge a Little 6947 Sweepstakes, c/o Prize Destination you wish that entry to be considered for, P.O. Box 1315, Buffalo, NY 14269-1315, U.S.A. or Indulge a Little 6947 Sweepstakes, P.O. Box 610, Fort Erie, Ontario L2A 5X3, Canada.

To be eligible for the San Francisco trip, entries must be received by 4/30/94; for the Alaskan cruise, 5/31/94; and the Hawaiian trip, 6/30/94. No responsibility is assumed for lost, late or misdirected mail. Sweepstakes open to residents of the U.S. (except Puerto Rico) and Canada, 18 years of age or older. All applicable laws and regulations apply. Sweepstakes void wherever prohibited.

For a copy of the Official Rules, send a self-addressed, stamped envelope (WA residents need not affix return postage) to: Indulge a Little 6947 Rules, P.O. Box 4631, Blair, NE 68009, U.S.A.

INDR93

INDULGE A LITTLE 6947 SWEEPSTAKES
NO PURCHASE NECESSARY

HERE'S HOW THE SWEEPSTAKES WORKS:
The Harlequin Reader Service shipments for January, February and March 1994 will contain, respectively, coupons for entry into three prize drawings: a trip for two to San Francisco, an Alaskan cruise for two and a trip for two to Hawaii. To be eligible for any drawing using an Entry Coupon, simply complete and mail according to directions.

There is no obligation to continue as a Reader Service subscriber to enter and be eligible for any prize drawing. You may also enter any drawing by hand printing your name and address on a 3" x 5" card and the destination of the prize you wish that entry to be considered for (i.e., San Francisco trip, Alaskan cruise or Hawaiian trip). Send your 3" x 5" entries to: Indulge a Little 6947 Sweepstakes, c/o Prize Destination you wish that entry to be considered for, P.O. Box 1315, Buffalo, NY 14269-1315, U.S.A. or Indulge a Little 6947 Sweepstakes, P.O. Box 610, Fort Erie, Ontario L2A 5X3, Canada.

To be eligible for the San Francisco trip, entries must be received by 4/30/94; for the Alaskan cruise, 5/31/94; and the Hawaiian trip, 6/30/94. No responsibility is assumed for lost, late or misdirected mail. Sweepstakes open to residents of the U.S. (except Puerto Rico) and Canada, 18 years of age or older. All applicable laws and regulations apply. Sweepstakes void wherever prohibited.

For a copy of the Official Rules, send a self-addressed, stamped envelope (WA residents need not affix return postage) to: Indulge a Little 6947 Rules, P.O. Box 4631, Blair, NE 68009, U.S.A.

INDR93

░░░░░░░ INDULGE A LITTLE ░░░░░░░
SWEEPSTAKES

OFFICIAL ENTRY COUPON

This entry must be received by: MAY 31, 1994
This month's winner will be notified by: JUNE 15, 1994
Trip must be taken between: JULY 31, 1994-JULY 31, 1995

YES, I want to win the Alaskan Cruise vacation for two. I understand that the prize includes round-trip airfare, one-week cruise including private cabin, all meals and pocket money as revealed on the "wallet" scratch-off card.

Name_____

Address _____ Apt. _____

City_____

State/Prov._____ Zip/Postal Code_____

Daytime phone number_____
           (Area Code)

Account # _____

Return entries with invoice in envelope provided. Each book in this shipment has two entry coupons—and the more coupons you enter, the better your chances of winning!
© 1993 HARLEQUIN ENTERPRISES LTD.   MONTH2

░░░░░░░ INDULGE A LITTLE ░░░░░░░
SWEEPSTAKES

OFFICIAL ENTRY COUPON

This entry must be received by: MAY 31, 1994
This month's winner will be notified by: JUNE 15, 1994
Trip must be taken between: JULY 31, 1994-JULY 31, 1995

YES, I want to win the Alaskan Cruise vacation for two. I understand that the prize includes round-trip airfare, one-week cruise including private cabin, all meals and pocket money as revealed on the "wallet" scratch-off card.

Name_____

Address _____ Apt. _____

City_____

State/Prov._____ Zip/Postal Code_____

Daytime phone number_____
           (Area Code)

Account # _____

Return entries with invoice in envelope provided. Each book in this shipment has two entry coupons—and the more coupons you enter, the better your chances of winning!
© 1993 HARLEQUIN ENTERPRISES LTD.   MONTH2